More praise for *The Last Chicken in America*

"[An] elegantly constructed web of stories about Russian-Jewish immigrants living in the Squirrel Hill section of Pittsburgh. . . . Warm, true and original, and packed with incisive, subtle one-liners. . . . Though Litman's stories unfold on a more contained, more domestic canvas than the novels of her fellow Russian expatriate Gary Shteyngart, they evince a similar appreciation for the ironies of American culture. . . . Masha and her family anchor the book, appearing in alternating stories, always slightly older than they were before." —Maud Newton, *New York Times Book Review*

"In Ellen Litman's quietly assured debut, the Russians have landed. Litman . . . renders her characters with a refreshing lack of sentimentality, coupled at times with wry humor. . . . Litman displays skillful restraint in depicting her characters' slow erasure. . . . In this insightful first book, Litman tenderly conveys that, fleeting and illusory as it may be, these immigrants must accept the smallest consolation." —Don Lee, *Boston Globe*

"These stories, spare, realistic, sometimes gently satirical, are told from various points of view of old widowers, middle-aged divorcees, unemployed engineers, and resentful college students still shackled to their parents by economic necessity. . . . Litman writes about their dilemmas with wit and sympathy. . . . Litman's book, with its large ensemble cast, offers the most expansive and most detailed view of Russian immigrants' experiences." —Elaine Blair, *New York Review of Books*

"*The Last Chicken in America* should be required reading for the entire planet: those of us yearning for a larger fate, those of us struggling under the loving burden of family, and, in particular, the various proto-fascists attempting to use immigration to scare decent Americans. Ellen Litman's stories remind us that the human soul is, in its essence, an immigrant: eager, rootless, searching tenderly for home. The depth of her insight, and the incandescence of her prose, is startling." —Steve Almond, author of *The Evil B. B. Chow and Other Stories* and *Candyfreak*

"A beautiful, complex portrait of an émigré community that, through its heart, virtuosity, humor, and unrelenting precision of vision, ends up being about America itself—about the complicated blessings that freedom, and the possibility of affluence, bring. The people in *The Last Chicken in America* struggle—sometimes meanly, sometimes nobly—which is to say, they struggle like real people. Litman's accomplishment is the compassion we feel for them. She is a wonderful, generous, immensely gifted young writer." —George Saunders, author of *In Persuasion Nation*

"A beautifully written, highly amusing and sobering look at contemporary Russian Jewish immigration to America. . . . Litman, a Russian immigrant herself, skillfully shows the clash of cultures and the learning process of assimilating into America." —*Library Journal*

"Litman joins Laura Vapnyar and David Bezmozgis in portraying Russian Jews stymied and inspired by the curious mix of abundance and emptiness that characterizes American life. Yet, Litman's pristine, entrancing interconnected short stories are distinct, given her light touch, crisp humor, and the push-and-pull of her characters' tidal emotions. As obdurate Russian transplants simultaneously cling and repel each other, Litman's many-faceted stories revolve around the search for a calling in life, the quest for love, and the tragicomic predicaments that thwart seekers and lovers. Straightforward in structure yet intricate psychologically, Litman's smart stories take measure of the confounding divides between cultures and generations, men and women." *Booklist*

"Ellen Litman's intelligence is fresh, tender and wonderfully alive."
—Mary Gaitskill, author of *Veronica*

"Litman does an admirable job of showing how the freedom to shape one's own destiny . . . can be as isolating as it is empowering. [She] is quietly insightful and extremely fair to each of her characters, who range from lonely senior citizens to stifled office workers and old-world parents mystified by their kids' quintessentially American aspirations. This smart, well-crafted book both documents a historical phenomenon—the recent experiences of a subset of immigrants—but also gets at something larger than America itself: universal questions about the choices we make and the stubborn elusiveness of happiness."
—Adelle Waldman, *Time Out New York*

"This is an excellent debut novel. The writing is crisp and sparse, and the characters are rendered authentically, flawed and often unlikable, but always sympathetic. Litman has given us the opportunity to see our community in a new way, through the eyes of those who are struggling to find their place. In this way, we may develop a deeper appreciation of this unique place we call home, as well as deepen our sympathy for those who still stand on the outside hoping we will welcome they in."
—Erik Rosen, *Jewish Chronicle of Pittsburgh*

"Permanently severed from a country that thwarted a sense of Jewish belonging, [the characters] are now forced to navigate a new outsider position as immigrants. In bringing their stories to life, Litman tenderly balances pathos and humor, and the result is a deeply sympathetic look at a community struggling to understand its hyphenated identity."   —Irina Reyn, *Moscow Times*

"It's Masha's 'delirious noble dream' of finding her way in her new world that gives the book its structure. In the first story, she's convinced that 'immigration distorts people'; subsequently, she pushes against those distortions even as she is molded by them. . . . The small community of Squirrel Hill comes alive through its immigrants, and eventually it is a place that Masha's heart fully inhabits."
                    —Carolyn Kellogg, *Los Angeles Times*

"Litman gives marvelous voice to a dispirited community tentatively absorbing American aspirations in her debut novel. . . . Through the voices of disaffected teens, disillusioned moms and ailing oldsters, Litman conveys a community in flux, always with dry wit and an empathetic heart. . . . Litman writes with admirable control sharpened by sardonic humor."
                    —Carole Goldberg, *Hartford Courant*

"Litman's strength is in showing the different ways people have adjusted, how the Russian immigrant world is not monolithic. Her work is a welcome addition to this Russian immigrant genre."
                    —Rabbi Rachel Esserman, *The Reporter*

The Last Chicken
in America

a novel in stories

Ellen Litman

W. W. Norton & Company
New York London

For my parents,
Josef and Mariya Litman

The following stories appeared in somewhat different form in the following publications: "The Last Chicken in America" in *Ontario Review*, "In the Man-Free Zone" in *Gulf Coast*, "Dancers" in *Tin House* and *Best of Tin House*, "Peculiarities of the National Driving" in *Vrij Nederland* (in Dutch), "When the Neighbors Love You" in *Another Chicago Magazine*, "Among the Lilacs and the Girls" in *Guilt and Pleasure*, "The Trajectory of Frying Pans" in *Ploughshares*, "About Kamyshinskiy" in *TriQuarterly* and *Best New American Voices 2007*.

For information about permission to reproduce selections from this book,
write to Permissions, W. W. Norton & Company, Inc.,
500 Fifth Avenue, New York, NY 10110

For information about special discounts for bulk purchases, please contact
W. W. Norton Special Sales at specialsales@wwnorton.com or 800-233-4830

Manufacturing by RR Donnelley, Bloomsburg
Book design by Anna Oler

Library of Congress Cataloging-in-Publication Data

Litman, Ellen.
The last chicken in America : a novel in stories / Ellen Litman. — 1st ed.
p. cm.
ISBN 978-0-393-06511-4
1. Jews, Russian—United States—Fiction. I. Title.
PS3612.I866L37 2007
813'.6—dc22

2007015563

ISBN 978-0-393-33357-2 pbk.

W. W. Norton & Company, Inc.
500 Fifth Avenue, New York, N.Y. 10110
www.wwnorton.com

W. W. Norton & Company Ltd.
Castle House, 75/76 Wells Street, London W1T 3QT

1 2 3 4 5 6 7 8 9 0

Contents

The Last Chicken
in America

The Last Chicken
in America

I THINK A SUPERMARKET is a poor place for a romance to begin.

We came to America in July, and now, in August, the supermarket is still a bit of a miracle, although our eyes are starting to adjust to the earnest pinks and yellows and blues in the packaging that spell out *foreign* to us. We don't have a car yet, and our trips to the supermarket are long processions along Murray Avenue past the BP gas station, the karate studio, and the funeral home. The Giant Eagle is at the far edge of Squirrel Hill, bordering on Greenfield.

Of the three of us, my mother is the most impressionable. While my father and I trail behind, she gets carried away with her shopping cart, marveling at the display of frozen pizzas, calculating the best price for a pound of apples. She follows the supermarket circulars as if they were a map to a treasure island, and soon we lose her. "Masha, where's your mother?" my father says.

We find her in the aisle of canned soups. She is talking to a wiry boy who looks my age—seventeen, maybe eighteen, twenty.

"Alick is from Moscow," she says. "He came to Pittsburgh all alone."

"An exchange student," explains Alick. He shakes my father's hand, and I step back a little. He looks to be the kind my parents adore. The best student in class, always in the first row. A geek, *a botanist*, as we used to call them at my Moscow school.

Alick smiles at me, and it's the unpleasantly wholesome American smile. It emanates charm and fluoride, good fortune and good breeding, and you either know it's fake and don't trust it, or you trust it too much.

"You're living all alone? It must be hard," my mother says. "You must be missing your parents."

Yes, confirms Alick, he misses them a lot, worries about them stuck in Russia with the Russian economy forever plunging, worries practically every day, sometimes can't even sleep at night. My parents give me quick, chiding looks—that's what children are supposed to be like.

HE LIVES BY THE UNIVERSITY, but his job is in Squirrel Hill. Four nights a week he works at Rosenthal's Pizza on Murray, a faded yellow building with blue lettering, nestled between the travel agency and Judaica Books. The following night he comes over, bearing a large cardboard box of leftover pizza slices—a move sure to win over my parents. At dinner, he tells us about his job, about the Hasids who come to the restaurant for their kosher pizza, sweating in their heavy jackets and hats, their beards and *payess* slick and unclean. They leave miserable tips or sometimes no tip at all. Goddamn Jews, Alick says, and smiles. He is, like the rest of us, unmistakably Jewish, with his squiggly looks and black curly hair. We don't like Hasids either.

To my mother Alick relates the hurdles of his solitary life; to my father he explains the advantages of Visa over American Express. We learn that he is twenty, studies business at the University of Pittsburgh, and that both of his parents teach economics at Moscow State University.

"He's got a good head on his shoulders," my father says, when Alick finally goes home. "Unlike you, Masha."

MY FATHER IS WRONG and he knows it: I've always been a good student. In our class in Moscow, I was the fifth best in physics and in math; my composition on *Fathers and Sons* was sent to the regional Olympics; and if it weren't for chemistry, I might have graduated with a silver medal. This is what I think as I sit in my daily English class and practice dialogues from the *Easy Steps* workbook.

"No man will ever notice you if you look so sleepy," whispers Regina. She is sixty and well-preserved. She wears her hair up, twirled into a crown, and her makeup is tasteful. It is unclear what men she is referring to; the only men in our High Intermediate ESL are worn-out middle-aged engineers with bratty kids in Allderdice High School and loud wives in the Advanced Beginner class next door.

"Brighten up, Masha," Regina orders me. "Look at Larisa, how her eyes are always shiny." Regina likes to maintain contact with the younger generation. In our class, the young generation is me, Lariska, and Mila and Yana, the twin sisters from Donetsk.

At lunch, Lariska and I take our sandwiches and yogurt outside. Lariska is two years older than me, with dusky fuzz on the sides of her face and eyebrows grown together in a loose checkmark. She wears turtlenecks from the $9.99 store, and I don't think she is all that pretty. She's been here for four months and she tells me there are no appealing boys among the new immigrants. She is in love with an "old-timer," a mysterious distant cousin, Zhenechka. He has a girlfriend, but Lariska is working to fix that.

"Any progress?" I ask.

"He still doesn't know what's good for him," complains Lariska. She shows up at Zhenechka's house unannounced and ready to seduce. His parents adore her. "He's melting too," she says. "I think he's melting." When she is upstairs in his room, his parents don't disturb them.

"Do you know if you're supposed to wait to have sex after a yeast infection?" she asks me. "Because I think I'm going to sleep with him on Thursday."

I say I don't know. She has it all planned anyway.

ALICK KEEPS COMING OVER for dinner. Not every night, but often, three or four nights a week. He sits at our dining room table, all smiles and good behavior.

"Loans are good," he tells my parents. "That's how you build your credit history." He explains to them how credit history is important and how loans are "the American way."

"Now, what did you do in Moscow?" he asks my father, and listens to him mumble about circuits and resistors.

"I think you'll be able to get a good job here," Alick says with the confidence of a fortune-teller. "Do you know how to do a résumé?"

I get up and go to my room, where I try to read F. Scott Fitzgerald without a dictionary. Then I walk outside, check the mailbox—a few glossy flyers from a furniture store, a *PennySaver*, no letters.

Later, my parents scold me for ignoring Alick.

"What's your problem?" my father says. "He's a good guy, so what's your problem?"

"Can't you be a little nicer to him?" says my mother. "The boy is all alone—show some kindness. How did you manage to grow into such a hard person?"

I tell them Alick bores me. I tell them I'm allergic to his cologne.

"You've never been allergic to anything in your life," says my mother.

IN SEPTEMBER Alick asks me out. He invites and I go. I don't even want to. It must be because I want to prove to my parents that it's me Alick cares for, not them. Or maybe it's because of Lariska's *shiny eyes* and Regina. Or maybe it's nothing at all; maybe I'm just lonely, missing my friends   it's only been two months, two months and two weeks, and every time we pass by the karate studio on the way to Giant Eagle I think of a particular classmate back in Moscow who was just starting to notice me at the end of the year, just before we left.

We have dinner at Burger King. Alick orders two cutlets layered between the bread buns. "You hold it with both hands, like this," he instructs me. "Then you bite into it." *Listen, genius,* I want to say, *my mouth doesn't open that wide.* I pick up the ungainly sandwich and try to preserve my decorous European ways. It falls apart, its soggy layers sliding, dripping mayonnaise, spilling shredded lettuce.

"I think I need a fork."

On the way home, Alick does all the talking—the quick succession of family history and useful information. He tells me jokes, old Armenian Radio anecdotes. He tries to imitate the Armenian accent:

Is it possible to build socialism in Switzerland?

It's possible, but why? What has Switzerland ever done to you?

I steal sidelong glances at him—his childish face, small body.

"So, Manya," he says, and I cringe at this unwelcome variation on my name, "what are *you* going to study at the university?"

"It's Masha. I hate it when people call me Manya."

"Come on, Manya is cute. My best friend in Moscow is Manya. Don't worry, I'll help you with your college applications."

Oh, the vexation. This is not what I want. Not this boy with his adolescent chicken-neck and his outdated jokes. What I need is somebody like my blond ex-classmate with his muscles and his karate, somebody strong and assured who would shield me from this world.

In our apartment all the lights are dimmed and blue streaks dance across the window in the room where my parents are watching TV. And all I feel is this unsettling longing. I sigh involuntarily. Now Alick will think it's about him, about our so-called date being over.

But he understands. He looks at me and his eyes are encouraging and quiet. He says, "Give it time. Things will turn out right." He says, "I'll call you. Tomorrow." I watch him walk back to the bus stop, the vague outline of his backpack melting in the dark, and I think it might be okay to be friends. I might need it.

AFTER ENGLISH CLASS I wait for my parents. They are in Advanced Beginner next door. Then we walk home together. Susan, my parents' teacher, hurries by, late for her bus. She's young and dark-haired and into bodybuilding.

"See you later, alligator." She waves to my parents.

"In a while, crocodile," my father grins back. It's a little rhyme they've learned in class this week.

"What did she say?" my mother asks.

"Nothing. She said good-bye." My father doesn't like to explain things.

"No, there was something else. I'm not crazy."

"She said good-bye. In English. Were you in class today? Were you listening?"

"Masha, you tell me. What did she say?"

"I don't know. I wasn't listening. Leave me alone."

I hate being in the middle. I hate being with them at all times, everywhere they go—classes, welfare, dentist's office, supermarket. I translate forms and letters; I interpret. This is my job and I'm required to go along.

Then there are tears. Right in the middle of the street my mother is crying; her lips twist helplessly and her face bunches up.

"You're hiding things from me. You hate me. You're ashamed of me because my English is bad." She takes off, walks ahead of us, tripping, smearing those tears.

I glance at my father—*Should we hurry up? Should we go get her?* His face says, *No, we shouldn't,* and we continue to walk, slightly behind, following my mother's uneven gait.

"WHERE'S YOUR BOYFRIEND TODAY?" says my father. He's recently taken to calling Alick my boyfriend, seeing how much it annoys me.

"A boyfriend?" mouths Lariska, who has stopped by on her way to a store.

"He's not my boyfriend," I say to my father. "Don't listen to him," I tell Lariska.

It goes like this: I come home from English class, lie down on my bed, face the wall. I wait for the phone to ring, and it always does, always at the same time. The clocks are doing their countdown, matching my own panicky heartbeat, whispering, rustling: *There's still time to escape—leave the house, think of a good excuse.*

I never say no. I take a bus to Shadyside, to Oakland, to downtown—wherever it is Alick and I meet. On the bus, I'm full of misgivings—I breathe in shallow, nervous gulps, and listen to my stomach churn. But when I see Alick, my wariness fades. Our companionship is effortless and easy. We roam Pittsburgh streets, together but unconnected. He doesn't take my hand, and this space between us feels safe. We have coffee at Dunkin' Donuts; we go to the Carnegie Museum; I am getting used to the smell of his cologne.

LARISKA AND I GO SHOPPING at Hit or Miss. It's pretend shopping. We pick out corduroy skirts and synthetic sweaters that we'll buy later, when we have money. Lariska talks about her Zhenechka. They sleep together now, but still he shows no initiative, and she's pretty sure he hasn't told his girlfriend yet.

On the way out we run into the twins, Mila and Yana from Donetsk. Mila needs a blouse for a birthday party tomorrow.

"Great," I say. "Whose birthday?"

You don't know him, they tell me.

They must hear a certain optimistic eagerness in my voice, because they rush to explain that they don't admit newcomers into their snug circle of cousins and friends.

"Our group is pretty big as it is," says Mila.

"It's a pretty solid group, you know," adds Yana. "It's not exactly up to us."

In English class, the twins are chatty and sweet; they hang with me and Lariska during lunch breaks; we joke together about boys and about the old rat Gretchen from the Career Development Center.

"Who needs them," I tell Lariska after we leave the store, and Lariska agrees that nobody needs them.

"You know," she says, "they are just afraid new girls will steal their men."

THIS IS WHAT'S WRONG with immigration. Those who could be your friends at home here become cautious competitors. Parents envy their children. Sisters become dangerous—all that private information they can unleash at a strategically chosen moment. It's about surviving. Immigration distorts people. We walk around distorted.

I tell this to Alick right after I tell him about Mila and Yana.

"But seriously, Manya," he says, "what did you expect? They are from Donetsk."

"It has nothing to do with Donetsk."

"Come on, you and I, we are two mature intelligent people talking here. Are you going to tell me about Donetsk? Have you been to Donetsk? It's small, it's provincial. Culturally it's just not the same."

"It would be the same even if they were from Moscow," I say. But silently I doubt it. With Alick, who is from Moscow, nothing feels distorted. He tells me about his friends back in Russia. They send him letters, tapes, videos of the parties he's missed. I start learning their names, then faces. They are not unlike my friends, except a little louder and bolder.

We watch the videos together, the new ones and the old ones Alick has made himself. They are a little wild back there, those guys pouring drinks and disappearing to the balcony to smoke, the girls in miniskirts and white ruffled blouses dancing to Roxette, the few boisterous couples making out in dark corridors.

I identify the girl who must be Alick's girlfriend. She wears longish dresses, the kind that little girls wear to birthday parties. She moves skittishly across the room to get away from the camera. She hides behind a piano. When the camera catches up with her, she blushes, and sometimes there is a tiny smile of embarrassed joy and, strangely, of gratitude, and then I know that the person behind the camera is Alick.

Her name is Katya, Alick tells me. She's in Philadelphia now, also an exchange student. He says she's an old friend. On another tape she's wearing a sleeveless dress and the two of them slow-dance.

"YOU DO NOTHING around here," my father says, when he finishes his soup. I set my spoon aside and look at him. We've just come home from the doctor's office where I filled out all the paperwork and then tried to explain my father's medical history, except I kept confusing the word for *kidney* with the word for *liver*.

"*Nothing*," my father repeats. "Every minute you spend with Alick."

My mother says nothing.

I tell them I can't believe it. I tell them that nothing I do is ever enough. I tell them they can stuff themselves with my unfinished soup. Then I run out of the room.

My mother comes onto the porch a minute later. "Masha," she says, "please go back to the table. You know how your father is; he is stressed."

I used to have this confused idea, this delirious noble dream— we come to America and I immediately begin to work, an unglamorous, hard job. I support the whole family and they are grateful, grateful and also proud of me because I go to school at night. But things are different. I can't get a job because of the welfare thing, and I can't go to school because of the financial aid thing. So instead I translate and interpret for my parents. I make all the phone calls too, while they argue over my head, pushing me to say contradictory things. I tell them that if they want to argue they can make their own phone calls. I tell them that I'm tired and nervous, and that my English isn't good, at least not good enough to deal with them screaming and with an American person on the other end not understanding me. They call me lazy and irresponsible and say that the next time they will have to ask Alick, a stranger, for help, because their own daughter is too damn selfish. Which is fine, they say, because the next time I need something from *them*, I better be prepared to wait a long, *very long* time.

ALICK HELPS ME with my college applications. He sneaks me into the computer lab in the basement of the Cathedral of Learning, and I am afraid that someone will identify me as a non-student.

Alick laughs and calls me a silly teapot. "Thirteen thousand students," he says, "and that's just the undergrads. Who's going to notice you?"

I am typing an essay for my applications—one to the University of Pittsburgh, another to Carnegie Mellon University. Alick is checking his e-mail. He gets e-mails from Katya, the girl on the videotapes. I know she is his girlfriend or ex-girlfriend, even though he doesn't say it and I don't know how to ask.

He talks about Katya with admiration. She's driven, and smart, and ambitious. She got accepted at Wharton. What's Wharton? A really great business school in Philadelphia.

"How do you spell *achievements*?" I interrupt, and he shows me how to use a spell-checker.

—

"MARIYA," SAYS REGINA, "I hear you got yourself a little special friend?" She calls me by my passport name, uses the formal *you*, as if to say, *See, I treat you like a grown-up*. It comes out condescending, and I always suspect she means it that way. And what is a *little friend* anyway?

I say I don't know what she's talking about.

"Oh, stop it," she says. "What's your boyfriend's name? Your parents told me."

The Donetsk twins are listening now. They say they know who he is, he is that little Russian guy who works at Rosenthal's Pizza and wears a yarmulke. I hate the Donetsk twins; they do these things—loiter on Murray with their cozy entourage, stop at random restaurants. And yes, Alick does wear a yarmulke at work; it's a kosher restaurant; he has to; it's like a uniform there.

HE COMES FROM HIS JOB at Rosenthal's Pizza exhausted and humiliated. He earns little. He has student loans and other debts. He says his throat hurts.

There's little I can do to help. I offer him minty lozenges and we play music on my tape player. A famous Russian rocker, hoarse and lonesome, screams his despair.

> *What is autumn—autumn is a sky.*
> *Crying sky under my feet.*

A strange, tender dependency has developed between us lately, and all the songs we listen to have become meaningful. I rewind the song to the beginning and he stands behind my chair. One day we'll be living in New York City, careless and sparkly, without a trace of sadness. "Rockefeller Center," says Alick. "I'll show you the Rockefeller Center. And Central Park. You'll love it in New York." His checks bounce and his phone bill is unpaid. We are not even a couple. He puts his hands on my shoulders, and I am not sure what this means.

> *Autumn, ships are burned in the skies.*
> *Autumn, I need to get up there*
> *Where all the sorrows are drowned.*

YANA, THE QUIETER of the Donetsk twins, now has a boyfriend. His name is Mike—well, Misha really, but everybody likes to say *Mike*, with a special influx of air, even pretty Susan who teaches the class next door, even Regina who is old and married. He is tall, with unkempt facial hair and bloodshot eyes. When he comes to class, he sits in the back with his head against the wall and his eyes closed. The girls go crazy for him; for weeks I've been aware of the complex arrangements—chairs shuffled, looks exchanged, giggles suppressed.

But now he is Yana's. From across the street we watch Yana and Mike walk up and down Murray, both looking ahead, their faces bleak and sober. Are they really together?

Yes, they are, confirms Mila, the loser sister. She yawns—a big lazy yawn, a show of indifference. The lunch break is almost over and it's starting to rain.

"You think she is upset?" I ask Lariska when Mila goes back inside. Lariska shrugs. Yana and Mike keep walking, not eating lunch, not smiling at each other.

"They look weird together," I tell Lariska. "Do you think they have anything in common? Anything to talk about?"

Lariska shivers and looks in her bag for cigarettes.

"And you know what else?" I say. "He smells. Have you noticed? I don't think he showers often."

"It's not like there are options," says Lariska. "You're lucky to have your . . . whatever . . . Alick. It's not like there's much to choose from." There is something wrong with Lariska today. She keeps fumbling for her cigarettes and when she doesn't find any, she curses and goes back inside.

The lunch break is almost over. Yana and Mike walk up and down Murray. There's something wrong with all of us.

MEN AND WOMEN shouldn't be alone. Not on overcast November nights, when it gets dark early and the wind accosts you as you walk nervously from the bus stop. How soothing it is to know that somebody is waiting for you, maybe pacing nervously, listening to the steps outside. He'll see me and understand immediately. Or maybe he already knows, heard something in my voice on the phone when I told him I'd take the 61A bus at a quarter to six.

"I hate this fucking country," Alick says when he opens the door. It's been a bad day for him. The restaurant cut back his hours; his boss said the customers don't like his manners—he has to work on being humble.

"I might just knock off all this stuff and go home. Go to Moscow to my family, my friends. And to hell with America."

I reason with him. It's just a bad day; he'll get another job, a better job. He's achieved so much already. In the refrigerator there's a chicken breast and an onion, and I don't think I can make a meal out of those. I boil pasta and mix it with shredded cheese. That's our supper.

"Things will get better," I say, "because they always do. Eventually." Nonsense, but what else do I say? That he can't leave because of me? Because he promised me New York City and it sounded like we'd be together for a while?

"I don't know, Manya," he says, "maybe I'm too tired to go on." I sit close and listen for the wavering softness in his voice, but I don't hear any and he doesn't touch me. He is sitting on the couch, hugging a pillow, and I stand in front of him, with all of my failed expectations, my jacket in my hands. And then, finally, he sets aside the pillow and takes away my jacket. He pulls me next to him, and it all pays off then—the pasta that I've cooked and my low-cut sweater. He holds me close. I continue to whisper the soft, soothing nonsense in his ear, and we sit like this, rocking slightly, until our lips tenuously touch.

I WAIT FOR HIM to say that he loves me. Isn't that what's supposed to follow, to accompany what we do, what we've been doing for weeks now? His chin, square and ragged, leaves scratches across my cheeks. When it's time to go home, my face always looks a little bruised and I am afraid that my parents will know. I use Cover Girl to hide the redness.

I don't like it much when we actually do it—the pressure, the weight, the pushing. Alick says it will get better once I am used to it more. I like what comes before—the teasing, the slow undressing part. He pulls down the straps of my bra. I watch him undo the zipper on my jeans.

He makes all the good noises, but no words of love are exchanged. Which is strange and disconcerting. Because we are so alike. Because people like us don't do it unless they love each other. We are the Moscow *intelligentsia*, the kids from good Jewish families. The other stuff happens among simpler people—pimply guys from trade schools, high school dropouts with chemically processed hair, the ones who always get in trouble.

He takes me by the wrists, presses me into the pillows. I shouldn't ask any questions. It's a matter of pride, a matter of being wise. I will not ask him any questions.

"What about Katya?" I say.

"What do you want to know?" he murmurs. His mouth is on top of mine, distracting, silencing me.

"No, seriously," I say, wriggling away. "Are you and her . . . ?"

"Katya is just a good girl," he says. His mouth moves away from my lips, down my neck, over my collarbone, between my breasts, down and away where I won't see his face.

HE CALLS HER *kitten*. He says everybody does. It's not even an endearment, he explains, so much as a derivative from her name: Katya—*kotyonok*—kitten. I don't know if I should believe him. She phones him a lot, I know, I'm aware of the situation. Sometimes he takes the call; other times he tells her he has a class to go to. He probably calls her back later, when I'm gone.

On the way to the bus stop, he talks about next year. We both will be in school. We'll take a class together, Russian lit or maybe astronomy. The bus arrives. He kisses me quickly, and for a moment his lips on mine are warm and reassuring. He walks away, not looking back, not waiting for the bus to close its doors.

LARISKA GETS A TEMPORARY JOB wrapping gifts at Kaufmann's department store downtown. I visit her there. Outside, the air is frosty and crisp, and the sky is a triumphant, overpowering blue. It's Christmas season, and my expectations are low.

"Angels or Santas?" Lariska says, waving the samples of wrapping paper. Then she waits for each customer to pick their perfect pattern and the perfect ribbon.

During her lunch break, Lariska buys herself a cup of coffee, and we go to Rite Aid next door. I tell Lariska how wonderful but difficult things are between me and Alick. I try to keep it abstract and hope that Lariska will say something encouraging.

She says it doesn't sound good.

I explain to her my theory: If I am patient, supportive, and sweet, if I avoid unnecessary questions, he'll be happy with me. And if he's happy with me, he won't need anybody else.

"If it's not good in the beginning, it will never get better," says Lariska. She has recently given up on her unresponsive Zhenechka and now there's a new Russian kid who's been courting her—I mean really a kid, still in high school, I think—and she, if not falling for him, is feeling loved and deserving.

For one dollar, left from some unused bus fare, I buy myself a new lipstick, Wet 'n' Wild. It has a deep, almost purple shade and leaves a plastic taste in my mouth. The new lipstick makes me feel like a tough, independent woman, as opposed to the sheltered houseplant that I am.

Lariska says something about playing hard to get, making them beg, making them suffer. She pulls out a copy of *Cosmopolitan* from her bag. "Go home and study," she says, handing me the magazine.

ALICK HASN'T CALLED ME in two days, and I'm not calling him either. I'm holding out, showing my character, the strength of my will. I've read Lariska's *Cosmopolitan* and then went out and bought this month's copy: *10 Tips for the World's Lustiest Lovers. Land That Man, Ace Your Job.*

So now I am not calling him and he is not calling me and it's snowing. In my room I study what it means to be an American woman: strappy sandals, skimpy suits, the hair—straight and shiny. A Russian woman is all about hardships, guilt, and endurance. She waits and forgives and then waits some more. But an American woman doesn't wait: she puts on a push-up bra and has meaningless sex whenever she feels like it.

Alick calls me at noon. He says his classes have been canceled because of the snow.

Look Your Best Ever, the magazine suggests, and I try. I put on my purple lipstick and a gauzy shirt that is kind of transparent. I practice the indifferent, slightly scornful look of the *Cosmopolitan* models.

I know I've done something right when Alick forgets to offer me tea. I like the way he steps back a little when I first come in. What does he see in my face? What kind of ruthless intent?

The clothes rip under our fingers—the buttons, the zippers, the impatience of it all. He leaves my shirt unbuttoned but hanging off my shoulders; he says the gauzy material turns him on—its whiteness, its presumed innocence.

Our bodies swing in a harsh, grinding motion. The phone rings—we pay no attention to the phone. Fingers grip, leaving imprints; teeth scrape against the skin. We do it the *Cosmopolitan* way—sex for the sake of sex.

MY PARENTS SAY I spend too much time at Alick's, but it's not true. There are now uncertain intervals between our meetings, some scheduling manipulations I don't understand. There are days of nervousness and days of apathy. I stay home a lot.

My parents are irrational, impossible to be around. There seems to be an angry electric current running through their blood. I understand. I try to be understanding. It's because of the jobs, there are no jobs in Pittsburgh. They've been to the résumé-writing workshops and to the interview-going workshops; they've memorized hundreds of sample dialogues and know how to write the perfect thank-you letter. But nobody wants a former teacher and an engineer with minimal English skills.

They take it out on me and on each other. We don't look much like a family anymore. But we have to stick together—there are still appointments, phone calls, and Giant Eagle.

We stand shivering in the meat and frozen-food section.

"Are you done yet?" says my father.

My mother idles, turns over the packages of frozen chicken, picks up one, then another, then both.

"Slow down, Lina. It's not the last chicken in America."

"I know what I'm doing," says my mother. "Today it's ninety-nine cents a pound, tomorrow it will be twice as much."

"We've been here for an hour, Lina. Enough already."

"You two can wait for me outside," says my mother. "I'll manage without your help."

"Bitch," he says, and storms out of the store.

It's a bad sign when my father blows up like this. He never used to curse in my presence, but now they both do and it doesn't even shock me anymore. I follow him outside. We watch flabby Americans load chickens into the trunks of their all-absorbing cars. My father smokes a cigarette. I walk the length of the sidewalk—from the soda machine to the uneven formation of the supermarket carts and back.

It's better to say nothing. It's better to be invisible. Otherwise he will remember everything he hates about me too: that I don't do enough around the house, that I haven't heard from the schools yet, that I spend too much time with Alick, that my English is good, that my English isn't good enough, that he still has to worry about me and my future, and that without a job there's not much he can do for me.

"I DON'T KNOW IF IT'S RIGHT that I've told you. But I thought you should know," says Lariska. She's sitting on the edge of a chair in our living room, stirring sugar into a cup of tea.

"When was it?" I say. "Are you sure?"

She says, Last week, at a party. Alick was there. With Katya. Lariska had never seen Katya before, but she's pretty sure that's how he introduced the girl. Everybody was there—Yana, Mila, Mike, snub-nosed Vika. I imagine the Donetsk twins whispering, exchanging knowing looks, laughing at me behind my back.

"Will you be okay?" says Lariska. She's going to New York with her boyfriend, the one who looks like he is twelve. Perhaps it's all a mistake, a rumor. Squirrel Hill is full of rumors.

"I think it's best to know these things," she says. "You're going to tell him, right? You're going to stop seeing him now?"

I shake my head: *I don't know.*

She says something about dignity and self-respect.

"I have to go," she says. She's busy these days, busy with her new boyfriend. And the twins, who approve of her current situation, now include her in their plans. She gives me a pack of little green pills. In case it gets bad and I can't sleep. She says she feels terrible she won't be around.

—

FOR A WHILE, Lariska's two green pills a day keep me subdued and indifferent, but then they are gone and it's bad again. When Alick calls, he says, "Manya, please! Don't create a tragedy out of nothing." When I call, he says he can't talk—Katya is in town for her spring break.

I am afraid to run into them, so I don't leave the apartment. I pace my room, hover over the phone, Alick's number pulsing in my fingers. My parents circle around me, afraid to come close. My heart is fast, my stomach is queasy. I envy people who smoke.

"Do you love him that much?" asks Lariska.

I say no, I hate him now, but it doesn't matter.

"It could've been worse," she tells me. "You could've been pregnant."

At first I think, *She's right.* Then I think, *What if I am?* Suddenly it all makes sense, the jittery feeling in my fingers, the question mark in my stomach, the strange flu-like fever I had two days ago—a bug, I said, but isn't fever also a sign?

I won't know for another week, and even then I might not know right away. I study calendars. I study *Cosmopolitan*s. But they don't tell me about the symptoms, and I don't want to ask Lariska. There's nobody to ask. The question mark quivers in my stomach, and I realize I've had slight but noticeable nausea since the previous morning.

I lie down on my bed, pull the covers up to my chin—now I'm a small, dying person. There will be no college; nobody will ever love me. I have ruined my life.

On the other side of the wall, I can hear the movie my parents are watching on TV (the muttering of dialogue, the dramatic splashes of music). They are arguing, good-naturedly, about whether we should find a cheaper apartment for next year and whether our landlord is a scoundrel. It used to be okay, our life before this moment, our English classes, our doctor's appointments. The welfare. The Career Development Center once a month. Even our fights were okay.

The movie ends (the credits music falling down in big piano chords), and they come into my room, my parents. My father is looking indecisive and gentle, like when I was seven years old and had mumps. He says, "What's the deal, rabbit?" And my mother is peeking over his shoulder, looking frumpy and a little out of it, like she's just had a nap. "Are you feeling sick, Masha?" she says.

And then, it's like I *am* a seven-year-old with mumps, and they have come to read to me and brought me mechanical color pencils. I know I shouldn't tell them, but—*It's over; it doesn't matter*—I start crying and tell them everything. My mother sits down on the edge of my bed, and my father on the chair next to it, and they comfort me, smooth my hair, ask questions. I explain about my stomach and about the nausea, and they call me silly. My mother tells me how she was pregnant with me during their honeymoon (in Pyarnu, in Estonia), how she kept throwing up every morning and completely ruined the honeymoon for everyone involved (a meaningful wink toward my father). It's probably nothing, they say, probably stress, but just in case we'll make an appointment on Monday. And Alick? We don't need Alick. My mother looks at me a little regretfully—she is the one who likes Alick the most. But my father says, Alick is a goat, and we laugh, and my mother laughs too. She shakes her head and says, "What should I make you for supper?"

And it probably won't last, the way the three of us are together like this and laughing. But tonight we are perfect. Tonight we're the way a family should be. It's warm and the heat is rattling in the basement like a high-speed train, sending puffs of hot air through the floor vents. There's plenty of chicken and frozen pizza in our refrigerator. And there's *Child's Play 2* starting on the Movie Channel, which we somehow get for free. After supper my mother will distribute the bars of Klondike ice cream and we will huddle together in front of the TV, shuddering and laughing at the horrors of Chucky the doll, feeling warm and fortunate in our American apartment. Feeling like we have everything.

What Do You Dream Of,
Cruiser *Aurora*?

LIBERMAN MET MIRA on the flight to New York. For twelve hours, they sat across the aisle from each other—stretching, lurching into bleary dreams, stirring awake when there was turbulence, sipping tomato juice from plastic see-through cups, not risking anything stronger—two ponderous old people, both traveling alone. He didn't want to talk to her. She was a chatterbox; he could tell by the way she'd been going on to her neighbor, an Armenian woman in the window seat. To avoid conversation, he kept his eyes closed. But eventually a restrained understanding developed between them. When Mira's earphones broke, Liberman offered her his pair. When he had to use the bathroom, he asked her to look after his things.

They were on a charter flight from Leningrad, an uneasy mass of immigrants, and everybody had a story to tell. The woman next to Mira had lost her two sons in the recent Armenian massacre: one was dead, the other was missing. She hoped to find him in America. Liberman was lucky compared to her. He still had his family, even if it was splintered. His son stayed in Leningrad; his daughter, Dinka, lived in Pittsburgh.

Most of the people traveled in families. There was one seated behind Liberman—a married couple with two children and their grandmother, Berta. He'd noticed them at Pulkovo airport. The old woman didn't seem right. *Where's Berta? Go fetch your Grandma Berta.* She kept wandering off, a stooped creature in a long woolen coat, her face scrunched up and bored. It was the same on the plane. She didn't seem to know where she was. *Grandma, wait! Grandma, where're you going?*

And where was Liberman going? He thought of his farewell party two evenings before. The whole mishpocheh had gathered to ready him for the trip—his son, Arkasha; his sisters-in-law, Tsilya and Fanya; their daughters, young soaring girls in spring coats; grandchildren and husbands. The little ones had given him a concert—a stumbling version of the Dance of Little Swans and a song, "What Do You Dream Of, Cruiser *Aurora?*" They sang slowly, painstakingly turning out melodious vowels: *Is it your sa-a-ailors, in black overcoa-a-ats . . .* Tsilya and Fanya furtively blotted their eyes. He chided them softly ("What's the matter? Tsilechka? Fanechka? No one's dying") and cuddled their small, callused palms.

To listen to Arkasha's wife, Tatiana, it didn't matter where he was going or whether he was going at all. "St. Petersburg or Pittsburgh, it's almost the same thing," joked Tatiana. "You'll come visit us in a year or two. In a big cowboy hat and boots with spurs."

"And pistols," said Arkasha.

Arkasha's girls giggled. They liked that, the image of Liberman with pistols. "Grandpa the cowboy," they said. "Grandpa the bandit."

He fell asleep during the last hour of the flight and woke up as the plane was swooping over New York, everyone craning to see the green goliath of the Statue of Liberty. They landed shortly afterwards. All the passengers stood and applauded their pilot and one another. They had arrived. It was the end of one struggle and the beginning of many others, though no one seemed to be thinking about that yet. They were hugging. The Armenian woman cried. Mira turned to Liberman and offered him her hand.

"I'm Mira," she said.

"Liberman," he said, "Mikhail Abramovich. My compliments." He even attempted a quaint little bow. How odd, he thought, surprised at himself and at her. What was the point of introductions now?

"Take care, Mikhail Abramovich."

They'd shared this twelve-hour journey, and they'd barely talked, and now they'd never see each other again. Was it the thought of another departure that bothered him, or was he afraid of being left alone? He pictured himself in search of his connecting flight, lost in the crannies of the New York airport. It didn't seem fair.

But twenty minutes later they were still together, crammed in a line to get their passports stamped, in a room tight and stuffy (so many of them!) and smelling of plastic partitions and carpet. Liberman and Mira stood next to each other; Berta with her family ahead of them. It must have been the smell or the hard stagnant air that made Berta faint. She swayed, her body slackened. Mira gripped Liberman's elbow. "Look," she said, and they watched Berta's slow collapse.

The line collapsed as well. An anxious circle formed around Berta and her family. *Prop her up! No, let her stay! Is there a doctor in here?* A bottle of ammonia was passed around. Berta sneezed twice; it seemed to make her better. Finally, a bald INS man appeared among them. The crowd parted, and he kneeled in front of Berta and stared harshly into Berta's blurry eyes.

"A hypnotist," Mira whispered to Liberman.

She was still holding on to his arm, breathing heavily through her mouth. People were dispersing, and it was clear now that Berta would be fine. She was sitting up, twisting her head left to right. Rumpled like a sparrow, alert again, embraced by her family— lucky, lucky Berta.

HE NEVER PLANNED to go America. It all happened suddenly, quickly, without his involvement. Phone calls, paperwork. He blamed it on sickness, too much sickness. First, Sara, two years ago, a silent ischemia aggravated by pneumonia, a week at the hospital, and she was gone. He'd seen her that morning; she'd been cheerful, busy, weaving a goldfish from old IV tubes; she sent him home and he promised to come back around suppertime, and in the afternoon he got the hospital call. Then, a month later, Liberman's brother-in-law had a stroke. Then Liberman himself, a heart attack. Then apathy. He didn't even know when it started, swept over him, opaque like a fog. That was when Dinka and Arkasha began their campaign to get him out of the country.

Dinka picked him up at the airport in Pittsburgh. In the five years since he'd seen her, she'd grown imperial, stout. Her dress, black with flowers, pulled tight against her belly and her butt. She brought him lilies. Her husband, Slavik, wispy, bespectacled, rapidly blinking, shook Liberman's hand. Pavlik was there, too—eight years old, soft and doughy. "Come give your grandpa a hug," said Dinka. He did. He said, "Hello, *Dedushka* . . . Grandpa." The stress was on the wrong syllable, and it hurt Liberman to know that the boy spoke Russian with an accent.

He spent the first week at Dinka's house in the suburbs, sleeping in the living room downstairs, on the red velvety couch. His first morning there, a Sunday, he woke to the shuffling noises of Pavlik sneaking into the kitchen. A sigh, a knock, a clink. Pavlik said, "Ouch, ouch." Then he was creeping back, his plate piled with waffles. Liberman watched him, feigning sleep. Pavlik looked so serious, so deliciously clumsy, a sweet roll of a child. Liberman couldn't help but give a wink. Pavlik was startled. For a moment, he stared at his grandfather, and then he squeezed his eyes shut and fled upstairs.

Was Liberman scary or just unfamiliar? He meant to ask Dinka. It didn't used to be like this, not back in Leningrad when Pavlik was three and he read him *Telephone* by Kornei Chukovsky:

> *And then crocodile!*
> *In tears he dialed:*
> *Do send us galoshes.*
> *For me and my wife and Totosha.*

Such sweet and joyful nonsense.

The following week, he moved into a furnished apartment on Beacon Street in Squirrel Hill. Other people's furniture made Liberman nervous. He dusted the surfaces of the cupboard and the nightstand. During meals, he sat sideways, trying to occupy only the tiniest corner of the dinner table. His third day there, he unpacked his things. The walls of the apartment were cream-colored and bare, and he decided what the hell, he'd decorate. He fixed two pictures of matching sailboats over the dinner table. Above his bed, he put a broken barometer, its needle now always stuck on *storm*. The centerpiece was a framed picture of Sara. In it, she was a young woman with a recklessly drawn mouth and eyes so bewildered it seemed she was asking what both of them were doing in this strange apartment.

Dinka didn't approve of his work. "You're such a punishment,

Papa. Look what you've done, you've spoiled all the walls." She came to see him every day at four o'clock. Dinka was practical, so practical it scared him sometimes, her thinking blunt, unsentimental. He studied the side of her face, her close-cropped hair, her crude and aggressive makeup. There was no airiness in her, no light. She looked nothing like Sara.

On the fourth day, there was a knock on his door. He thought it might be his landlord, coming to see the spoiled walls, but when he opened the door he saw Mira.

"You?" he said. "What are you doing here?"

The last time he'd seen her was at the airport in Pittsburgh. He hadn't thought of her since, but here she was, in slippers and a housecoat, as if she lived in an apartment next door.

She did live in the building. "Didn't you know?" she said. "Here. I brought you a housewarming gift." She gave him a packet of cookies and a small crystal vase in a box.

He looked at the box. "Where did you get it?"

"Where do you think? I stole it?" said Mira. "I *brought* it with me."

"You brought it? From Leningrad? You brought a vase? We had a luggage limit, two bags, one carry-on."

"You had your limit and I had my limit. What's the matter? What did *you* bring?"

He wasn't sure anymore. Books? Pictures? Clothes? He remembered some things he'd been told not to bring—Sara's silver pin (too old, he wouldn't get it past customs), or the handcrafted replica of the cruiser *Aurora*, his retirement gift, thirty-three inches from bow to stern, complete with eight lifeboats.

"How did you know I lived here?" he said.

"I know things," said Mira. "I saw your daughter coming in. I saw your name on a mailbox downstairs."

She lived in the apartment below his. It was identical, she said,

except she liked his kitchen floor better. His was parquet. Hers was
spotted linoleum. "I can hear you walk," she said.

It was true: he walked, he paced, he had silent conversations
with himself (sometimes not so silent). Had he made a mistake?
Could he go back now? Or was it too late? He'd left his Leningrad
apartment to Arkasha, which meant he would have nowhere to
live. He could live with Arkasha, but Arkasha's wife wouldn't like
it. He wondered now if Mira had ideas like that. Of course they
weren't acquainted enough, so he couldn't ask her.

They went for a walk instead. It was April and already too
warm, much warmer than in Leningrad. He wore his army green
trench. She put on a winter coat with fake rabbit fur. There were
no cowboys in Pittsburgh, no bandits. Instead, there were orderly
streets full of churches and synagogues, dark Gothic structures.
Bearded Orthodox Jews in black hats roamed the sidewalks.

"Your children live here?" said Liberman.

She told him she had none. She had a sister and niece in Mount
Lebanon.

"My daughter's in Monroeville," said Liberman.

"That's not so far," said Mira. "Have you been there?"

He said, "Of course."

"You have?"

It was as if he had offended her. They walked in silence for a
while. But with Mira, he was learning, you could never have long
silences. She told him about the stores they were passing. Rite Aid
was cheaper than Thrift Drugs. Giant Eagle was okay if you used
coupons. The street was uneven and hilly, and it made Mira breathless with air and words. She kept checking her watch.

"Where are we going?" he said.

"JCC. Jewish Community Center. They have lunches for seniors. We get a membership for free, because we're immigrants."

The JCC was on Darlington Road—a sprawl of red brick, an arched entrance, a hallway that smelled of chlorine. "There's a swimming pool downstairs," said Mira. And it was true, they could see it through a big picture window, its water turbid and gray, brimming with swimmers.

In the lunchroom, Russian seniors were clustered to the right. You could recognize them immediately: men in ill-fitting brown trousers, women in cotton dresses and knitted cardigans, all of it purchased a long time ago and altered repeatedly. Lips pursed sternly, faces stiff. Compared to them, the Americans (mostly women) looked like careless parakeets—bright, excessively painted, and cheerful.

Mira led him to one of the big round tables. A man, angular and slender, was reading the *New Russian Word*. Across from him sat a tiny old woman.

"Greetings, Boris Alexandrovich," said Mira. The man nodded to her and folded his newspaper. She sat next to him, and Liberman sat on the other side of her.

"How's your health today?" Mira asked Boris.

"The heart's fooling around."

"Such tsoris," said the tiny woman. "No health. No health at all." *God's Dandelion*, Liberman thought of her. She turned to him and Mira. "And you?" she said. "Who are you? Where are you from? I haven't seen you two before."

She seemed to think that he and Mira were together, and it embarrassed him. He liked women with lilting voices, with the complicated scent of lotion on their hands. Mira's hands looked rough, and her voice was full of soreness and moisture.

He said he was from Leningrad.

"We're from Kiev," said God's Dandelion. *We*, she said, and he knew she had come with her family. That was how the people at

JFK Airport had talked—*we*—perched on top of their orphans' bags, each family banded together, spreading like a Gypsy encampment. That was the proper way to emigrate, so you wouldn't feel like an intruder later, so your grandson wouldn't get afraid.

On the way home, they walked down Darlington. "It's more scenic," said Mira. It was. They walked slowly, ogling the queenly colonials and their less fortunate neighbors, which, Mira explained, were split into apartments and rented out. At one of those rental houses, she stopped abruptly.

Liberman looked at the house. It had a porch with an intricate iron grating, and there on the porch stood Berta, the woman who'd fainted at JFK Airport. He said, "Berta, my God!"

Her housecoat had snaps instead of buttons, and her shoes were unfastened. She moved haltingly, like she was tethered to the porch.

"It's time to go back to Leningrad," she said. "We're going tomorrow, by train."

"She thinks she's back in Russia, at their dacha," Mira explained.

"I know," he said. He thought it was easy to make such a mistake, what with the provincial streets, two-storied houses, backyards full of squirrels and birds.

"This is America," Mira said loudly.

"What rubbish you're talking." Berta twisted her mouth.

Liberman said they should leave her alone.

"We'll see you later, Berta," said Mira. But Berta's attention had already been diverted by the voices inside the house.

"Must be sclerosis," Mira said to Liberman, when they resumed their walking.

"She's lonely here," he said.

"She barely knows her name. She'd be just as lonely back home."

"Maybe," he said. "Maybe not." He hated it when elderly people were treated like babies, as if they didn't have souls, as if all they needed now were food and rest and medical support. He hated it when Dinka called him *a punishment*. He knew it was just an expression, she didn't mean it, but still, *a punishment*? He was her father.

"You know," said Mira, "that's what I fear the most, to grow like Berta, senile."

LIBERMAN DREAMT HE WAS IN Leningrad. He was taking Arkasha's girls for a walk along the Neva embankment. They were looking at bridges, and he told them how at night the bridges came to life, rose like magnificent animals to let tall ships pass. The girls' laughter was fragile like wind chimes; it filled him with astonishing tenderness, and he knew then that his love for them was absolute, not at all like the critical love he'd had for Arkasha and Dinka when they were growing up.

Dinka seemed pleased he'd found the JCC lunches. She said she would've taken him herself, except she'd been completely spinning lately. "It's all such a hustle," she said, and he wasn't sure whether she meant work, family, or him. He was trying to be self-sufficient. He went to free English classes for seniors, another bonus from the JCC. Four times a week. The classes were taught by a fidgety woman from Russia, Lilya Glikman. She volunteered at the JCC. In Moscow she was a geography teacher.

There were eight of them there. Boris Aleksandrovich had the best English, and God's Dandelion the worst because she never did her homework. Lilya's own English wasn't very good, so she used a tape player. She put them in pairs and made them do dialogues ("What are your plans?" "I want to go into Manhattan." "It is a great town, New York!"). She also had a tape with songs.

In May, the JCC arranged a trip to the Carnegie Museum. The

trip was for seniors, both Russian and American. It was free, spaces were limited, and they had to sign up in advance. There would be a bus and a tour guide.

"We're going," said Mira. She'd heard about the museum. It had a cardboard box of ketchup on display, and some pictures by Andy Warhol. Did Liberman know who Andy Warhol was? He didn't. "You'll like it," she said.

But Lilya had a different idea. She made a list, in which she ranked them by their language abilities. If you were at the top of the list, you should go to the museum. If your English was poor, you shouldn't be wasting a space. Liberman and Mira, for example. They weren't on the list at all. They were too recent.

"It can't be helped," Liberman said, relieved. He didn't think a ketchup box was art. In general, he didn't like museums.

But Mira said it was discrimination, and threatened to complain to Lilya's superiors. This wasn't Russia anymore, she said, and Lilya, a mere volunteer, had no power to restrict them like that.

The list was canceled. They all signed up for the museum trip. Mira, victorious, said she'd only wanted what was fair. Lilya said she might quit. Liberman felt bad for Lilya.

This was on Wednesday, and it took him two days to remember that he couldn't go on the trip at all. He had a doctor's appointment that day.

"What's wrong with you exactly?" Mira said contentiously, as if she thought he was shirking his duties. "Is it you're sick?"

He said he had a checkup at Falk Clinic. Dinka was taking him.

"Why can't you go to Knutchek? He takes Medicare like everyone else. Plus he speaks Russian, so you could go by yourself."

Dinka, he said, didn't like Dr. Knutchek.

"Can't she reschedule?" said Mira. "If she's so busy, I can take you. I can translate."

He was getting frustrated with Mira. Why was it so hard to understand? His health was more important than museums. He wanted his daughter to take him; he didn't want some stranger. Of course, Mira wasn't a stranger per se, but she wasn't his family either. He valued her friendship and so on—he didn't want to seem ungrateful—but maybe it was good to take a break. He said he didn't think she could translate for him.

The day of his doctor's appointment, Liberman waited for Dinka in the courtyard. He'd waxed his shoes, ironed his shirt, and brushed his one good jacket. He'd wanted to make a good impression, but Dinka was late, and now he stood there stiff like an effigy, conspicuous, dressed up as if for a parade.

Dinka's green station wagon appeared, fifteen minutes late. In the back was Pavlik—a surprise, a startling addition. He'd had a stomachache that morning, Dinka explained. She'd kept him from school, but couldn't find a babysitter. "He might've been faking," she said. "He's capable. Pavlik, sit up straight!"

Pavlik was sprawled in the backseat, not looking sick at all, his stocking feet dangling in the air. "Hello!" said Liberman, twisting to look at him. "Hello, Cruiser *Aurora*!"

"Who?" Pavlik said.

"Don't you remember?" said Liberman. "We used to sing it together. *Dozing lies the becalmed northern city*."

"He doesn't remember," said Dinka. "He was three."

Liberman turned to her. "Why can't *I* be his babysitter?"

"Because," she said slowly, "we're taking you to see a doctor."

"Not now." He winced. She knew perfectly well what he meant. "I mean in general. On other days."

"Well," said Dinka, "for one thing, it's not practical. You live here, we live in Monroeville, and Pavlik is at school until two—"

"I could move to Monroeville."

"You couldn't," said Dinka. "It's too expensive, and besides, you'll miss your friends."

"I don't have any friends," said Liberman. Dinka had been visiting him less and less, counting, he guessed, on Mira. He could sense her reluctance to see him. Even this morning she'd been late.

"Why do I need these doctors anyway?"

"We don't want to take any chances," said Dinka. "It's why I brought you here. So we can look after your health."

Nonsense. He was in fine health.

"I see it all the time," she said. "These poor elderly people arrive, barely walking, barely holding up. And then they come here and *bloom!*"

She looked at Liberman. He wasn't blooming yet.

"Papa," she said, "please don't be cranky. I'm doing all I can."

Cranky, he thought. Another one of Dinka's little words. A *child* is cranky. He looked at the car clock, and wondered how long the appointment would take. He wondered when Mira would be coming back from the museum. She, too, was full of nonsense, and they quarreled occasionally, but someone had to set the poor woman straight. It might as well be Liberman.

THEY TRIED TO VISIT Berta every couple of days, whenever she was out on the porch. They never went inside her house, never talked to her family, though surely the family must have noticed them by now, must have remembered them from the plane. Even Berta herself was starting to recognize them. Mira did her interventions, trying to jolt Berta's memory awake. *What's your grand-daughter's name? What did you have for breakfast?* Liberman felt that Berta liked him better. He never bothered her with questions.

He was feeling a little foggy himself. At his doctor's appointment, nurses had poked his arm with needles, had taken his EKG. It was all normal for his age, the doctor said, though he had to be careful. He wrote him prescriptions and sent him to specialists—a gastroenterologist, a dermatologist, an oculist. "A dermatologist!" Liberman joked to Mira. "They need me to look pretty in my grave?"

If anyone needed a doctor, it was Mira. Summer came, and she discovered shopping. She went after class, every day, almost obsessively. She studied bus schedules, then traveled to Edgewood and Homestead. The shopping was wearing her down, clearly, and he had told her so. "Look at your face," he said. But did she listen? No. "Why are you wasting your money?" he said. "Well, it's my money," she said. "What else should I do with it?"

In truth, she only went to dollar stores. He saw her returning with bags full of naphthalene garments, cheap kitchenware, china dolls. One time she brought him a radio ("How can you live without a radio?"); another time it was a shirt. Used clothes made him squeamish, so he never wore it. He told her the sleeves were too long.

He waited at home for her while she shopped. He'd see her from his window and put the kettle on. By the time she limped upstairs, the tea was ready, along with a plate of butter-and-cheese sandwiches and a saucer of raspberry jam from Three Bears, the Russian store.

They ate and then they did their English homework. Liberman was forgetting the simplest vocabulary words, the dialogues they'd learned some weeks before. She said it was because he didn't practice, but he knew that it wasn't his fault. It was the medicine his doctors kept prescribing him. So much medicine! Dinka got him a special plastic box, with several compartments for each day of the week. The pills made his head thick and cloudy.

Dinka visited him once a week. She took his blood pressure and asked him if he needed anything. Otherwise they had nothing to say to each other. She squirmed if he told her how much he missed and loved her. It was nothing but one of his grievances, she seemed to think. "I can't be with you every minute, Papa. I have to work. We *all* have to work." It was safer to talk of his maladies, simple and clinical things, the burning sensation he felt after meals, the tingling in his feet, the numbness. At the JCC lunches, he listened to the medical complaints of others, and later he found he had all their symptoms as well.

By the end of the summer, they were learning about American holidays in English class ("What do you do on Labor Day?"), and then one afternoon, Lilya, their teacher, decided that Mira needed a more advanced partner. She paired her with Boris Alexandrovich, and told Liberman to sit next to God's Dandelion, who was as bad as Liberman himself.

He couldn't do without Mira. She used to write all their dialogues down. She rescued him whenever he got stuck. They were supposed to make a new dialogue now, using the one in their workbook as an example, but God's Dandelion was whispering to him in Russian. She wanted to know how much he paid for his apartment and whether it was subsidized.

Lilya heard them. She made them stand up and say their dialogue in front of the class, but of course they didn't have one ready. She said they wasted everybody's time.

"You ought to be ashamed," she said. "We're not playing at spillikins here. You, Mikhail Abramovich, I'm especially surprised at you. Why do you bother coming back if you don't want to study?"

Oh, how she hated him! Why did she hate him so? He'd never challenged or bad-mouthed her. In fact, he had defended her sometimes. This puny thing, this peewit! She had no right to speak to him this way. She had no right to take away his Mira. And what about Mira? She just sat there, shoulder to shoulder with Boris Alexandrovich. She wouldn't even raise her eyes.

In the end, he said nothing to either of them. After class, it was raining, and he and Mira stopped under the brick entrance arch. Mira was unfolding her big black umbrella.

"Come to Edgewood with me," she said. "There's a clearance at Pharmor."

Was this her idea of showing remorse?

"I'm busy," he said. "My daughter's coming." That was a lie. Dinka wasn't coming till tomorrow, to take him to the dermatologist. He'd be missing tomorrow's lunch, but Mira didn't know that yet. Nor would he tell her.

She narrowed her eyes, as if suspecting something, but he'd already stepped from under the arch. He was walking away from her now, raindrops settling heavily into the shoulders of his jacket.

"Don't you have an umbrella?" she asked. "How can you not have an umbrella?"

He tried to walk faster.

"I'll get you one, never mind. You can get it for a dollar in Edgewood."

She'd do it too. She'd knock on his door in a couple of hours, bringing him radios, umbrellas, all kinds of junk. Except this time he wouldn't answer.

The next day, at the dermatologist, Liberman's face was numbed with two injections, and two suspicious spots were removed, one from the area below his right ear, and another from the side of his nose. The wounds were then stitched and concealed under Band-Aids. It didn't hurt at the time, though later he felt some discomfort, the Band-Aids sticky on his skin.

In the morning, Liberman inspected his face. It looked lopsided, and he decided not to go out. He didn't call Mira but she showed up anyway, demanding to know what had happened to him.

"It's nothing," she said, after she saw his bandages. "We're going to lunch. Get your things."

He'd been ready to end Mira's punishment, but now that she'd spoken to him so dismissively, with such disregard to his condition, he felt wronged again. His wounds and his face weren't nothing. She could go ahead. *He* wasn't coming.

She left. But she returned that afternoon and told him news: The lunch had been atrocious—some soup with rice and barley. Lilya had gone completely mad. Next week, there would be a concert at the JCC. She'd bought a ticket. She was going with Boris Aleksandrovich. "It's classical," she said. "I didn't think you'd like it."

She brought homework too, but Liberman refused to look at it. "Go study with Boris Aleksandrovich."

"Stop it," she said. "You're not all that sick."

"I'm sick of your English. It's the pain in the rear I don't need at my age."

"You want to rely on your children instead?"

He was silent.

"I won't beg you," said Mira. "Sit here and feel sorry for yourself. Just don't expect I'll keep you company."

"Thank God," he said. "If there's one thing I'm sick of, it's your company. And what's it to you anyway? Why do you always have to interfere?" His face was itching, his every nerve quivering with frustration, and he wanted to say something insulting. "At least I *have* my children."

Mira left and didn't return. Not after supper, not the next morning. At first, he was glad. He could use a vacation from her. He figured it would take her two days to cool off. He watched TV and

read two issues of the *New Russian Word*. It was a little boring. He
called Dinka twice at work and one time at home. "What's going
on?" Dinka said finally. He told her he was worried: his heart had
been bothering him, plus there were the stitches. "Don't worry,"
she said. "The stitches don't come off till a week from tomorrow."

Friday morning, Dinka, Slavik, and Pavlik left for the Riviera
Maya. Five days, all-inclusive, a four-star hotel. It was something
he'd known for a while but had forgotten in the last couple of days.
Such unfortunate timing. And Mira had no idea they'd left. If only
she could find out by accident, she'd instantly come to his aid. Not
that he needed aid, but their quarrel was making him tired. Maybe
he'd run into her on the street. In the afternoon, he walked almost
as far as the JCC, telling himself he might look in on Berta, but in
the end it was just too embarrassing, so he turned around.

That night he felt worse. All of his symptoms intensified—
arrhythmia, heart murmur, whatever they were. He went to bed
early but couldn't fall asleep. It was the same the next day, and the
day after. He stopped eating. He developed insomnia. On Sunday
night his chest constricted, and after that he was afraid to sleep. He
spent the night in a living room chair, across from Sara's portrait.

He told her everything. She used to say he was too proud, he
never once apologized for what he did, like the time he thrashed
Dinka for playing a prank on their neighbor Arina Aronovna (hiding her grocery bag). He locked Dinka in the pantry for an afternoon (a guardhouse, he called it—he was a navy man). Later he
learned it wasn't her fault, so he bought her a wood-burning set
for her birthday—not an apology exactly, but close. Or maybe that
wasn't what Sara had meant. Maybe she'd meant the year he'd
served on Sakhalin Island. He'd had a woman there—what was her
name?—a beautiful woman. To this day he didn't know why Sara
hadn't divorced him back then.

In the morning, he called Mira. He was nervous. A sniveling boy, that's how he felt. What would he tell her? Should he invite her over?

"Hello?" she said. "Who is it?" Her voice was hoarse and low. He wondered if she'd been asleep.

"How many winters, how many springs!" he said. It was stupid. He was the one who called her. "What are you doing?" he said.

She said she was packing, she was going to New York City for two days.

"Alone?"

"No," she said. "It's a group tour."

"Who else is going?" *It is a great town, New York!*

"Oh, I don't know." She paused. "Boris Aleksandrovich is coming too."

He should've known.

Dinka returned on Wednesday. She took one look at him and gave him a terrible scolding. He must have been a sight by then: a shrunken figure in a bathrobe. She made him take a shower. He was weak from not eating, wobbly, so she had to go in and help him, too. "Why didn't you eat anything?" she said, squirting shampoo into his hair. "You want me to put you in a nursing home?" He was ashamed of her hands, of his body parts, his dribbling skin. When he tried covering himself, she stopped him. "No one's looking at you, Papa. Please stand still."

That night she stayed in the apartment with him. She made mashed potatoes and hot dogs for supper, and it was just what he'd wanted: rooms full of warm electric glow, her flat shambling footsteps. Something frayed and familiar, like the rotary phone with a chipped plastic corner that used to stand in their Leningrad hallway.

One thing was clear: it couldn't go on like this, this disgraceful feud between him and Mira. He knew she was back from New York. "Are you still bickering?" Dinka asked him one morning.

"Who's bickering?" he said. He was fine in the mornings. It was in the evenings he felt bad again.

And then it was another day. He was alone, dressed and clean, eating an apple. Somebody knocked on the door, and his heart leaped up, pleading. "Just a minute," he said, placing the apple on a plate. The knocking continued. His hands shook a little as he unlocked the door. "Hold on," he said. "Hold on. What is it, a fire?"

Mira was standing in the hall. Finally: Mira. But something was wrong. Her glasses looked blurry, her face smudged and giant like the surface of the moon.

"Berta's gone," she said. "Didn't you know?"

BERTA'S FUNERAL WAS ON Thursday. Liberman wore a suit with his war accolades on the lapel. His stitches were gone, but the scars were still visible. Well, he said, it was a funeral, not a beauty pageant. Mira agreed. Her eyes were red. She was dressed in a black knit dress, her sleeves stuffed with balled-up tissues.

Berta had died unexpectedly. Tuesday morning she woke with a stomach pain, and by noon she was in surgery. There was a tumor in her stomach, another one in her brain. She'd never risen from anesthesia. "At least she didn't suffer long," said Dinka. But who could tell for sure how long?

From the funeral home, Dinka drove Liberman and Mira to the cemetery. She grumbled how far it was, somewhere in *the devil's antlers*. Mira said it was awfully good of her to take a day off to drive them. She didn't seem angry with Liberman anymore. The night before, they'd split a quarter liter of Stolichnaya to honor Berta's soul, and so far, neither had mentioned their argument.

The cemetery was a poor loamy slope strewn with small stone tablets splattered with dirt and halfway grown into the ground.

There was a group of Berta's relatives, and two or three women from lunch, who'd come because Mira had asked them to. The ground was slick. Mira and Liberman stepped cautiously, supporting each other. The funeral was free, provided by the Jewish Family & Children's Service because Berta's family was still new to the country. A rabbi was provided too, a confused man himself, mixing Polish and English. They could barely hear him.

From years and years ago, Liberman remembered some things: the tearing of Kriya, some Kaddish in snippets. There wasn't much tearing happening here. The rabbi used a small pair of scissors to make a discreet rip in Berta's son's shirt. He called Berta "Freda" and no one dared to set the man straight. They stood there, shrinking beneath their umbrellas, diminished, every one of them. Except for Mira.

She was a striking presence in the rain, a lonely and powerful vessel, the folds of her raincoat flapping like sails. It would be just like this, Liberman thought, his own funeral, a drizzly day, a meager group of relatives, some bored onlookers who could make it to this distant cemetery. And Mira would stand in the back. He was certain she'd be there. If the rabbi bungled his name, she'd be the one to correct him.

"I'm sorry," he said. "I'm sorry."

But Mira only pressed his elbow, as if to say it didn't matter, they had years still, years ahead of them.

Charity

I GOT THE JOB from the Donetsk twins when they didn't want it anymore. It was at the end of the winter, our second year in Pittsburgh, and we were still on welfare. The job paid in cash, and after a week of pleading, I persuaded my parents to let me take it. "You don't need a job," they had said. It was technically true: we bought groceries on food stamps, paid rent with the welfare money, and my college expenses were covered by loans and grants. If I needed new clothes, we drove to Gabriel Brothers, a huge ugly store by the Century III Mall, where poor people shopped and where a four-dollar pair of jeans with holes was considered a "value-priced item." "Your job is to study," my parents always said, but I'd grown sick of asking them for bus fare, cosmetics, or snacks. All my jeans had holes in them.

The job was in a nicer part of Squirrel Hill, on Northumberland, a clean, slow street, with slanted lawns and tidy brick. The house—when I found it—was prim and narrow, its walls like a new chocolate bar. I'd been told to use the entrance on the side, facing the driveway. Pamela let me in. She was holding a bowl of noodles, stirring them with a fork. She was big and goofy looking: sweatpants droopy at her knees, a pink candy wrapper trapped in her hair. "Tell me your name again," she said.

She led me through parts of the house, the labyrinth of freshly painted rooms, parsley and lavender. When we got to the kitchen, there were buckets of spackling compound on the counter. The floors were covered in plastic. "We're expanding," said Pamela, and she stretched out her arms as if to show how rapidly they grew. We went into the family room, vast and mostly unfurnished. The kids were in there—the boy on the floor in front of the TV and the baby asleep on the love seat.

Pamela said, "Guys, this is Marsha."

The baby didn't move.

The boy looked at Pamela quickly. "Is she from Russia like the others?"

"She is," said Pamela. "She's Marsha from Russia."

"Masha," I said. "No *r*."

"They might call you Marsha anyway," said Pamela. "It's their aunt's name."

She asked me if I had a driver's license. I didn't. She asked me what my parents did. I told her they were unemployed. She asked me if I was in school. I said yes, I was a freshman at Pitt, studying computers. It seemed to surprise her: "Not Carnegie Mellon?" and I could imagine the rest of it: *A bright, hardworking Jewish girl like you?*

I said I didn't like Carnegie Mellon's attitude.

It wasn't exactly true. Carnegie Mellon didn't want me. There'd been a barricade of tests. On the TOEFL, which I took twice, my scores turned out mediocre. On the SATs, I did okay in math but lapsed on logic questions, and my reading section was a wreck. I'd gone to the admissions office to explain: I wasn't a bad student; in Russia, I used to be one of the best. They said I should consider other options.

Pamela said Carnegie Mellon was an excellent place.

She put on her parka, which was purple and stained with traces of sawdust and plaster. "If somebody calls, take a message," she told me. Then she left, and I stayed with the kids—one asleep, the other ignoring me. This was a horrible mistake. To get along with kids you needed something—confidence, liveliness, earnestness—something the Donetsk twins must have had. I had none of these qualities. The only thing left was to huddle on the floor at the foot of the love seat and wait. The boy watched cartoons and snacked on pretzels; the baby slept. After a while, I thought perhaps this wasn't so bad: the TV softly muttering, the room turning murky. We all might stay quiet like this, for an hour or so. And then Pamela would come back.

It only lasted twenty minutes, though. The boy abandoned his TV, and I followed him into the kitchen, where he perched on a chair and seemed to be waiting for me, his eyes bright like cherries, searching, beseeching. I didn't remember his name. Either Pamela hadn't told me, or she had and I'd forgotten it in my nervousness. "Let's order pizza," he said. I said I didn't have any money. "Let's put it on your credit card," he said. I didn't have that either. "Okay," he said, thinking, "okay."

I asked him his name. He said, Kevin. He was in first grade. His father was a doctor; his uncle was a doctor too. His mother wasn't anything. He would go to Yale, like his father and uncle—they'd been roommates in college. In their dorm they had a little fridge, because their food had to be kosher. "Do you keep kosher?" he asked me. I didn't. It had been different in Russia, and I tried to explain in a way a first grader might understand. He said, "Jews *have* to keep kosher."

—

I WAS HAVING a difficult winter, and I didn't know why. I had meals with my family, salads with sour cream, microwavable pizzas from Giant Eagle, hot dogs swelling in boiling water. After dinner, I studied. By ten o'clock I usually was asleep, which, my father said, wasn't normal for a college girl of eighteen. I rarely went out.

I used to look forward to college life. I would picture a small beautiful campus, full of benches and sculptures, with students lounging on freshly cut lawns and falling in love with one another. But at Pitt, the campus was crisscrossed by traffic, scattered, and the students were in the thousands. They traveled in streams in between the classes—from Langley to Hillman, from the Benedum computer labs to Litchfield Towers. At the center stood the Cathedral of Learning, skeletal and tall, with long lancet windows, pointed arches, and a vaulted lobby like a cave. It was where I had most of my classes, where I studied during breaks and ate my sandwich-and-banana lunches. Sometimes I went up to the thirty-sixth floor, which was as high as you were allowed to go and where tourists appeared in clusters to take in the view. I'd sit with my back to the windows and read Russian classics.

My life consisted of the shuttle rides to the campus and back. The university shuttle that circled Squirrel Hill carried a good deal of Russians. Most of them, like the Donetsk twins, worked at the hospital cafeteria in the upper part of the campus and studied computer science or accounting. They gossiped on the way to classes and generally kept to themselves, and by the end of the day they were back at the shuttle stop, smelling of grease and wet paper towels. I envied them. Aside from my best friend, Lariska, I didn't have any friends, and as for Lariska herself, she was never around; she had a new beau from Boston and a job at the Benedum computer lab.

My schedule at Pamela's was flexible, which is to say I came whenever I was told to, at two, or at three, or sometimes in the morning when I didn't have classes, and I stayed until Pamela said to go home. The pay wasn't great, four dollars an hour. I knew that others in similar jobs were paid better. But the work was so easy I couldn't complain. The kids didn't involve me in their games. Sometimes I had to change the baby's diaper or put a slice of pizza in the microwave. Also, the basement was being remodeled, and I had to make sure the kids didn't go in there. I used the time to study. When I needed a break, I went into the kitchen to find some Styrofoam containers with popcorn chicken, egg rolls, and, my favorite, the mushroom-and-chicken dish called moo goo gai pan. I'd pick from each container, though not so much that the loss might be noticed later. I'd eat right there, standing by the open refrigerator, cringing, ashamed of myself. Afterwards, I'd wash my hands and return to the kids in the family room and watch cartoons with them.

They were an odd family. The boy seemed a little unstable: on a bad day, forbidding; on a good day, needy, almost delicate. But the baby was worse, the beautiful two-year-old with silk ringlets of hair. Every week, he left bite marks on my arms and my wrists. Pamela said, "No biting," but you couldn't reason with a baby. You couldn't prevent it either. He was surreptitious—cuddly and dear, so you couldn't really foresee it until you felt his teeth, closing and pinching.

I never understood why Pamela needed me there. She didn't work. She said they could afford it, her not working. She told me the price of their house, and all the things inside it, and how much her husband earned. At night, the husband came from work, his eyes behind thick, foggy lenses, his hair, like the baby's, in thin, sweaty curls. Pamela went to meet him at the door. They hugged.

Together, they looked enormous, like two magnificent white bears. He was a psychiatrist and spoke in a thin, clinical voice. I watched him and Pamela: they were unbeautiful, but they made sense. I wondered how they'd met. It couldn't be just money. They had to be in love, at least a little, to become so big, so twinlike, so oblivious to the rest of the world.

Friday nights they had Shabbas. Pamela prepared a meat dish, her special, and served it in small metal pots. She found some candles, cleared one end of the dinner table, enough for two to sit in comfort—the kids and I weren't involved. I loved to watch the preparations. The dinner itself. The moment when she closed her eyes, lit the candles, recited a blessing. She said to her husband, "Shabbat Shalom, hon." I thought it was a beautiful tradition, the sort I'd be keen to take up, except that I had no one to make Shabbas meals for.

THE YEAR BEFORE, we'd lived in an apartment across from the Jewish Family & Children's Service, and as new arrivals, we were required to report there. At the first appointment we were told that the Jewish Federation would pay our rent for the first ninety days. In return, we'd work on our résumés, attend tutorials and ESL, meet periodically with the Career Development counselors. We'd behave like Americans by washing every day and dressing appropriately, in variedly colored clothing. We were encouraged to affirm our faith by frequenting one of the synagogues. Ever since then, I showered incessantly, and daily changed my turtlenecks. I had seven of them, in all colors of the rainbow, except instead of green I had black.

We'd gone to a synagogue once. On Yom Kippur, in September. We walked to Beth Shalom on Beacon Street. The entrance was crowded. My father was handed a spare yarmulke and something that looked like a towel. Inside, the synagogue was big like a theater, with tiers of upholstered seating, stained-glass windows, and bright round lights embedded in the ceiling. The service had already started. It was mostly in Hebrew, which neither of us knew. I had a hard time concentrating. I waited for it to feel meaningful. When the cantor started singing, I felt sad. He had a luminous voice that went up to the skies and made my insides clench with loneliness. I glanced at my parents. My mother picked at the prayer book. My father sat shriveled under an unfamiliar prayer shawl. They were filled with stifling discomfort.

American Jews had it easy. They all seemed well-off, and except for Hasids, they weren't too conspicuous; in the proverbial American melting pot they could pass for Italians or Greeks. Not that they had any worries. They took pride in their Jewishness, they celebrated it by building community centers and synagogues, and by sponsoring immigrants from Eastern Europe.

We never went back to the synagogue. On the way out, my father forgot to return the yarmulke and tallit, and a yeshiva boy had to be sent after us. At home, my father said he was tired of living on charity. My mother said we didn't have a choice.

"Your parents have jobs yet?" asked Pamela.

It had been three weeks since I'd started working there.

I said no, not yet.

"What about your boyfriend? Do you have a boyfriend?"

I said yes and yes. Two jobs, plus some translations he did for the Slavic Languages program. What I meant was, he was my ex-boyfriend, we'd broken up last spring, and he was now seeing a Japanese girl who majored in speech pathology. He still called me, though. He said he felt responsible for me, which was exactly what he'd told me last year about his previous ex-girlfriend.

"Slavic Languages." Pamela shook her head.

"She doesn't keep kosher either," said the boy.

"It's none of our business."

We were driving on Murray—we often did—Pamela at the wheel and me with the kids, buckled up in the sticky backseat. She wouldn't say where we were going, but the kids seemed to know, and I tried to deduce it from Kevin's moaning and the baby's weak bleeps. Sometimes it was a restaurant, Mr. Ying's or McDonald's. Other times, it was a building supplies superstore in Monroeville. I was hoping for Mr. Ying's.

"You don't want to marry too early," said Pamela.

She herself married late, close to her forties.

"How old is Masha?" said the boy.

I said I was eighteen. Pamela yawned. "Eighteen," she repeated to the boy. "I hope she gets her driver's license soon."

We had to drive slowly. It was February, and the streets were bleary and covered with sleet. We stopped by a kosher store across from Giant Eagle.

"Wait here," said Pamela.

The boy released a howl. No way was he staying with me and the baby.

"You're being a nuisance," she said.

He pounded on the window. The car, he said, was suffocating him.

"You can wait outside," said Pamela. She unbuckled the baby and locked all the doors.

I was left on the sidewalk with Kevin and the baby and no idea how to restrain them. I felt stranded. I held the baby while he squirmed, and Kevin ran circles around us. I asked him to stop— he was colliding with pedestrians. He paid no attention. "We don't have to listen to you," he said, after I'd raised my voice. "Our mother's paying you."

I considered quitting on the spot. But I couldn't, I prided myself on being persistent and responsible. I didn't want to give my parents the pleasure of gloating and saying they'd warned me about the job. I stared at the traffic, at the pedestrians on the other side of Murray, elderly women in plastic kerchiefs, plump yeshiva boys in their unbuttoned coats. I saw a couple stop: bundled-up, middle-aged, their faces drab, a hint of discontent and kidney stones. My father saw me first. He prodded my mother, who at first looked startled and then elated. They waved to me. I made a brutal face that meant *Go away!* But they wouldn't, to them this was a great entertainment.

"Those people are waving at us," said Kevin, when Pamela came out of the shop.

It didn't take her long to understand who "those people" were. She waved to them: "Hello, Masha's parents!"

My mother smiled gratefully. My father scoffed. It was their turn to be embarrassed. They were dwarfed by their Russian-bought coats and by the absence of jobs, humbled by Pamela's attention. We watched them withdraw into a side street, two comical figures, stepping timidly on the icy sidewalk.

"Your parents are cute," said Pamela.

MY PARENTS SAID I looked like Pamela. There was something in the shape of our faces, the fleshiness of cheeks, the heaviness of jowls. I was humiliated. In my opinion, Pamela was messy and not like the rest of Americans. She had a porous, sprawling body, and her face was wide and hardened into a permanent smirk. She often looked distracted.

By March, I stopped eating at home. The way my schedule worked, I usually managed to miss dinner completely. By the time

I came home from Pitt, my parents were leaving for their evening classes at the community college. My father was taking Computer-Aided Drafting, and my mother was taking Microsoft Word—Expert Certification. My mother would say, There are cutlets in the plastic Land O Lakes container, or There's soup with meatballs. But I couldn't eat anything. I thought it had to do with our apartment, the smell of it: the garbage overflowing, the dollar-store tablecloth with its odd whiff of vomit. I couldn't tell my parents. They loved that apartment. They'd found it the previous fall, and the rent was affordable. If they asked me, I told them I'd eaten at McDonald's.

Instead, I ate at Pamela's—the stolen food, leftovers. I got really good at it. The key was not to get too greedy. You went for small, discreet things, something you could pop in your mouth while watching TV, something you picked from the fridge while getting a carton of juice for the baby. Or else you waited till the children had their dinner, and then you cleaned their plates.

Pamela didn't seem to notice anything. The house on Northumberland Street kept growing—drafty, incongruous, spreading at awkward angles. Contractors came every day; they were building a new bedroom with a skylight on the second floor. They were sullen, plainspoken, and I could tell they didn't like Pamela, who was exploiting us all.

At the end of each evening, she paid me in old crumpled bills, which I counted and straightened at home. Having money, she told me, meant you could do whatever you wanted, no matter how odd. You didn't have to act contrite or mince your words, not in front of your neighbors, nor your sister (Aunt Marsha), nor your parents-in-law. She pointed at the chandelier in the family room: "Guess how much?" I had no idea. She told me the price, and it seemed like a lot. Her husband had bought it for her. A chandelier.

The husband was forever late from work. We'd be waiting for

him at Mr.Ying's, the Chinese restaurant, the family's favorite. Mr. Ying would deliver our plates—popcorn chicken for Kevin and the baby, moo goo gai pan for Pamela. For her husband, she ordered Mongolian beef. I ate whatever I was given, fried rice and the pieces of chicken Pamela doled out for me. An hour later, the plates would be emptied, except for the beef, getting cold on the table. Mr.Ying's wife would refill our teacups. Was there anything else we would like? The Yings were nice to Pamela, though they seemed to shrink a little whenever she arrived. Pamela was complicated: she was loud, she took up a couple of tables, and she stayed for a very long time. The longer we stayed there, the more untamed the children got—running and irking the customers, stealing fortune cookies from the employees-only area—and the harder it was to contain them. But we couldn't leave, we kept waiting, and Pamela was trying to call the husband on her cell phone. "He must be on his way," she'd say to us.

On Shabbas he was late as well. By the time he got home from work, it was long after sunset, so it wasn't really a proper Shabbas. They ate hastily, without joy, and mostly talked of payments and repairs. Afterwards, they drove to Hechinger's. Or else they went into another room and fought, the husband's voice rising to a wispy falsetto. The home improvements were endless, the contractors were late. He said to hire different contractors. "Do whatever it takes. Ask your sister for help. She's the orderly one in your family."

The nights they fought, Pamela usually forgot to pay me. Sometimes, she was a couple dollars short. She said she'd give me the rest of it later, but she never remembered and I was too embarrassed to mention it. Not that I ever spent the money. I kept it in my desk, in a plain white envelope. I thought of all the ways I'd spend it later. In my free time, I went for long walks. There were restaurants I never ate at and stores where I never shopped. I walked to campus. There were food trucks in front of the library, and the William Pitt Union with its student cafeteria, where the American kids from my classes gobbled up their meal plans. I missed being at Pamela's.

One time I accidentally walked to Shadyside, to the Catholic school where my ex-boyfriend, Alick, had a night job cleaning the gym. I told him about my job, and he said he was proud of me. He always knew I'd make it. We stood in a locker room for trainers. I pushed up my sleeves. There were bites on my arms, from the baby, pink stretchy areas, achy. Alick leaned in to examine the blemishes, to nudge against the thickening of skin. Then I was splayed on the narrow bench by the lockers, and we had to be quick, because his supervisor could come in at any moment.

AND THEN IT WAS Passover. Pamela would need me every day that week, a busy week, with two Seders (one at Aunt Marsha's, one at Pamela's), and a children's pageant at Beth Shalom. There was work to be done in addition to babysitting—cleaning, polishing silver, unpacking Passover dishes. All the polishing and unpacking made Pamela talkative. She located old family photos. In one she was in her twenties, at a grad school party, a boisterous, round-faced girl. In another, it was her and Aunt Marsha, both with long hair, in long skirts, poised next to their Orthodox parents outside Poli's restaurant.

I'd never met Aunt Marsha. She lived in Upper St. Clair, in a house much bigger than Pamela's. I didn't even know where Upper St. Clair was, though I'd heard it was rich and had the best school system in the area. Pamela said it was the goyim area and the schools in Squirrel Hill were just as good, especially the private ones. Her kids, she said, belonged in Jewish schools.

She asked me what my parents did on Passover. I said we almost never celebrated it in Russia. The holidays we were accustomed to were secular and sharply marked: November 7—Great October Revolution; March 8—International Women's Day. Passover wasn't in our calendars.

I thought she'd invite me to stay for the Seder. She'd unearthed her Passover recipes—brisket and matzo ball soup, baked fish with olive relish—each dish a marvel, bubbling and boiling in the kitchen, making me famished. But it was more than just the food. She had told me about her mother (who'd died of lung cancer), her husband, her master's degrees (from Carnegie Mellon in psychology, Duquesne in education). I asked how she'd met her husband, and she told me it was through their relatives. "Not too romantic," she said. "But what matters is our shared background and values." These days he was never around. Whenever she called him, his cell phone was off. Not that it seemed to bother Pamela.

She didn't invite me to her Seder. She said to tell my parents Good Pesach and to try Rodef Shalom synagogue, which was Reform and more accessible for immigrants. She herself had always gone to Beth Shalom. "And don't forget the pageant on Wednesday."

On the day of the children's pageant, the baby was in new overalls, the boy in black pants and a white shirt with a collar. Pamela emerged from upstairs, slimmed up in a green silky suit, her legs shapely in nylons. A headband, a pair of shoes with square buckles. She even wore some makeup. I myself had come directly from my classes, and I had on a turtleneck, a sweater, and a pair of jeans tucked into ugly boots I got for when the streets were slippery and I had to wade through snowbanks.

In the car, Pamela asked why Jews celebrated Passover. Kevin said it was because of the Exodus from Egypt. Pamela said that was correct. We must never forget the bitterness of slavery. Nor must we forget about the Jews in Russia, who were still enslaved and couldn't pray or celebrate High Holidays. It was why they came to America. Because American Jews rescued them.

"Has Masha been rescued?" said Kevin.

"Of course she has."

"She doesn't seem very grateful."

"I'm sure she's grateful. She just hasn't learned what it means to be Jewish yet."

"Maybe she'll learn at the pageant," said Kevin.

"Let's hope," Pamela said.

I wanted to tell them I knew what it meant. It meant classmates calling you names. It meant a line in your passport, schools that would never accept you, jobs you couldn't have. It meant leaflets and threats and a general on TV promising pogroms in May. It meant immigration.

At the pageant the baby was cranky, trying to sneak away, crawling between the aisles, and me crawling after him. It was embarrassing: all the other children well-behaved, attended by their babysitters, competent, sturdy girls in skirts—they studied at Hillel Academy and knew about Jewish holidays.

When the show ended, we staggered into the hall. The children dispersed. Outside, there was a parents' reception. They all knew one another from college, junior high, kindergarten, or else they were related. There was Pamela's sister, Aunt Marsha, skinny, impeccable, nothing like Pamela, her lips in a tight, feral curve. She'd brought along her boys, two brutish juniors, and from the way they scowled and stomped in their high-tops, I knew that Pamela's kids would get trampled.

Pamela looked frumpy compared to the others. A run in her stockings, a spot on her blouse, a slant in the hem of her skirt. Something was off with her makeup. She tried to be a good sport.

She laughed at jokes and talked to everybody. She had a trumpet of a voice. Everything was *hunky-dory* and *okeydokey*—that inane childlike talk—*You go to Colfax? We go to Community Day, yep still at Shadyside, his own practice, usually on Sundays, ha-ha, no we don't see him much—pardon? You're going now?*

The lobby was getting quieter. Most of the children were gone, taken home by their babysitters, who, unlike me, had driver's licenses. The parents, unencumbered, were making dinner plans, twining around Pamela's pretty sister, the popular one, the center of the crowd. It was eighth grade all over again, and Pamela was the dorky hippo girl in glasses, who annoyed everybody with her perfect grades. She was ahead of them now—with her house, her husband—at least, ahead of some of them. But what did it matter? The night was winding down, and her husband was late. Aunt Marsha said, "I don't think he's coming. Look at your children, Pam. They're tired." They both turned to us: me sitting down, the baby asleep in my lap. The boy was twirling in the middle of the lobby, his arms spread like an airplane. No one paid attention to him. His eyes were closed. It was the loneliest thing you'd see, this blind endless twirling, over and over.

IN APRIL, I TURNED NINETEEN, and Alick surprised me by taking me to a Chinese restaurant for an early dinner. We went to Mr. Ying's. I ordered moo goo gai pan, which I said I would share with Alick. But I didn't, I ate the whole thing. The fortune cookie promised me prosperity. I figured it was true. I'd been spending most of my evenings at Pamela's.

We were like regular Americans, eating dinner and acting relaxed. I wore heels and a black turtleneck dress I'd bought at Gabriel Brothers the previous week. I wished desperately Pamela could see me. But when I tried to picture it—the surprise on her face, her inquiries—it made me ill at ease. She hadn't paid me since the pageant.

Alick said I should either confront her or quit. I said Pamela was well-meaning. She employed me unofficially, and I believed she would give me good references if I ever needed them.

Alick said, "You won't need them. I can get you a cleaning job for cash."

I said I'd think about it.

We'd already finished our dinner. Alick had asked for the bill, when the restaurant door tinkled and Pamela's husband walked in. I stopped breathing for a minute, but he didn't see me. The woman that followed him wasn't Pamela. She was younger and thinner, decked in a burgundy dress, and if I didn't know better, I'd think she was Aunt Marsha, Pamela's sister. He was holding her hand. They asked for a takeout. Mr. Ying said they could wait at one of the tables. They picked the one by the bathroom, farthest from the entrance.

Outside Mr. Ying's, Alick said he'd enjoyed having dinner with me. Incidentally, his roommate was away, the coast was clear, we could rent a movie and make a night of it.

I said I had to work at Pamela's that evening.

"On your birthday?" he said.

I told him she really needed me.

I wasn't due at Pamela's that day, but as I walked home, I knew I had to see her.

Pamela didn't seem perplexed by my appearance. She often made mistakes, scheduling me on the days she didn't need me. She stepped aside, letting me into the kitchen. The house was still. The children, she said, were at their cousins' for the evening. Her husband was at work. There were no contractors either.

"I fired their asses," she said. "They think I'm a bitch."

I couldn't tell if she was kidding.

"Sit down," she said. She had a pot of boiling water on the stove. I watched her crunch some pasta into it. "So," she said, "what's the story?"

I said I'd gone to Mr. Ying's.

She asked me what I'd ordered.

She stood with her back to me, stirring her pasta on the stove, her sweater stained, her hair dry and overgrown. A starchy aroma was filling the kitchen, linguine, olive oil.

"You're hungry?" She glanced over her shoulder.

I nodded.

She said that was the problem with Chinese.

She made two bowls of noodles, placed one in front of me. We sat at the opposite ends of the tall marble counter. I tried to eat slowly, taking long sips of tap water. The noodles were perfect, soft, supple, salty, mixed with thick tomato sauce. We didn't speak. We were messy and ravenous, with smudged orange circles forming around our lips. We scraped at the last bits of food in our bowls.

I thanked her and rinsed our dishes in the sink.

Then I cleared my throat and told her what I'd seen at Mr. Ying's.

At first, it seemed she hadn't heard me. She checked the dishwasher. She picked up her keys and moved them to the shelf above the cutlery drawer. She whistled an opera tune. Eventually she turned to me. "It wasn't him," she said.

She handed me my coat.

I was at the door when she spoke again.

"You're not very good with the kids, but I like you because you're honest. But even honest people make mistakes. That's normal, as long as you're willing to learn from them. I think you're learning. You've made a mistake. One day you'll have a family of your own, and then you'll know what I mean. It's not what you imagine at eighteen, but then it's not so bad either."

"Nineteen," I said. "I am nineteen."

She gave me a roll of twenty-dollar bills. I knew without counting that it was more than what she owed me. She told me they'd see me next week.

I walked home. The air smelled like tree bark and loose soil, the wind was riffling through my sleeves. In my pocket I had two hundred dollars, enough for a dozen meals, enough to buy a wardrobe full of clothes. I went into my room and fell asleep and didn't wake up until the following morning. I never returned to Northumberland Street.

In the Man-Free Zone

ON JANUARY 15 I celebrate my thirty-ninth birthday. The guests—only a few close friends—are invited for six o'clock. I am making a roast duck with honey glaze. I've already made two salads and bought a Kiev cake at Three Bears. Andrey presents me with a paper collage (cute and clumsy, something he's made at school) and a small box of chocolates (his father sent him money). I hug him and say, "Thank you, dear." Then I make him collect the video games he's strewn all over the house.

Galka and Lyonchik, my former classmates, called last night from Chicago. Chicago is a long way from Pittsburgh, they said. Lyonchik is studying for his CPA exam, and Galka never travels anywhere without Lyonchik. But Happy Birthday anyway. My ex-husband Vadim has sent me a card; my sister Lyudka has called from Moscow; my classmates are not driving from Chicago.

At five o'clock Dinka Gurevich marches in with a meat thermometer. She is an expert in roasted ducks. Dinka's husband,

Slavik, is carrying a bottle of wine—the wrong one, says Dinka. She shoos me away from the stove, yells at Slavik for being an idiot, sends him back to the liquor store. She tells me, "You're so lucky, Natasha." Lidka from Mellon Bank rings the doorbell at ten after six. She is with her second husband, Grisha, and her mincing daughter, Allochka. They bring me Obsession, the perfume, and an ugly teapot with a rooster.

We quickly feed the children and send them upstairs to play. They are noisy and careless there, tussling over the laptop I bought for Andrey, arguing in quick, high-pitched English. Games! They want more games! It is fortunate that they are so close in age: Andrey is now ten; Dinka's chubby Pavlik, nine and a half; Lidka's Allochka, eleven. From downstairs we catch their chirping insults—*Not fair*, screams Allochka, *you're not playing fair*. We'll never be so nimble in English.

"To you, Natasha," says Lidka's Grisha, and we drink. We've already drunk to me, to my parents (heavenly kingdom to them), to my health (knock on wood), to success in my professional life and happiness in my personal affairs. Grisha, the profligate, winces as he drinks. He has a smoldering Moldovian handsomeness—the thick shoulders, the heaviness in the eyelids and lips.

"What you need, Nataliya, is a man," he says, his voice a coarse singsong. "You know what I mean?" He winks at me. "A big and sturdy man."

"Eat, Grisha," I tell him. "Drink and snack."

"Go ahead, make fun of Grisha. What does he know!" says Grisha.

"Have some salad, Grisha," says Lidka. "Have some little fish."

"My wife doesn't respect me," he says. "But seriously, where're we going to find Natasha a man?"

Lidka giggles. She is pretty in her purple cashmere sweater, snug and low-cut. I could be pretty too if I tried, but my eyes are paltry without makeup, and my chin is weak. I show up at work with my hair tightly braided and wet from the swimming pool, my eyelashes colorless behind the glasses. Lidka likes to scold me for being careless this way. You've got to use what God's given you, she says. I wish God gave me Lidka's sumptuous form, but unlike her I've always been narrow like a boy.

Lidka tells me there's a new *interesting* man in Tech Services. "Russian," she says in her confidential voice. "No ring."

"There are no *interesting* men in Tech Services," I tell Lidka.

"Nonsense," says Lidka. "We can stop there on the way to lunch on Monday, tell him your screen is flickering."

"It's not good for a woman to live alone without a man," says Grisha. He is squeezing Lidka's thigh under the table.

"You're drunk, Grisha," says Lidka. She shoves him away.

"But you like it, don't you? You like your man drunk." His hand is now pressing on Lidka's shoulder, kneading, pulling on her sweater. Deliberate, greedy movements. Lidka looks embarrassed but proud. It's belittling, but as I watch them, my body starts to tingle, and I say I need to go check on the duck.

Dinka follows me into the kitchen. "What are you doing?" she says. "Let me." She gets her meat thermometer, and we both crouch in front of the oven, peering through the glass. Dinka is stout in a matronly, inveterate way. She doesn't bother herself with diets. We met years ago in an English class. I was still married back then, and Vadim, though short-tempered and critical, wasn't cheating on me yet. Dinka says she never liked Vadim, with his sneering, scientific eyes.

"Grisha is drunk like a cobbler," says Dinka, "but he's right— you *do* need someone. What about Vova? From my New Year's party? You remember Vova. Wasn't he nice?"

"He was divorced, Dinka. Twice. Both of his wives left him." I remember Vova—small, balding, opinionated. I remember other candidates culled by Dinka—a man with no job, a man with no green card.

"You're divorced too." Dinka balances the skillet on top of the stove while I look for a carving knife. "I mean, look at your Lidka. Smart, attractive woman, and her Grisha is—"

"Her Grisha is a butcher."

"But look at them together. They have a nice little life."

I say, "Fine. Tomorrow I'll find and marry your Vova and we'll too have a nice little life. Will this make you happy?"

"Do what you want," says Dinka. "You think everybody else is a fool."

She leaves, her silk-covered chest heaving. I will apologize tomorrow, and she'll forgive me and start spinning another wire-ribbon of advice. That's how it works. Dinka makes suggestions, and I make jokes. I'm good at jokes. At night alone in my bedroom, I might turn into a sad sack, a blubbering slush, a plate of noodles. But during the day nobody wants to see your noodle nature. So you throw a party, you cook a duck, you make jokes about the phallic-looking meat thermometer. Another couple of hours and my guests will file out of here in pairs—husbands supporting their wives, wives supporting their unsteady husbands. They'll say to each other, *Isn't she brave, our Natasha? Isn't she funny? Isn't it a pity that she's so unceasingly alone? And what did she do to drive away her clever biologist husband, all the way to Southern California, where he's now given up on biology and instead sells real estate?*

"Mom, are you all right?" Andrey is standing in the doorway, sweaty and agitated. "Are you okay, Mama?" He mostly speaks to me in English, except when he senses I'm about to stick myself with a carving knife.

He comes closer and I straighten his rumpled hair, brush it away from his eyes. We are both due for a good haircut.

"Everything is normal," I say in Russian, and make a clown face.

"Can I have some juice? We need some juice upstairs."

He is beautiful and smart; he does well enough in school; his classmates like him. When he flies to California to be with his father, I worry and down tranquilizers.

"No food upstairs, Andrey," I tell him. "Better get everybody down here. The duck is ready and there will be a cake soon."

AT MELLON BANK, I work as a programmer. I am responsible for benign maintenance tasks—monitoring batch jobs, poring over thick yellow printouts, folded along the perforation. Sometimes I have to carry a pager on weekends. In Moscow I was a biologist, like my ex-husband, but that life now seems a million years away.

The Monday after the party, I sit in my cubicle and write out checks: gas, electricity, Visa. It's a quiet Monday—my manager is out sick—and Lidka has been badgering me to call the man in Tech Services. She's even dictated his extension number, and I've written it down on a Post-it note and stuck it to the bottom edge of my computer screen. His name is Oleg.

When my coworker June pokes her head over the cubicle wall, I cover my checkbook with the perforated printouts. She says, "Happy Birthday, Natasha." June is big and amorphous. She wears caressing colors—lavender, pink. She is the kind who remembers birthdays. "You look tired," she says.

I tell her that life is supposed to be strenuous for single mothers. Single mothers are bad for the economy.

June squints at me. "You've been watching Fox News again?"

June makes me feel like I can handle Americans. We have long conversations about politics and National Public Radio. We understand each other's jokes. We watch independent movies that no one else in Squirrel Hill wants to see. June herself is unmarried and childless, living with another woman, Vicki. There's a picture of the woman, tucked in the corner of June's cubicle. They've been together for fifteen years—met in college, in a literature class. There aren't many couples among my friends who've lasted that long.

"We're having a brunch next Sunday," says June. "Vicki's got a new job. Will you come?"

"Fabulous," I say. "Fantastic." I'm proficient in basic American pleasantries.

She e-mails me the directions to their house, and I think of all June's friends that I will meet: friends who listen to National Public Radio, donate money to protect the environment. And what if June wants to set me up with someone? She must know some straight, single men. As I think about that, the idea of Oleg from Tech Services becomes less frightening. He is just one of many possibilities. When I feel sufficiently brave, I unpeel the Post-it note, dial the number, and say, "This is Natasha from Asset Management department. May I speak with Oleg?"

I GET HOME AROUND SIX. My house, half a duplex on Phillips, near the synagogue, is a neat square box. I bought it a year ago, and for that, Dinka and Lidka still call me crazy. They say, You have a child and no husband. What if there's an economic crisis? What if you get hit by a bus? I tell them that if I get hit by a bus, the child has a father in California. Free oranges and lots of real estate.

In the living room, Andrey is on the floor doing his homework. The TV is on. It's too loud. He shouldn't be doing his homework in front of the TV.

"Mom," he says. "Check this out, Mom." Mrs. Edwards liked his science project, he wants to try out for the Math Olympics, he needs five dollars for the trip to the Carnegie Museum. I drop my coat on a chair, wade into the kitchen.

"Did you eat, Andrey? Didn't I tell you to eat?"

The Olympics, he says, and I'm thinking: *What Olympics?*

"Did you forget what you got on your history test?"

"You never support me, Mama," he starts whining. "Why can't you believe in me?"

I wonder if they teach him at school to talk like this?

"Parents and children should respect each other," he says. "For example, I respect you, Mama."

I say, "That's enough, Andrey. I'll respect you when you start getting better grades."

But the whole thing makes me feel lousy, like I'm a backward Russian parent. For God's sake, the child wants to try out for the Olympics. Why do I always expect him to fail?

I don't exactly apologize to Andrey, but I tell him that the Math Olympics might be okay, provided he stops blasting the TV and does something about his history grades. Then I order pizza and we eat in the living room and watch a sitcom.

Pizza is not the healthiest dinner, but it's the best I can do today. Andrey prefers junk to homemade food anyway, although he likes to watch me cook, says it feels *homey*. Homey! The truth is I used to try harder—perfect mother, perfect wife, starchy aprons, freshly prepared soups, tea served in a favorite mug. We had "Best Mom" and "Best Dad" mugs. We rented an apartment on Alderson. Vadim returned from his lab, his face like a storm cloud, and I fawned, fluttered around him like a bird of goodwill. Here's your dinner, Vadimchick. Here's a clean towel. The first time Andrey flew to California, I smashed the "Best Dad."

When the pizza is gone, I set the pizza box on top of my head and try to walk in Lidka's sauntering way.

"Watch me," I say to Andrey. "It's a good exercise for your posture." I giggle, and he smiles at me indulgently. Then I stumble and the box falls off my head, scattering crumbs everywhere. I sit on the floor, laughing and gathering the box and the crumbs.

"It's going to be pretty hard for you to find a man, Mom," says Andrey. He sounds sensible and a little regretful.

"Why, Andryusha? What makes you say such a thing?"

"Admit it, Mom, you're pretty weird. Walking with a pizza box on your head." He is smiling now, being a silly kid again. He slides from the couch and starts helping me with the crumbs. "But I love you anyway," he says.

I want to promise him crazy things—that I will reconcile with Vadim, that I'll find myself another husband. I want to tell him that I have a date with the man from Tech Services, but it's not the kind of thing you tell to a child.

ON WEDNESDAY I have my date with Oleg, the Tech Services man. It's not exactly a blind date—Lidka has pointed him out to me in the cafeteria—but still I am nervous. He is right on time, and I watch him from my bedroom window as he parks his car, a battered Chevrolet, fitting it in front of my garage, a little to the side, adjusting it, backing out and trying again. I think: *What is his problem with parking?* Then he rings my doorbell.

Dinka tries to set me up from time to time; she forgets to tell me and I get phone calls from confused Russian men. I've had some stern conversations with Dinka, about checking with me first, about consideration and respect. To her it's all like water off a goose. She thinks she's helping me. This one, however, is my own mistake.

We blunder through introductions. He is not bad-looking, Oleg, tall, but soft-spoken and anxious. He has a leather jacket on. It seems too large in the shoulders and he is wearing it with hesitation, like maybe he isn't used to wearing bold things like that.

"My eyesight got bad here," he says. "Well, not really bad, but just so. Worse. From the hard American life."

I understand that the last part is meant as a joke. A sad joke. But I don't understand why he's telling me about his eyesight.

He explains that his sense of direction is no good in the dark.

I say, "No problem. I'll drive."

He doesn't argue. I don't know what he's had in mind for our date, but I don't want to stay in Squirrel Hill, where everybody knows me. We get into my Jeep and I back out slowly, trying not to hit his car, which, despite his efforts, sticks out awkwardly. He says he likes my Jeep, but there's something in his voice that makes me think he doesn't approve, finds it excessive.

A man like that is a find, says Dinka. Insecure, true, but also open to improvements. She says she's seen it happen: a starveling of a man in the hands of a bright, capable woman straightens up, assumes confidence and force. You can breathe life into him, says Dinka. I tell her I don't have time to be that kind of woman. I have a job. I have a son to raise.

I take Oleg to a little café in Shadyside. He says he's lived in America for the past two years, worked at Aaron's Bakery, delivering bread and pastries to local supermarkets. He speaks slowly, and his eyes are beautiful and doleful. He used to be an engineer in Russia. And now, he says, now is this job. Though he's only a contractor, and there are rumors of layoffs.

I ask him what he's planning to do in the future.

"Ah, what are you talking about?" he says. His hand does a little dismissive wave, and from his voice I know that he is annoyed with me now, annoyed with my optimism, so American. "What future?" he says. "Lucky to be making it from one day to another."

I tell Dinka they are weak, these men. Dispirited. Damaged by the immigration.

Not all damaged, says Dinka. You can still sleep with him. When was your last time?

I tell her I can't make love to a weak man.

THE NEXT NIGHT, Andrey and I are having dinner at the Gureviches'. Dinka's kitchen is a man-free zone, and Lidka and I are watching her slice vegetables for the salad. She had initially invited us for a quiet, girls-only night. But then Pavlik and Andrey's hockey practice got canceled, and now all three of them—Pavlik, Andrey, and Slavik, who was supposed to take the boys to the practice—are home, crowding us. The boys, impatient for dinner, try to sneak into the kitchen, but vigilant Dinka sends them away. Slavik comes in to ask if his shirts are back from the dry cleaners.

"Would you leave me alone?" says Dinka. "Can you manage anything by yourself? It's not a husband; it's some sort of punishment."

Slavik says nothing. He's been strange and absentminded lately—working long hours, leaving home on a Sunday to buy a quart of milk and returning home after midnight, his excuses muddled and unconvincing. Dinka seems vaguely worried, but mostly annoyed.

The men are clearly a nuisance, she says, but she's glad that the practice got canceled. She wants to pull Pavlik off the hockey team anyway, but she hasn't decided what to subject him to instead. Pavlik is already taking extra math—American schools are so lax, and there's a Russian immigrant offering advanced math classes—but that doesn't seem enough to Dinka.

Her hands are quick and methodical, and the blade of the knife falls on the cutting board with a thump. The salad seems healthy, but it's just a decoy for the heavy items—cabbage soup, veal cutlets, vermicelli, bread. Everything is garnished with oil and butter and sour cream. Pavlik is overweight. He needs more exercise, but there's no delicate way of saying this to Dinka.

"Music?" says Lidka.

"No, music is definitely out," says Dinka. "All those boy musicians grow up to be gay. Pavlik has tendencies. You should see him prancing in front of the mirror, brushing his hair. No, no flutes, no pianos for us."

I don't come to the defense of gay boy musicians. I don't tell them about my fiasco of a date or about June and the invitation to the brunch. They'll say I am becoming too American. They'll say, *What do you want with them, Natasha?*

During dinner Dinka is talking SAT classes (it's never too early) and expensive boarding schools (nothing prepares a child better for the Ivy League), and I think it's ridiculous because our children are nine and ten. But maybe it's me, being an underachiever. In college I never cared enough for biology, though the student life was fun, with weekend parties, electric trains, guitars, and mandatory stints at potato farms. After college, they assigned you somewhere, and you began your life as a junior research assistant. It was the same for everyone, and not unlike working at Mellon Bank. Same business every day—dinner breaks, smoke breaks, collecting money for the boss's birthday. My boss encouraged me to finish my candidate dissertation, and I tinkered with it, haphazardly. By then I was married, safely tucked into my own society cell.

The boys are eating in the kitchen. "So that we can have our food in peace," says Dinka. Slavik is struggling to open a bottle of wine. Dinka takes the bottle away from him. *"Ubozhestvo,"* she says, "a cripple." Slavik doesn't argue. His cell phone starts ringing and he goes upstairs to take the call.

We leave Dinka's house around nine. Andrey is half asleep in the back, and Lidka (I'm giving her a ride) is in the passenger seat.

She whispers, "Do you think Slavik is having an affair? If he is, it's Dinka's own fault. She needs to lose some weight and do something with her hair. Her head looks like an egg."

I say I don't know. I am the wrong person to ask about affairs.

Lidka says, "I didn't mean it like that."

Vadim was visiting us last month. Visiting Andrey, I mean, but he stayed at the house, because it would be foolish, he said, to pay for a hotel. Impractical. On the last night, late, he came into my room, and I haven't told anyone.

It's not like he was a stranger. He'd picked up some new techniques there in California. Exciting, but not tremendous. Mostly he was the same. I thought that maybe he still loved me, regretted leaving. He was cheating on her, the other woman in California. Did it mean he wasn't happy there? I thought of how we used to be—the two of us driving to the Sam's Club to buy paper towels in bulk and having nothing to say to each other. Back then he was having work-related troubles. I was taking computer classes at the community college, but my head was full of houses and lawns and picket fences.

In the morning I said, Let's all go out to Gullifty's for breakfast. Vadim didn't like the idea. He said, This is not what I'm sending you money for. You can't make your own omelet and a couple of hot dogs? You have to pay for your tea? I said, It's not your money. He still thought it was a stupid idea. Finally he agreed when I told him Andrey loved Gullifty's and going out.

At breakfast, I told Vadim what I thought about primary elections and how arts and education were underfunded. We'd never had a conversation like that before, and I thought maybe that was why he left me. Because what had I been? A housewife? I was something more now. And maybe I'd get a graduate degree in information management. Learn Spanish or French—both beautiful languages—and then travel extensively in Spain and in France.

He said, "Can you stop now? My head is splitting. Do we have to talk about this?"

ON SUNDAY MORNING I find an old pair of contact lenses and try to accentuate my eyes with taupe shadows and black mascara. I'm wearing a long skirt and dangling earrings. I don't know why I'm trying so hard; it's only June's brunch.

Andrey is watching cartoons and not paying me much attention.

"Child," I say, "are you going to be okay?"

"Uh-huh," he says. I feel guilty for leaving him alone, and because of that I promise him a dinner out and maybe even a movie if it's not too late.

I drive slowly around residential Penn Hills, blinking at the street signs and stopping to check directions. It snowed the night before and the streets are narrow and uneven. I almost pass June's house. On the porch, I pause before pressing the doorbell. What's the point of trying? Shouldn't I be home with Andrey, making coffee, prying him away from the TV?

June opens the door, soft and calming. She takes my coat, directs me upstairs, toward the buffet-style table. There are pancakes and waffles with syrup. Breakfast fruit cut in dainty squares, green, yellow, and orange, sprinkled with blueberries and grapes. A woman comes in, carrying two glasses and a carafe of orange juice. "Natasha, this is Vicki," says June. The woman says hello. She sets down the carafe and the glasses and shakes my hand. Her eyes are gray and perceptive. She is skinny. Her hair is pulled back with a rubber band.

In the living room, I meet the other guests: Christine and Mike, just married and in search of their first perfect house; downstairs neighbors with their toddler, Luke. There're no single men. There is another woman couple; they look like sisters—lanky, short-haired and dark, with intense equine faces.

I tell Andrey he would have liked them, June, Vicki, the guests. They all had interesting professions. He's been asking me lately about jobs people have. He has to pick a good one, he says. He's already rejected biology and computer programming. I tell him one of the women was a professor at Pitt. She teaches women's studies. And Vicki now writes for the *Pittsburgh Post-Gazette*. Were there any kids he could play with? I tell him no, no one his age. He wants to know if the guests were funny. Funny? I say. I guess some of them were funny.

I sit by the bay window, concentrate on my food, prepare to have a serious conversation. Local politics. Picasso at the Carnegie Museum. A couple of the usual questions about the collapse of Communism in Russia. Jazz is playing in the background, low and surreptitious. It worries me, puts me on edge a little. Vicki comes over, asks me whether I like my job, and whether Andrey likes his school. (A silly question, scoffs Andrey.)

I try to figure out what the rest of the guests are talking about. They are talking *Star Trek*. Eighties rock bands that didn't stay together. Vampire movies. June brings coffee and brownies. She says she has a crush on a blond vampire girl that appears weekly on TV. (She's a slayer, Mom, Andrey says, not a vampire.) Vicki says, That's because the girl is anorexic and June has a thing for anorexic chicks. Poor June blushes. The guests laugh, June and Vicki laugh, and nobody tries to be especially sophisticated. I don't know the shows they are talking about, can't participate in the jokes they make. I can only laugh along, and really, that's all that is required.

Growing up, I had an obsession with couples. I observed them at my parents' parties, in stores, inside metro trains. I asked my mother what she thought these people were like alone at home, whether they argued, whether they really loved each other. I would point out an especially glamorous item: a man and a woman in long autumn coats. They are young. They are returning from a theater date. Her hair is tousled like after a party, and she is holding a flower. She is tired and leaning against him, and he is holding her hand. "Stop staring," whispered my mother. "You're embarrassing me." She and my father always fought at home, even though they stayed together until my father passed away. But there were times when my mother would look at the couple I'd chosen, squint wistfully, and then we'd share a beautiful fantasy, our own fairy tale.

Later, when the coffee is served, Vicki and June are sitting next to each other. June is peeling an orange. Vicki is leaning forward, talking to one of the equine sisters, her fingers absently drawing something between June's shoulder blades. Outside, the snow is sparkling and melting. A new record starts to play, the violins full of big, old-fashioned hope, and I think, *How long can this last? How long can they stay this way?*

I tell Andrey I looked at each couple and thought of the old game I used to play with my mother. "What was it?" says Andrey. We are at the Eat'n Park on Murray. He is having a milkshake with a smiley-faced cookie, and I'm having a Caesar salad. The restaurant is crowded. "What's the game?" he says. For a moment I'm tempted to point out a couple and ask him. But I stop myself. He is twisting his milkshake straw, trying to make a popping sound. I tell him, It doesn't matter, honey. It wasn't a very good game.

Russian Club

IN THE LAB on the seventh floor, mice were being slaughtered. Mice dripped into test tubes and retorts, into the machines that smothered shivery mouse-heartbeats. The heartbeats would become signals, signals would become data, an article in a medical journal, a paper presented at a conference on physiology and cell biology.

I knew nothing of biology. I was a computer science major and my job was to write computer programs that would process the heartbeats and turn them into spiky, life-affirming graphs. It was my second year at the University of Pittsburgh, and among other things, I'd taken Algorithms, Data Structures, C++, and three Russian literature courses. Too much Russian literature, not enough math, my advisor at the Thackeray Hall had warned me.

My days at the lab were Tuesdays and Thursdays. I showed up at nine in the morning, a slouchy work-study in leggings and a sweater with unraveling sleeves. I brewed myself big mugs of coffee, which I drank with lots of sugar and cream. Most of the day I sat in a tight, lightless room in the back of the lab, alone with my computer. There were four of us at the lab. Lakshmi, the director, was from India. JT was Chinese. I was from Moscow. The only American among us was Gary, a junior researcher from Georgia, who joked, "Woe is me. I'm trapped with immigrant overachievers." It was true, except I was one immigrant who couldn't achieve anything. Maybe the signals were faulty, or maybe the problem was me, but the graphs came out wrong every time I ran my programs.

I waited for JT to rescue me. He appeared toward the end of my shift, slim and limber like a schoolboy, with a thin leather bracelet wound tightly around his wrist, and he fixed up my code for me. Computers were his hobby. He was working on his Ph.D. in biology, which I found hard to believe. He seemed too frivolous. His desk was strewn with action figures. He had a pet ferret that lived on his shoulder, though on the days of the experiments he put it in my room. He called the ferret Rat. Afterwards, he would offer to buy me a burger, but I always said no.

The problem was I never had the time. In the fall, I had joined the Russian Club, a group of Russian majors, mostly juniors, supported sparsely by the Department of Slavic Languages. The club met on the days I worked, Tuesday or Thursday, at five o'clock. There was a parlor on the fourteenth floor of the Cathedral of Learning, across from Slavic Languages, and that was where we gathered each week. Sometimes there was pizza. We ate and planned activities: a potluck, a film series, a costume party on Soviet Army Day—the sillier the better. The Russian Club people were nice to me. I explained to them Russian slang, which they appreciated, and sometimes I helped them with their homework. I'd hoped our friendship would extend beyond the meetings, but so far, it hadn't. In the end, their conversations always turned to dorm politics, roommates, and sports, and I had nothing to contribute. And even if I did, I was too quiet, too unsure of my English.

VICTOR HARLAMOV, thirty-five years old, looked like he'd just stepped off a Communist poster: sun-bleached, blue-eyed, trustworthy, dressed in a checkered shirt with rolled-up sleeves. He was a visiting professor of philology from Moscow State University, and the first time I saw him was at the Russian Club meeting in early December.

The moment I walked into the parlor, I knew something uncommon was going on. All eyes were on him. He sat to the right of the door, looking amiable, mild-mannered, with a hint of a smile twinkling around his lips.

Monica, our secretary, introduced him as Professor Harlamov. She'd spent a semester at Moscow State University, where she'd been a student of his. She was pretty and quiet, with smoky eyes and dusky, almost Indian skin. She kept glancing at him as she read us his bio. His article on Acmeism was a classic, and his book on the poet Nikolai Gumilev a masterpiece. In the spring, he'd be teaching a class on the silver age of Russian poetry. It'd just been added to the schedule, and if we hurried, we could still get in. She herself had signed up earlier that afternoon.

Afterwards, it was his turn to speak. He said to call him Victor and to quit flattering him, because one thing he couldn't stand was flattery. He had a few words for the Russian Club: "I've taken a look at your calendar, and what I've seen astonished me. Amateur talent activities. Potlucks and films. Dull is your life, dear comrades. Narrow is your reach. You can do more with your resources. How many of you've been to Russia?"

Two people raised their hands.

He said, "You're not being serious."

I didn't think he noticed me at that first meeting. I didn't raise my hand or speak, and he was too busy enticing us with his Soviet-style wisdom. After the meeting, the Russian Club members went to Hemingway's for drinks. I assumed Victor went with them. I told myself I didn't like him. He was too phony, too presumptuous, with his folksy simplicity and Communist looks; his class would be a travesty. I'd promised my advisor no more Russian classes. I'd signed up for a whole array of math and general requirements, and the registration period was over for sophomores.

But Victor hadn't gone to Hemingway's. A few minutes later, I saw him at the shuttle stop, waiting for a Squirrel Hill shuttle. His shoes and jacket were too thin, he kicked his feet against the sidewalk, and he carried his things in a torn paper bag. I waited beside him.

He shivered and said, "Firs-and-sticks! They're not in a rush here, are they?" He was speaking in Russian. To me.

I said, "They call it service with a smile."

We both laughed, and a few minutes later the shuttle came in.

The next day I went to the registrar's office and wheeled my way into Victor Harlamov's class.

THE CLASS WAS ON Thursdays at midday and it lasted three hours, which meant I had to leave the lab and then come back. Most days I didn't, but instead worked a few extra hours on Friday, easy enough since no one was there except for Gary, who didn't care what I did. I sat in the back and read poetry for Victor's class.

Poetry, Victor had said at the first class, was a serious business. He spent most of his life studying it. "I presume you feel strongly about

it too. Or else you would be at the movies. Or at a baseball game."
There were laughs and noises of approval. Most of the Russian Club
members signed up for the class, and most of them were women.

"Who is the most important Russian poet?" Victor asked.

One girl said, "Pushkin."

Another one said, "Blok."

"Nikolai Gumilev," said Monica.

"Well, maybe not the most important, but definitely worth your
time. Monica's been to my lectures; she knows."

He talked about the silver age, how it was magical, the two
decades at the beginning of the century, the hungriest years, when
poetry was more important than bread. Poetry flourished,
branched into new directions: Symbolism, Acmeism, Futurism. The
poets gave readings and met in places like the Stray Dog Café and
the Tower. It ended with the Russian Civil War. Some poets emi-
grated, while others stayed and were later imprisoned or even mur-
dered by the state.

I was impressed with Victor's lecture. He spoke with real passion.
When the class was over, I went to introduce myself.

He smiled when he saw me. "It's Masha, isn't it?"

I nodded. I said I loved the silver age.

"Good to speak to a like-minded person," he said. "Americans
are so goddamn joyful, it's messing with my head."

"There are quite a few of us here. Russians, I mean. But everyone studies computers, and nobody takes Russian lit unless they
need an easy credit."

"This one won't be easy," he said.

I knew that. I, too, studied computers, but unlike everyone else,
I took Russian for pleasure. I hadn't declared my major yet.

"Minors, majors . . . You're wasting your time," Victor said.
"You either dedicate yourself or else you're just dabbling. I don't

care for dabblers. I'll teach them if I have to, but it won't be a productive relationship."

I promised him I'd dedicate myself.

"You better," he said. "I need a person I can talk to in this waste-
land."

I became Victor Harlamov's best student. He called me "Mariya
the Artisan," after a character from a Russian fairy tale. My first
paper was covered in red, because of poor grammar. "What are
they teaching you here?" he said. His English, I thought, was
impeccable, and his grammar was better than that of the American
TAs who taught Basic Writing. He gave me an A–. The paper I did
was on Anna Akhmatova's *Requiem*, a sequence of poems about
Stalin's terror she wrote after her son was arrested in 1935. I called
it "groundbreaking." I argued that it showed heroism and strength.
Nineteen thrity-five wasn't the silver age exactly, but her earlier
poems were all about love. I felt that in Victor's class, heroism was
a more appropriate topic.

Nikolai Gumilev was his favorite poet. He hunted lions in Africa,
fought in the First World War, and in 1921 he was charged in a con-
spiracy and shot by Bolsheviks. He was also married to Anna
Akhmatova, but their marriage hadn't worked. He wrote about her:

> From the town of Kiev,
> from the serpent's lair,
> I brought not a wife but a witch.

and she wrote about him:

> He didn't like crying children,
> tea with raspberry jam,
> and hysterical women.

Victor was popular with college women. After class, there was always a crowd of them gathered around his desk. He greeted them cordially. They knew not to trouble him with anything banal. He had a wife and son at home. He showed us a picture from his wallet—a thin-faced blonde in a cable-knit sweater, and next to her a little boy. It was a common story: college, exams, kisses in staircases, civil registry office, and a few years later, a pram. Now they were in their Squirrel Hill home while Victor was at work, lecturing, grading, instructing undergraduate girls.

The ones that stayed the longest were Monica and Daria from the Russian Club. They were smarter and prettier and more exotic than the others. Daria was vaguely Ukrainian (her parents came from Argentina). Monica was from New York. They worked for a couple of professors at the Slavic Languages program. I liked Daria the best. She was the least self-righteous. Leggy, foulmouthed, with long corkscrew curls. Her plans involved a Ph.D. in Russian and Ukrainian, although in case that didn't work, she might become a flight attendant for United.

They treated Victor like a friend, their manner intimate and flirty. I thought if he were to enter an affair, it would have to be with one of them. They told him jokes, shared departmental gossip. I waited in the back. I wasn't as articulate or confident, but I had something neither of them had. I was Victor's compatriot.

After they left, we walked to the William Pitt Union for coffee. The campus was snowy and cold, and, as in Russia, we were wrapped in scarves and coats. He wore a long woolen coat and a fur hat with earflaps.

"What do you miss the most?" he asked.

I said I missed walking in Moscow, traversing old boulevards, the sidewalks glistening in the night, Pushkin Square, the lovers clutching flowers beneath the poet's statue—*the sentinels of love.*

He said he also liked the boulevards, and Eskimo ice cream sticks for twenty-five kopeks.

What Victor missed was Russian brokenness. He said it was the core of the Russian soul. "You see it in poets: Tsvetaeva's suicide, Esenin, Mayakovsky. But it's not just the poets. We're sensitive, foolish, illogical. We live in a state of turmoil, on the brink of being destroyed, steps away from the next drunken bout."

I knew what he meant, I had my own brokenness. I felt it at the lab, in front of my computer. The whole place smelled of phenol, and I thought I could hear the squeaking of mice in the front part of the lab. I never witnessed the experiments. JT kept telling me they were important and had to do with finding a cure for heart problems.

Day after day, I did nothing. I read. I was afraid to ask JT for help, because then he'd uncover the truth: I didn't understand my programs. I did well enough in my classes, but at the lab I felt worthless.

"I'm not smart enough for computers," I'd said.

"You're smart enough," JT had told me. "You just have to apply yourself."

IN THE MEANTIME, the Russian Club members decided to go to Moscow. It was Victor's idea, but Monica became its champion. They should go this summer, she said, before their senior year, before they started looking for jobs. *This* was the moment! She spoke of Russia as she'd seen it: its hardships and its spirit, the turmoil of corruption and reforms, and the first thrill of freedom.

The others supported her: Daria; Mark with an earring, who worked in a Squirrel Hill coffee shop; short, bumptious Alicia, her hair heaped up in a high ponytail like a tiny palm tree and spilling.

And me? I was supportive too, in theory, though the Russia I remembered, the Russia of less than two years ago, was a cheerless place, punctured and cheated. The metro trains at rush hour, the lines in front of empty stores, the mobs of tired people, their faces like stone and loam.

At first, it seemed like an impractical idea. I didn't have the money for the trip. I'd need a special travel document and a visa. My parents wouldn't understand. They'd come all this way to rescue me from Russia. How could I go back? What hadn't I seen there?

I didn't think Victor was going either. He was on an H-1 visa, and I assumed that, like everyone else, he wanted to stay in America. But Victor said he'd supervise the trip. He told me the Russian Club needed me. He needed me too.

I said I was taking two classes that summer, Calculus II and File Systems.

"I thought you were switching to literature."

"Computers," I said, "is a good job for immigrants."

"But not for you," he said.

He was convinced that had I stayed in Moscow, I would've applied to Moscow State. He was mistaken. Philology was too prestigious, the competition rigorous, with tens of applicants contending for each space, and a Jewish person with no connections would've been felled. That's what we called it—*felled*—when you did well on the exams, but the committee tricked or failed you.

"This doesn't happen anymore," said Victor.

He seemed discomfited by my suggestion. There were topics we never discussed. My Jewishness, for example. He never asked about my parents or why we had come to America. I wanted to tell him. I thought he'd understand. He was open-minded, intelligent, a boy from a little Siberian village who'd made his way up, first to Moscow, then to America.

But he never asked, never shared his own reasons for leaving. He spoke incessantly about the trip to Moscow, and the more I resisted, the more forceful he got. He hinted at the honors research possibilities. He even said he'd make me his assistant to help offset the costs. I promised to consider it.

FOR A MONTH OR SO, the Russian Club bubbled with its idle Moscow talk: no particulars, just pouring it on, from an empty bowl into a hollow one. I thought they'd never pull it off. Then, in the last week of February, they had a breakthrough. They found a hospital there, in Moscow, affiliated with Magee-Womens in Pittsburgh. The hospital would let them volunteer for six weeks. They could stay in the dorms of a nearby university. Of course, they still needed the funding for the trip, and Monica was drafting a proposal.

The costume party, so lovingly planned for Soviet Army Day, turned into a simple potluck and a meeting at Monica's house. There were chips and salsa and a couple of casseroles. No one had dressed up, except for Daria, who wore a green soldier's blouse. Monica said it felt wrong to dress up, in light of all the suffering in Russia. To celebrate anything Soviet would be blasphemous. She'd done some studying. She had statistics and photographs—patients in poor striped robes, linoleum hallways.

They all had been studying. It was all they could talk about—the conditions in Russian hospitals, the babies with AIDS and hepatitis C, the blankets and toys and syringes. Hospital buildings with no hot water or heat. Was it true? they said. How could it be?

We sat in Monica's living room—ramshackle couches and chairs, lamps pleasantly shaded, a table with food. I was waiting for Victor. I'd dressed up in my mother's best sweater and a corduroy skirt. I'd given much thought to his offer, and now that the trip was taking form, I was starting to want it. I'd spin it to my parents as a job.

"The way we see it," said Monica, "this trip is for juniors and seniors." She glanced at Daria for support. They both were finishing their junior year. "We think it's fair," Monica continued, "but we expect the rest of you to be involved. We're going to need some volunteers."

"Excuse me," I said, and they all looked at me, because I hardly ever spoke. "Do you have any medical experience?"

"It's not important," said Monica.

"It's not?"

"We'll bring supplies, we'll raise some money—"

"Your money?" I said. "They'll take your money. They'll tell you thank you very much, and then they'll turn around and buy some office furniture or maybe build a summer cottage for their child."

"You'd rather do nothing?" said Monica. Like a clever orator, she turned toward her real audience. "*This* is the problem"—she pointed at me—"this kind of apathy. I mean, children are dying—"

"Leave her alone," said Daria. "She's got a point."

The rest of them acted appalled. Here they were, burning to save my old country, spoiling for a fight. Didn't I care? Didn't I love it?

But it wasn't my country anymore. I'd never really belonged there, in the Russia they imagined, among its fields and chapels, the clamor of its bells, the beggars in black shadows along the walls, the golden light bleeding from tiles, candles, and icons. It had been the fall of my senior year in high school, our class trip to the Troitsky monastery, and the boy I liked was crossing himself by the icon of Nikolai the Miracle Worker. He had a silver crucifix under his shirt, which probably meant nothing, except it was what nationalist patriots wore in those days, when they went on TV at midnight and talked of planned pogroms. No, I didn't miss Russia.

After the meeting I took a shuttle to campus. I tried Victor's office and the nook at Hillman Library where he sometimes worked. It was Saturday, nine o'clock, and like all normal people, he must have been at home with his family. And what of my family? Light thinning, my mother asleep, my father playing solitaire in the living room. I came home late, and they never asked me any questions, except maybe about my grades. It was easy enough to mislead them.

I tried to picture Moscow. I liked it the best in the summer, golden and green, the air rippling, the asphalt pulsating from the heat. I saw myself and Victor. The city unfolded before us, revealed its parks and streets, Pushkin Square, Moscow State University. Then Victor disappeared. It was suddenly winter, and I was lost in a distant part of Moscow, among identical apartment blocks.

I walked back to the campus shuttle stop. It was cold, almost unbearable. The shuttles were rare because it was the weekend. I waited and waited. After a while, a white Honda hatchback parked next to the sidewalk. JT rolled down the window. "I thought it was you," he said. Inside, the car was warm and smelled of candy, and the stereo flashed HELLO! spelled in blue and red letters.

"How are you feeling?" he said. I'd called in sick a lot in the previous weeks.

I said I was feeling much better.

"You're coming back to us?"

I said, Of course.

"Lakshmi's been asking about your code. I didn't know what to tell her. Do you mind if I tinker with it in my spare time?"

I shook my head to say I didn't care. I was feeling nostalgic for something. It wasn't the lab or the code. I didn't know what it was. I said I might go to Moscow in the summer.

"To see your folks?"

I told him my parents were here in Pittsburgh.

He said, "You lucky dog."

I'd never asked JT about his family. He was well-adjusted and playful; it seemed unthinkable that he might feel alone. He had his friends, he had his ferret.

He kept talking about the ferret. It had been acting strange, and maybe being at the lab was getting to be too traumatic.

I said, "Poor Rat." I'd keep him company next week. And then we'd get some burgers at the cafeteria.

But the following week I had midterms, and I forgot all about my promise. I never made it to the lab. At the end of the week, I stopped at Victor's office. His desk was piled with photocopies and student exams. He was shuffling through them. His briefcase was open. He said he had a dentist's appointment the next morning but he'd misplaced his insurance card.

My question was whether or not I could go to Moscow. It had been bothering me since the meeting at Monica's, since she'd implied I didn't qualify.

"For God's sake," said Victor, "don't listen to Monica. You're going. You'll meet some excellent professors at Moscow State. In the fall, you'll declare your major, and in the spring we'll arrange an exchange."

I didn't know what to say. It seemed a little drastic. As far as my parents knew, I was still a computer science major, and then I'd have a job at Mellon Bank. I was afraid to disappoint them. I was afraid to disappoint myself. More than anything, I didn't want Victor to drop me. On my second paper he'd given me an A. It was on Gumilev and the influence of French Symbolism, and he said it was better than the drivel he got from his graduate class. He might even include it in a book of essays, provided I expanded it. This, of course, was no accident. I'd spent hours in Hillman Library, reading criticism, poring over grammar manuals. I lived in a blur of rhymes and stanzas, daydreamed in the rest of my classes, read books at the lab. It was thrilling to think I was finally good at something.

I told Victor I had a great plan for our final paper. It was broad, it was challenging, it could be turned into an honors thesis, and I hoped that Victor could help me with that.

He said, "Don't talk of your ideas in advance. You write, we'll take a look at it later."

AT THE RUSSIAN CLUB MEETING the next week, we learned that we got the money for the Moscow trip. Five thousand dollars, enough for the lodging and fees and maybe some gifts. But everyone would have to pay their own airfare. Most of the members seemed to be willing. For those with money problems, Monica said there were travel grants. They were merit-based. Your teacher had to nominate you.

In my checking account at Dollar Bank, the balance was two hundred fifty. It was my own blunder. I had all but abandoned the job at the lab. My time card last month listed less than twenty hours. I was certain Victor would recommend me for a grant, but all the same, it didn't mean I'd get it.

The following Tuesday I went back to the lab.

There were no smells, no sounds, no traces of mice; the floors were swept clean, the counters were spotless. Even the coffeemaker seemed to shine. I found JT in the back of the lab, playing a game on my computer.

I asked him, "Where's everybody?"

It took him a moment to answer. He said Gary was on vacation, Lakshmi was finishing her article. "We're done," he said. "You've missed the celebration. We even had champagne."

I said, "What about the graphs?"

"Finished. Done."

"But my programs . . ." I said.

"I had to rewrite them. You said you didn't mind."

He showed me the new programs. They were clean, neatly formatted. They ran. The graphs they produced looked solid. JT explained the meaning of each graph.

I said I had to talk to Lakshmi.

"I wouldn't," he said. "She's on deadline. And anyway, it's over."

"What's over?"

He looked at me like I was being dumb.

There wasn't too much to collect: two library books, a notepad, my coffee mug. I was supposed to feel regretful, but instead I was buoyant. No matter how badly I needed the money, it felt great to be done with the lab.

JT was back at my computer. He was playing a shooting game, cheap and oddly discolored, with dull explosions coming through the earphones.

He took the earphones down. "You'll be better off somewhere else. Doing something you actually care for."

"I know," I said. Then I paused, looking around. "Where's Rat?"

"Gone," he said. "He stopped eating one day. Eventually we had to put him down."

"You're kidding."

"I think he had cancer. These things never really last."

"He was your pet," I said. "I know you loved him."

He shrugged. "I'm a biologist. Biologists don't get attached."

He clicked some keys, and on the screen the enemy collapsed and the enemy's blood poured out. It was dull, pixelated, the color of a swamp.

—

I DIDN'T TELL MY PARENTS I got fired. To Victor, I said I'd lost some of my hours, which, actually, was for the best. I knew what I cared for, and I hoped that Victor could help. I thought I could start in advance as his assistant. My ex-boyfriend once did some translations for the Slavic Languages program. I told Victor I, too, could translate. I could make and collate photocopies, pick up books from the library, prepare coffee—whatever Monica and Daria did for their professors.

We spoke after class, toward the end of the semester. There was maybe a month of it left, and everyone was acting stressed and coming down with fevers and aches. Victor's son had an ear infection.

Victor listened to me, unconvinced. He said the department was full of bureaucracy, and as a visiting professor, he didn't merit an official assistant. In other words, he couldn't pay.

"Why don't you ask your folks for help?"

"They don't have any money," I said.

"You want me to believe that? That they don't have some emergency dollars squirreled away?"

I told him a Moscow trip was hardly an emergency. More like a holiday.

"You know what I think?" he said. "I think you never told them. Do they know about our plans?"

I said nothing.

"Have you told them?" he asked again.

"I haven't."

He got up from his chair, his face controlled and hollow, the face of a fighter pilot performing under stress. He brushed his hand against his desk. It was splintered and heaped with papers, some of which shifted and fell. I tried to collect them. "You're wasting my time," Victor said. "I warned you I didn't like dabblers."

After that, Victor mostly ignored me. He wouldn't call on me in class, and afterwards it was impossible to talk to him. The Russian Club had extra meetings—a task team, a benefit-planning committee—and Victor was involved in all those things.

JT hardly talked to me either. I ran into him a few times. He was friendly, but distant. The work, he said, was all right. They were preparing for a conference in England. The weather was a drag. He had a girlfriend who went to school in Meadville.

As for me, I had picked up a couple of cleaning jobs through my best friend, Lariska. They were infrequent, and the money still wasn't enough. I'd been toiling on my final paper for Victor. I wanted to be his best student again, his favorite assistant.

It was just before finals week that I heard about the travel grant. I was at the Russian Club meeting; the members were discussing it. Victor had kept it a secret. He nominated Monica, not me. Daria said, "Fucking typical." She'd been wanting the grant for herself.

"Did Monica get it?" I asked.

She said, "What do you think?" And where was Monica now? Having a one-on-one meeting with Victor. "He's always had a thing for her."

I couldn't believe it. I'd seen them together, of course, but I thought it was innocent, the way our meetings were. I remembered one afternoon in particular: Victor and I were at the shuttle stop, and she stood outside the Cathedral. She waved to us. She wore bright orange mittens, and Victor said, "She's such a show-off."

Later that day, I went to see Victor.

He was grading. He sat with his head bowed low, and I could see that his hair was sullied and thinning on top. We'd handed in our papers the previous week, and now he gestured toward them and said they were crap. He asked me what it was I wanted.

I told him I wanted to go to Moscow, but the money was still a problem. I'd hoped for a travel grant.

"I picked the most deserving candidate. It happened to be Monica."

I almost asked him, *What about our plans?*

"You should take a loan, if you still want to go. That's what you Americans do anyway."

I said I was about as American as he was.

He whistled and said, "No way. You're here to stay, dear comrade."

"Aren't you staying as well?"

"I'm not insane. I can't raise my son in a soulless society."

"It's not soulless," I said.

"Keep telling it to yourself, and maybe you'll believe it. You're already becoming like them. I think you should stick with computer programming. I'm told it's a good job for immigrants."

"Maybe I will," I said.

He didn't understand. He was a product of our homeland— sensitive, foolish, and scornful, full of lavish ideas and puzzling complaints, but unlike me, he had always belonged there.

He was the first to look away.

"My office hours are on Wednesday, if you have other questions."

I had no questions, I said.

MY FINAL PAPER was on the poets of immigration. They left in the early twenties and went to Germany or France. There they tried to re-create the silver age, started salons and publications. But it wasn't the same. They were alienated. Despite the riches of Berlin and Paris, their spirits were poor and drained. Some struggled to get published, and others struggled to support themselves. Still, many of them managed, perfected their craft, and even took it to a higher level.

At our last class, Victor said the silver age outlived itself. The best poets perished in Russia, while those who escaped were nothing but pale imitations. He wrote on the back of my paper, "For a true Russian person, immigration is death. A Russian poet can't survive in immigration."

He gave me a B–.

This was the last Russian literature class I would take. I had fulfilled my literature requirements, and for the next two years my textbooks were the only things I read. In the fall I declared my major. By the time I graduated, I'd gotten to be pretty good at computer programming. I even got some scholarships.

I heard the trip to Moscow never happened. Maybe the money didn't come through, or the hospital reneged, or maybe the Russian Club members lost interest. Sometimes I saw Daria on campus. We nodded to each other from a distance. I wondered what'd become of Victor. Was he with Monica? Was he in Pittsburgh? Or did he go back? I knew she'd tell me if I asked her. But I never asked.

Dancers

THEY WERE TALL, good-looking, and careless. They arrived unexpectedly, descended upon Tanya's life, took up residence in her apartment. They seemed instantly comfortable there, as if it were the most natural thing for them to settle on the living room couch of somebody's apartment in Pittsburgh. They were dancers and nothing could be done about it.

Petya had told Tanya on Tuesday morning. He was eating the oatmeal she'd fixed for him, and she stood leaning against the microwave, coffee mug in her hands—she didn't eat breakfast. Petya said his high school friend Senya was going to visit them for a couple of days. "You remember," he said. "I've told you about him. The ballet guy."

She didn't remember, but that was all right; she liked company. To others, she seemed like a solitary person, with her shyness, her eyeglasses, her quiet, concentrated look. People were afraid to disturb her; even Petya was afraid sometimes. She could tell he was a

little worried now. She smiled to reassure him. It was good that this
friend, this Senya, was arriving. They might all take a drive somewhere, go to a restaurant once or twice. Petya didn't like to eat out
unless it was a special occasion. They did okay, moneywise—he was
an engineer and she clerked at the medical center—but they were
also saving for a house. Tanya's parents, too, always saved, ate out
rarely and only at buffet places, and now they had a little house in
Squirrel Hill. They called Petya *a sensible fellow*, and were glad
because Tanya needed someone sensible. Tanya believed them and
was also vaguely glad she had Petya.

Where was Petya's friend coming from? How long was he to
stay? And what on earth were they going to feed him (their refrigerator in such a despicable empty state, you could roll a ball in
there)?

"Don't you panic, *starushka*," said Petya. He called her that sometimes, *starushka*, a little old lady. She had recently turned twenty-
six.

But Tanya panicked anyway. On her way to work and later at the
office, she felt the sweet and tugging anticipation of something, an
event. On her lunch break, she ran to the supermarket. She wanted
bright holiday food: a frosty bottle of champagne, chocolates indi-
vidually wrapped in crinkling foil, an enormous winter basket with
ribbons. But the holidays were over, and she wound up instead
with a splintery box of wilted tangerines.

The next night, Tanya and Petya drove to the Greyhound station. The New York bus had just pulled in, and there was Senya,
sparkling with good-natured energy, rangy and blond, in a silvery
winter jacket. He hugged them both. Tanya felt swept up by the
earnestness of Senya's hug. Then she saw the girl. She stood apart,
watching the commotion with cool, guarded eyes. She wore a long
leather coat. Her red hair was gathered in a classic knot at the nape

of her neck, the beautiful long neck with the fatigued tilt that Tanya had always associated with ballerinas.

"Why are you standing there, Ksyusha?" Senya said to the girl. "Look, this is Petya and this is Tanya."

She approached hesitantly, as if she knew they hadn't expected her.

"Nice to meet you," she said in a clipped little voice. She offered Petya her hand and introduced herself—*Oksana*. They were to call her by her full, formal name.

ON THE WAY HOME, Tanya learned that Oksana was from Ukraine, that Senya had met her in Las Vegas, where both danced for six months in a Russian show called *Caviar*, that soon they would sign another contract—an agent from California had expressed interest, and also the artistic director of *Caviar* wanted them for his next show. They brought with them the tape of *Caviar*. After dinner Oksana suddenly spoke up and insisted that they must, *simply must*, watch the tape. Tanya served tea in the living room. They all sat in front of the humming TV and watched.

There were women in long sarafans and beaded kokoshniks. Cossacks with fake mustaches strutted in their dashing sharovars. Someone showed up dressed as a bear. There were modern numbers too, meant to represent the new, uplifted Russia: men and women in stark suits, marching pointedly and swinging their briefcases. At the end, girls in bright little skirts danced the cancan.

"Look at them," Tanya whispered to Petya. "Their legs grow from the same place as their teeth."

She meant it as a joke, the kind of joke Petya usually made himself. But Petya shrugged and even moved away from Tanya a little. Maybe he thought the legs were nice to look at, or maybe he was afraid that Senya and Oksana would overhear. But Senya and Oksana heard nothing. They were watching their *Caviar*—pointing, arguing, and blushing, agitated Oksana saying that, *no, such and such was a good dancer . . . and once in the makeup room, Lida Gruzdeva told everybody . . . but it was a huge secret, like that time she got in trouble with Tikhonov, you remember that, right?* They were like two children just back from summer camp, still attached to the loud and communal way they had lived in Las Vegas.

Oksana's trunk stood in the hallway by the front door. The next night, coming home from work, Tanya bumped against it; it was the kind of dumb, clumsy thing she did a lot. The trunk was black and sturdy, with heavy metal patches around the corners; it had an old-fashioned bulk to it. Oksana said she never went anywhere without the trunk, not since her ballet school days.

"Tell me about the ballet school," Tanya said, rubbing her bruised ankle.

"School like school," said Oksana. "Classes every day. Bad food. Cold bedrooms."

"You lived there?"

"The locals got to go home," said Oksana. Her home was three hours away by bus, and week after week she stayed at the school, returning home only during long breaks.

Oksana spoke with a teenage abruptness, like somebody forced to constantly explain boring and obvious things. She *was* a teenager. Barely eighteen. The way she spoke made Tanya feel old.

"I tried to get into ballet once," Tanya volunteered. "When I was seven. They didn't take me, said I had flat feet."

"The requirements are very specific," said Oksana. "Feet have to be well-arched. Toes of equal length." She raised her foot and wiggled her toes to demonstrate. "Also the hips, wide so you can turn your feet to point outward."

She gave Tanya a quick once-over. "You've got the hips. But you're not tall."

"Well, nobody in our family is tall," apologized Tanya.

But Oksana wasn't listening anymore. Senya came into the room, and she half rose from her chair. Their love was in the annoying, devouring stage where the rest of the world was a mere nuisance. They needed each other all the time and urgently. They touched a lot; it was probably a dance thing.

Could Tanya love with such audacity, with sinking of the stomach and shaking in the knees? She had been seventeen when her family came to Pittsburgh. A plain, timid girl, she was virtually invisible. There was one excruciating year in high school, then college. Tanya had desperately wanted a boyfriend. She wanted a boyfriend to invade her life, to take control, to make her rare, unavailable, and thus desirable to others. She had seen it happen to her girlfriends.

Later that night Petya said that dancing was a bullshit profession. "No steady jobs," he said. "Look at them hanging, waiting for a contract. And Oksana? He'll dump her in a month."

He and Tanya were getting ready for bed. Tanya brought a basket of soft and toasty bed linens from the laundry downstairs. Sheets, pillowcases, a blanket cover. It smelled of safe, flowery confinement. No one was dumping anybody in their home.

But Petya said there was a couple in Montreal who had sort of adopted Senya. "You know," he said, "bored, wealthy people. Don't know what to do with their money. Get into silly matters, like the symphony or pictures or ballet."

"Maecenas," said Tanya, "patrons of the arts."

"Whatever. *Senya's* people. He's one clever comrade, our Senya. They have a room for him up there, in their house in Montreal. Wallpaper, flowers on the table. Everything's proper. Money for college, too."

"And Oksana?"

"What Oksana? I'm asking you, *starushka*, is Senya insane to spoil a sweet situation like that? To bring along some girl, a silly Ukrainian broad, one meter seventy centimeters?"

Tanya took one corner of the fitted sheet and Petya took another. They pulled in opposite directions.

"Still," said Tanya, "I think they're in love."

"*In love*," he mocked her. "Don't you muddle honest people's heads, Tatyana."

That was Petya, practical, unsentimental. Nobody could muddle Petya's head. Relatives had introduced them when Tanya was a senior in college. He told her that he worked at Westinghouse. He made jokes about American incompetence. He seemed bored with his job, bored with America, perhaps even bored with Tanya. They went on four dates and she was growing bored with him too.

Then one day Tanya met Petya's cousins, two slovenly guys, drinking beer from plastic cups at the bowling alley where Petya brought Tanya—*the American pastime, Tanyusha*. The cousins said it was a pleasure to meet her—Tanechka-Tanya—such a nice lady, too nice for a fool like Petya, and in college too! They said they didn't go to college. They were going to open a restaurant in Squirrel Hill. With a catering service.

Empty talk! said Petya. All of it! Dumb empty talk! He was taking Tanya home, and his voice kept breaking, he was so upset. He told Tanya that the cousins had been working in pizza joints, making minimum wage. They refused to understand that you were nothing, *nothing*, without education. Two young, strapping guys, and not half-wits either . . . Tanya timidly pressed Petya's hand. And her heart, her poor heart, tired of waiting and being invisible, it faltered, it paused. But the next time she saw Petya, he was again his smug, catlike self—he made sleepy jokes and took Tanya to the

movies at the Manor. She married him anyway, after a year of dili-
gent dating, and the relatives said they were well-matched.

THE APARTMENT BEGAN to carry traces of Oksana's presence.
There was a plush toy dog she liked to cuddle; there were her lace-
up boots with shapely heels; there was a nylon ribbon she tied to
the brass vanity in Tanya's bedroom. This was Oksana's peculiar,
undeveloped idea of beauty, and Tanya was both frustrated and
moved by it.

On Friday night Petya took Senya to the bowling alley, and
Tanya and Oksana sat in the living room with a bottle of Baileys
and a Victoria's Secret catalog. The *Caviar* tape was playing—those
Cossacks again—and there was Oksana in her short lime skirt and
her dance shoes, tall and red-haired. One of the three prettiest girls
in the show, she said.

A dancer in black elastic tights began a classical number. "Look,"
said Oksana. "That's Volodya."

By then Tanya knew the trajectory of Oksana's wayward past:
the ballet school, then the corps de ballet at a theater in Donetsk,
and finally the American tour. It was during the tour that she had
an affair with Volodya, the principal dancer. He was the one who
persuaded her to stay.

They watched muscular Volodya do a robust pirouette. "Such a
man!" said Oksana. "Such a wonderful, wicked man." And she
groaned in a languorous, sexual way. After the tour ended, she and
Volodya stayed in Philadelphia, in a ballet house with a dozen other
unemployed dancers. The house belonged to Mickey the connois-
seur, homosexual Mickey, who loved the dancers, kept them for
free, and even helped them get jobs. Poor *gomic* Mickey, said
Oksana. Come back anytime, he told her and Volodya, though he

seemed to understand that they wouldn't. Not together anyway.
After four months in Vegas, Volodya returned to Donetsk. He had
a wife and a daughter there, and the wife was fed up with Volodya's
touring.

"You didn't know?" said Tanya. In spite of herself, she was drawn
into this little adolescent drama. "He didn't tell you about the
wife?"

"I knew," said Oksana. "Everybody knew."

She spoke of men with the same assured precision she would
use to explain some interesting pas de deux. Here was this girl, this
creature, callow yet experienced in ways that Tanya would never be.

A week went by, and the dancers showed no intention of leaving. But Tanya had already fallen under the spell of their artistic
charms. With them around, life became brilliant and unpredictable.
They did spontaneous, expensive things, like going to the Russian
restaurant, Moscow Nights, or, at Senya's insistence, trying sushi for
the first time. There was a weekend when they all went to the zoo,
and there was a night when Oksana suddenly decided she needed
a present for her godmother in Donetsk and they all got up and
went to Monroeville Mall, even though it was after eight and Petya
had an early meeting the next morning.

In the morning, Tanya, pale and light-headed from lack of sleep,
cooked quick, soundless breakfasts. At work, she talked about the
dancers—that's what she called them, *those crazy dancers*—and what
they'd done the night before. The girls at the office thought it was
all very exciting. They wanted to know if the dancers were about
to perform anywhere locally and if so would there be free tickets.
Tanya tried to remain vague about that.

What the dancers did during the day was a mystery. Petya had
taken them around Squirrel Hill, showed them a couple of cafés,
some fancy boutiques on Forbes, a library. They could take a bus

downtown. But the dancers never went anywhere. When Tanya returned from work, they were always snuggled on the couch, napping or watching TV.

At night Tanya and Petya could hear them on that creaky living room couch. Tanya imagined their supple, capable bodies bending in all kinds of pleasurable positions. The sounds traveled from the living room: a trickle of laughter, Oksana's high-pitched, excited sobs. And next to Tanya was Petya, tossing, breathing heavily through his stuffed nose.

Petya couldn't sleep either.

"Have you seen her underwear hanging in the bathroom? What do you call those things anyway?"

"Thongs," said Tanya.

"Yes, thongs. Red. What's the deal with the red? What's the deal with the thongs? Don't they tear into your ass?"

"She likes them. It's sexy."

"One pair is sexy. Ten pairs is stupid."

"You're the one who's stupid," Tanya said, turning away from Petya. She had an urge to tell him that the gold chain he'd taken to wearing around his neck looked tasteless, that he'd gained weight, that the way he strutted around made him look like a small-town thug.

Something happened to Tanya whenever she watched Senya and Oksana together. They'd be standing by the window, pressed against each other—just the two outlines in the twilight—his body absorbing her small curves. Tanya's face grew hot. She noticed things about Senya: his hands, his bare feet, the way his jeans creased around his crotch when he sat. When he looked at her, she felt weightless and pretty.

After dinner, Senya would help Tanya in the kitchen. She washed the dishes and he stood ready with a dish towel. They worked side by side, silently, and their elbows sometimes touched. Tanya would say, Sorry. She could tell he was watching her—her neck, the side of her face. She would pull her hair back, tie it with an elastic—let him watch. He stood so close. Sometimes he stopped drying the dishes and just stood, looking at her.

"Were you really friends at school?" Tanya asked Petya one night. "You and Senya? Tell me how it was when you were kids."

Petya shifted in bed. "Settle down, Tanya. It's late and I don't remember."

"Come on, tell me," she said, reaching out and stroking his neck. "*Te-e-ell* me," she teased. She leaned on her elbow and let the strap of her nightgown slide down her arm.

Petya was not an inventive lover. He was straightforward with his needs and didn't know her body well. She believed it wasn't for lack of generosity. He was too shy to explore or ask, and she was too shy to show him.

"You're obsessed with your Senya," said Petya.

She pulled back, right away feeling ridiculous. *Remember who you are. Retreat into your poor, pudgy body—not fat, just poorly defined.* She felt ashamed. Was that because Petya had unwittingly spoken the truth? Her playfulness, her fascination were misplaced.

"Go to sleep, Tatyana." He patted her shoulder reassuringly and fixed the strap of her nightgown. "I'm exhausted."

She pulled the blanket over her head.

SHE BEGAN TO WORRY about the dancers leaving, going to California or Montreal. It was the end of their second week in Pittsburgh, and so far nothing had been mentioned, there were no signs, although they were now doing their exercises on the living room carpet every evening. Tanya stayed out of their way. She liked to watch them from the adjoining dining room, the way they crouched next to each other, checking out angles and curves.

"Before thirty your body looks gorgeous," explained Senya, "but if you haven't been taking care, you turn thirty and it all begins: injuries, strains, onset of arthritis. Next thing you know, you have to go for a hip replacement. Right, Oksana?"

Oksana was on the floor with her legs up in the air, a perfect forty-five-degree angle.

"And one, and two, and three . . ." counted Senya.

Petya was there too, right in the midst of it. He sat on the couch, his feet in ratty slippers almost touching Oksana's arm. Tanya called him aside, whispered how he was probably distracting the dancers. He said it was his home, and if they were distracted they could go someplace else.

"Abdominal muscles are especially important," said Senya. He got on his knees next to Oksana, inspected the angle. "Nope. That's too high." He lowered Oksana's legs to thirty degrees.

"I can't anymore," said Oksana. She dropped her legs and covered her face.

"Come on. Let's go," said Senya. "One, two, three."

"I told you I can't." Oksana got up from the floor.

"That's because you've been doing nothing," said Senya. "And eating crap."

"Look at yourself first," said Oksana. She picked up her toy dog and went to hide in Tanya and Petya's room. They heard her click the latch.

"She refuses to understand." Senya turned to Tanya. "It's different for male dancers. We don't gain weight the same way."

That night, Tanya cooked them a healthy dinner. Chicken breasts, broccoli. She didn't want Senya to think she was feeding them bad food.

"Is this all we're having?" Petya poked at his broccoli. She gave him a look, which he received stubbornly, blankly. He wanted fried potatoes and herring and a special salad with mayonnaise. And beer.

She went and got him a beer from the fridge. "Happy now?"

"Happy."

"Tanya should take ballet lessons," said Senya.

Petya chuckled and choked on his beer. "Ballet," he said, clearing his throat. He and Oksana exchanged sniggering looks.

"I think she would enjoy it," insisted Senya. "She's got a graceful step."

"Graceful step," muttered Petya. "You hear that, *starushka*? We're sending you to do ballet!"

Tanya stared at her plate and tried to remember that this was Petya, that he didn't mean it, that he actually loved her in his own morose, idiotic way.

"Don't listen to him, Tanechka," said Senya. "What does he know? He's a boorish little fool."

She looked up slowly. Senya was waiting for her, his eyes were waiting, they were saying: *It's* me. *Don't you* trust *me?*

And she did. There was nobody else she could trust.

IT WAS AT THE BEGINNING of the third week that it dawned on Tanya that the dancers weren't going anywhere, that they had money problems, that there was, in fact, a whole money situation going on. She overheard hushed arguments; she saw Senya frowning over his checkbook. The four of them had stopped going out. Now at night, they watched Russian films, the ones Petya had rented from Three Bears and copied illegally using his cousins' second VCR.

They had gotten into the habit of arranging themselves in a certain configuration around the TV. Petya and Oksana were both on the floor, Oksana on her stomach, Petya with his legs crossed, all of the remote controls gathered in a heap before him. Tanya and Senya were on the couch; it felt awkward at first to be so close together, but he eventually got her to relax—stretch out and rest her head on his lap. Nobody seemed to care. Not even Petya. They were all dancers, all used to each other by then. Senya ran his fingers through Tanya's hair, massaged her neck. She told herself it didn't mean anything. It was just Senya, creative, uninhibited. Sometimes, during funny moments, she looked up at him and they laughed together. And there were other moments when his fingers tentatively and stealthily touched her face. Then she didn't know what to think.

One evening after dinner, Senya sat at the table looking through the Sunday paper. Tanya was finishing up in the kitchen; she could see him from there, tracing inky listings of the help-wanted section.

"Tomorrow we're going to the Pittsburgh Ballet," said Senya.

"You are?" said Tanya. It wasn't really a question; she just felt like responding to his voice.

"To see if we can get a job for Oksana. Here, it says Liberty something."

"Is that East Liberty?" Tanya said worriedly. East Liberty was a rough neighborhood.

"I know where it is," called out Petya. He was in the living room, reading about real estate.

"He knows," Senya said, entering the kitchen. His palms were stained with print, and he held them up to Tanya. He had a small smudge on his cheek too; she pointed it out. He turned his cheek to Tanya, as if she could, with her bare fingers, take care of the ink.

The next day Senya and Oksana went to the Pittsburgh Ballet. At dinner, Oksana said she'd had an interview and later watched a class. Nobody had offered her a contract.

"They said I can come to the classes."

"You should," said Senya.

"They are terrible," said Oksana. "Girls just stand there slack, and the teacher doesn't correct them."

"It's a different system," said Senya. "Anyway, I'm sure the troupe itself is very good, and that is what's important, Oksana, getting a contract with the troupe."

"A system?" said Oksana. "Don't talk to me about systems."

Tanya listened, embarrassed and strangely satisfied. They had been quarreling a lot lately. And Petya was quietly gloating too; he'd never liked Oksana.

Oksana went to three more classes that week.

"If that's how they teach ballet, then I don't know," she said on Thursday.

"That's not the right attitude," said Senya. "*Learn* from them. Take from them everything you can. If they see you're good, they'll give you a job."

"Nobody's giving me a job," snapped Oksana.

"Because you're not trying. They see the attitude."

"Shut up already with your attitude," said Oksana. "Nobody likes American ballet. Except for inept dancers, like yourself, who can't do good jumps."

"Inept?" said Senya.

"Yes! And everybody in Las Vegas knew."

Tanya wanted to take Senya's hand, show him that she was on his side. But Petya led Senya away, probably to the bowling alley, where his cousins drank and said harsh things about women. Oksana started the *Caviar* tape. It couldn't be true what she had said about Senya. He was beautiful, he could jump. And even if he couldn't, it didn't matter, he was Senya.

On Sunday morning at breakfast, Senya said he was going to Montreal. He had to see his adoptive family; there was some business concerning his immigration status. He would leave first thing Monday morning, come back in a couple of days. Oksana was to wait for him in Pittsburgh.

From that announcement Tanya concluded that the adoptive family didn't know about Oksana, and this made her happy. She had big plans for this Sunday: had talked Petya into driving to the House with a Waterfall, a little road trip, with apple cider and a picnic basket. She thought of all the secret gestures she and Senya would be able to exchange.

But after breakfast Oksana and Senya started fighting. They went into Tanya and Petya's bedroom to argue, and Tanya waited and paced the living room. Their trip arrangements were falling apart, and Petya, who didn't want to go in the first place, was now annoyingly happy. In the afternoon it started to rain and there couldn't be any more talk of picnics and road trips. Oksana and Senya came out of the bedroom. Senya left to pick up a rental car. Oksana slept.

ON MONDAY AND TUESDAY Oksana went to her class. Her mood didn't improve. She hated the instructors, and without Senya around, she had to travel to the theater alone. At night she called Senya in Montreal and cried. On Wednesday she stopped going to the theater. "It's a waste of time," she said. "There are no professionals there." She watched talk shows and slept on the unfolded living room couch. In the evening, she refused to eat dinner and instead sat in the bedroom at Tanya's vanity, putting on elaborate, predatory makeup.

Without Senya, Oksana became an encumbrance, an obstacle. Every time she went into the bedroom with the phone, Tanya found a reason to linger behind the closed door. She listened deliberately and didn't feel ashamed for listening. She hated Oksana's voice, small and stifled, full of little hysterics. "You asked me to come with you," said the voice. "You know I hate it here." Tanya imagined walking in and taking the phone away from Oksana. What would Senya think? He'd hear the pause, the different pattern of breathing. She'd say, "Hi, it's me." Or something else. Of course there would still be Oksana to deal with, her prickly love, her mincing affectations. Still, Tanya didn't want her out. As long as Oksana was there, Senya would come back.

A week went by. "How long is she going to stay with us?" said Petya. "I'm not a millionaire to feed an extra mouth. I'm not a charity."

"Don't ask me," said Tanya. "He's your friend."

"Friendship is friendship. But hey, grandma, this crosses all the boundaries. This is simply insulting."

"He's *your* friend," Tanya repeated. It pained her to pretend that Senya was a stranger to her.

The days dragged on. Senya wasn't coming back. Tanya sank into apathy. "You've been kind of dull lately, grandma," said Petya. But Petya didn't bother her. He wanted the usual things: meals, an orderly apartment, their weekly trips to Giant Eagle. They drove to Monroeville, to furniture stores. He wanted to look for a new couch. Petya liked big, pompous stuff, chairs and couches that promised a long, settled life. Tanya in her coat, huddled on the edge of a leather love seat, yawned, looked around. Everywhere was monstrous furniture: sticky leather, loud print, something with flowers.

"This one? Or maybe that?" Petya rushed among couches. "Are you paying attention, Tanya?"

"Isn't this all terribly expensive?"

"I want to get the real thing," said Petya, "something that will look good in the house when we get one."

This is what she wanted to tell him: She didn't care about the couch or the house. Didn't want them. Didn't want Petya. The long, scheduled life, all its stages charted in advance by a committee of relatives. She didn't want *that*. I might not be around to share a house with you, Petya.

"You don't know what the real thing is," she said instead.

That night Petya got sick with a cold and Tanya had to care for his sore throat. She stood in the kitchen boiling milk in a small pan and thinking about Senya.

She and Senya would have to move away, thought Tanya. Pittsburgh wouldn't do. Perhaps they would settle in Montreal. Somebody else would have to bring Petya his boiled milk with honey and a dash of mineral water. Tanya imagined herself in Montreal. She would dress smarter there, let her hair grow longer and wear it in a French braid. She'd get a job at some kind of office.

Senya had been gone for two weeks.

The milk began to boil. She turned it off and kept standing there, rocking slightly and aching.

"What's wrong with you?" Petya said, stepping in front of her. He wanted his milk. "What are you? Sleepwalking?"

The picture in her head got blurry: Montreal and Senya; her hair in a braid; she would have to learn French. "It's nothing," she said to Petya, and walked out of the kitchen.

HE CAME BACK ON FRIDAY, early in the evening. Tanya had just returned from work and Petya wasn't home yet. She heard him from the kitchen: a knock on the door, the rustling of the coat,

Oksana's little squeal. Oksana hadn't told anyone he was coming. Tanya stayed where she was; she didn't want to watch them together.

"Hello, Tanechka," Senya said, coming into the kitchen moments later.

"We didn't expect you," she said, and stopped, realizing it sounded wrong. "I mean it's great that you're here. We just didn't know. How are you?" She was stumbling.

"Good," he said brightly, and she heard something smooth and fake in it. He wasn't looking at her, was looking instead at the window, at the stove, at the pages of the week-old *Pittsburgh Post-Gazette* on the counter. "How are you guys?" he said. "How is Petya?"

"As usual," said Tanya. Her voice was sinking and she was suddenly dull, an old housewife in the kitchen. "Everything is as usual."

Back in the living room, Oksana emitted a polite little cough, as if to say, *Your assistance is required here, Senya.* He said, "Just a minute," and ducked out of the kitchen. He didn't return.

Forty-five minutes later Petya came home from the office, and they had dinner with a Canadian beer Senya had brought from Montreal. Very brown and bitter. He'd had a good time in Montreal. The immigration business was settled; his surrogate family had missed him; he'd gone to see a hockey game.

Tanya took a sleeping pill and went to bed early. She said she had a headache, which was partially true. In the middle of the night she woke up and thought what a fool she was. Everything in her life was imaginary. She grasped at the tiniest signs of flirtation: a pause, a gesture, a tenuous smile. She pasted those together, convinced herself she had something whole. In the end, it was always a fluke, a delusion. She was invisible again. Next to Tanya, Petya was asleep and snoring, and she cried quietly until the tears exhausted her.

But the next morning Senya took Oksana to the Greyhound

station. It was a Saturday and he was sending her to Philadelphia. Oksana, her shoulders rigid with anger, had repacked her black trunk. She hugged Tanya and Petya like it was a formality. She thanked them, but there was something defiant in that too, as if she thought they were kicking her out.

"Should have done it a long time ago," said Petya.

"But why?" said Tanya.

Petya shrugged. "Got tired of her whiny ass?"

And just like that, Tanya had hope again. An idiot, she called herself, but the hope was already there, ringing in her ears, rippling before her eyes. She needed Petya to leave for a while. She tried to think of an errand for him, but Petya wouldn't move. Finally one of his cousins called, something about a car, a rusted muffler.

She was alone when Senya returned. He dropped in a chair, rubbed his eyes.

"Tired," he said. "All this driving."

She didn't know how to start, so she asked, stupidly, about Oksana. Senya said that Oksana would be all right in Philadelphia, that Mickey would take care of her.

"I'm sorry," said Tanya.

"Don't despair, Tanechka."

She suggested he have something to eat or take a nap, although she didn't really want him to sleep, she wanted to be with him like this, talking. Something important had to be said while it was just the two of them.

"That's okay, Tanechka. I need to head back."

"Back? Back to Canada?"

"To Montreal. I've got a job there."

"Dancing?"

"No, at a bank. Anyway, where is that bastard Petya? I want to say good-bye before I go."

"Don't," she said. "Please don't go yet." She looked down at her feet and waited for him to understand, her face an excruciating crimson.

"Tanechka," said Senya, "you're one terrific girl."

He sat across from her, polite and regretful. Not a dancer. A clerk at a bank. Your balance has been exceeded. Nothing else would be said, she understood, no matter how long the two of them sat like this together, no matter how long she waited. She was still for a while, taking shallow, labored breaths, trying to deal with this final disappointment. Then she went to get the phone and the cousin's number.

THAT NIGHT, AFTER Senya left, she found herself alone with Petya. The apartment felt dead, as if some devastating force had come and shaken it. Tanya sat in the dining room, her shoulders hunched. There was laundry to do and a meal to prepare.

"Oh, so good!" Petya said, stretching. "So good when all the guests go home. What's for dinner, Tanya?"

She said, "I don't know," and started crying. I'm so tired, she kept repeating, so tired.

He was startled to see her cry like that; she almost never did. He came over and gently touched her shoulder. "That's okay," he said, "I know you're tired. They were here for a month. Longer even. Please, what do you want, Tanyusha? Do you want to order Chinese for dinner?"

She continued to cry, now because it was so unlike Petya to be gentle, and because it didn't make her love him any more. And yet she knew this would go on. This was what she had, what she would always have. The long succession of meals and couches and rooms, the sleepy murmur at the dinner table. And the slow, insipid feeling, swathing her, erasing her from the inside. She was wise and old enough to know that in the long run people didn't change.

"*Nu, starushka*, stop this silliness," said Petya. "Come summer we'll drive to Montreal. Would you like that? We'll let Senya entertain us."

She nodded okay and tried to wipe her tears. She gave him her soft, reassuring smile. He was good and clueless. Come summer he would forget both Montreal and Senya. They both would forget.

Peculiarities of the
National Driving

THIS IS OUR everyday route. Me at the wheel, my dad in the passenger seat. We start on Wendover Street—it's where we live. I adjust the mirrors the way he tells me. To my left, the road. To my right, the curb, littered with tilted garbage cans. The sidewalk and five almost identical apartment buildings, brick with tarnished trimming. There's one with all the crazies: at night they come out, sleepwalking and howling. Joe Berman, who lives across the street, says they give him nightmares. Joe studies for his Ph.D. in Russian. Some nights, I see him sitting outside in his Tercel, listening to the songs by Vertinsky: *I am madly afraid of your shimmery shackles.* Sometimes I sit with him in there and translate.

"Are we driving today?" says my dad.

"We're driving."

I check for the cars on the left and ease back just a little.

"Careful," he says.

I'm careful. We are parallel-parked between a Subaru and Joe's Tercel.

"Wheel all the way to the left. Wait. Go. Wait." It's taking us forever to get out. In fact, it's taking so long that my mom, who's been watching us, leans out from our second-floor window and asks if everything's okay. She herself can't drive because of her migraines and overall nervousness.

My dad waves her off: "Don't interfere."

We drive to the corner, turn right on Beacon, then stop again and wait for our neighbor Liberman to cross the street. He is slow. He is returning from Three Bears, a jar of herring in his string bag. He likes to ask me when Alick and I are getting married. I tell him we're not even together anymore, it's been years, Alick is history. But Liberman never remembers. "Can he be any slower?" mutters my dad. Liberman's hesitating, squinting at our car. He'd like to talk to us, but he can't see against the glare.

Left on Wightman. This is better; no pedestrians. We fall into a slow line of cars. "Don't get too close," says my dad. I don't. He tells me I'm improving. He wants to turn on the radio but I tell him not to, it kills my concentration.

Straight on Wightman, cross Forbes at the light, then right on Northumberland, where I used to work for Pamela. "Shouldn't we visit your friend?" My dad's voice is snaky, like an insult. Of course, she's no friend of mine. No more lackey jobs, I tell him. Next year, I'll graduate and move to New York City to be a programmer analyst at an investment bank.

Lariska tells me I'm probably not ready. She thinks New York isn't far enough. "If you really mean it," she says, "you'll move farther." Farther where? She herself is ahead of me, graduating this spring, having transferred a year's worth of Russian credits. She's interviewing with the "Big Six" consulting firms, and it's making her competitive. She says, "You're just afraid to leave your parents."

From Northumberland, we turn right on Beechwood. I like driving here: it's wide and leafy and full of sweeping, leisurely loops. I sail through them loosely and gracefully.

My dad says, "You're wavering. You're all over the place."

I tell him I'm not.

He says I'm so off I'm in the biking lane.

"The stop sign!" he says.

"I see it."

"Your foot should be on the brake pedal already."

There are park areas, school areas, cemetery areas, and every time we pass one of those, he tells me to slow down. He also tells me to slow down when we pass one of the houses where he and my mom work. They have cleaning jobs this year, mostly in Squirrel Hill, plus one or two in Monroeville: a woman who used to sell steel, an Indian doctor and his family. My parents bring cleaning supplies and a vacuum cleaner, because, they say, you never know what people don't have. My dad vacuums, my mom does bathrooms, the rest of the tasks they split evenly. They are an excellent team, and their employers like them and pay them well and give them things, like old issues of *Reader's Digest* and *Good Housekeeping*. There's no more welfare for us, but at least we still get Medicare. To which I say, Thank god, since my mom's been in a pretty bad shape lately and we've had to call an ambulance twice for her headaches.

I have a job as well, looking after an elderly Polish lady. It's in the morning. I help her get clean, and then I make her breakfast, Sanka and oatmeal. But my parents won't touch my money, so I've been saving it for when I graduate, move to New York, and rent my own place. Lariska keeps saying I'm fooling myself. She says it's

either my parents or else it's Joe. "Joe?" I say. "Joe's just a neighbor."
He has a girlfriend anyway—red hair, skinny wrists, and freckles.
They live together, though for the past couple of months they've
had fights every day. Afterwards, Joe sits in his car and broods to
the songs by Vertinsky. "Why is she doing this?" he says. He's dark,
frat-boy handsome, and you'd never suspect this in him, this secret
frailty, this fondness for Vertinsky, a Russian singer-émigré (tail-
coats, top hats, an effete Pierrot with long, tremulous fingers).

I park on a side street (so tiny it has no name), and roll down
the windows. My dad gets out to smoke a cigarette. He circles the
car to make sure it's still okay—why wouldn't it be?—the bumper,
the "Proud to Be a Pitt Parent" sticker. He makes me flick the
lights on and off (high beam, low beam), and also the blinkers. He
seems convinced one of these days we'll have an accident. He likes
to tell the stories of our driving to his and my mom's friends, when
they come over on Friday nights. "It was a close call," he'd say, even
though we've had no close calls so far. The friends shake their
heads, relieved that their children are still too young for driving.
My mom makes sandwiches with eggs, sardines, and sprats. My dad
gets a bottle of cognac and crystal shot glasses. Then they watch
Russian films, either some stupid comedy (*Peculiarities of the
National Hunting*) or something completely depressing about a
parental sacrifice (*To See Paris and Die*).

My dad gets back in the car. *"Nu,"* he says, "start this goddamn
barrel organ." I start it. We usually go all the way around Beechwood, and then we duck into the parking lot of a squat, two-story
office building called Buncher Corp. No one knows what Buncher
Corp. does, but the lot is empty in the evenings, perfect for prac-
ticing parallel parking. In the trunk of the car, my dad keeps a pair
of orange cones. Sometimes we're there for an hour or more, until
I get dizzy from driving backwards.

Lately my dad's been really dedicated to teaching me. He used to be, No way, you'll smash the car and we'll have nothing; but now, all of a sudden, it's every night: Are we driving or not? Of course we are! I'm puzzled, but I don't ask any questions. I'm getting better too, except we're still avoiding highways, and the parallel parking is a hit-or-miss situation. The times when I manage it, my dad says, "Even a rabbit can be taught to play drums," by which he means don't get too proud, don't get your hopes up. Most of the time, he acts like I'm driving so badly it's giving him a heart attack. The other day, he said someone should make a movie of it, a cautionary tale. I said, "Sure. *Peculiarities of the National Driving.*"

Today, it looks like we're not going to Buncher. We turn back on Beechwood and get as far as the cemetery, and then my dad tells me to take a left on Forbes and follow behind a 61B bus. We've never gone this way before, so it's a little nerve-wracking, plus I'm tired, plus it's hard to stay behind the bus. I try to maneuver around it. We turn on Braddock, and then after a while, we reach the Edgewood Towne Center. My dad tells me to go ahead and find parking. I park all the way in the back of the plaza, in the row that only has three cars.

The plaza is huge. It has a Kmart, a Giant Eagle, a couple of clothing shops, an Office Depot, and a Pharmor, which was supposed to go out of business years ago, but is still around. At first, I think it's another one of my dad's cigarette breaks, but he tells me we're getting out. I follow him to Office Depot. He goes up to the counter with the "Business Center" sign. He takes a floppy disk out of the pocket of his shirt. To the bubble-gum girl behind the counter, he says, "I need to print this out, and also I need fax."

The girl, who must be still in high school, inserts the floppy disk into the desktop on the counter. She tilts the monitor toward my dad, and he points at a file. She nods and turns the monitor away from us. "How many copies?"

"Just one," he says.

She prints it out. "You want to fax it, too?"

He gets out a wrinkled strip of paper, and she takes it away from him and punches in the number.

"What's this area code?" she says—not that she needs to know.

"Kansas."

When the fax goes through, my dad says thanks and pays. On the way out, he crumples the printout and drops it in the trash.

"What's in Kansas?" I say.

"Nothing."

"Seriously, though?"

"Nothing," he says.

"Dad!"

"Borya Glikman, my old boss, is working in Kansas. Cook Composites and Polymers. They're looking for people, contractors."

"You're moving to Kansas?"

"Do you see jobs around here?" he says.

"So this is it? You and mom are going to Kansas. Were you planning to tell me?"

"We haven't decided yet," he says. "Besides, it's just me, not your mother. It's contracting, for God's sake, no benefits. Can you imagine, your mother with her migraines? I might go ahead, stay with the Glikmans for a while, and then if my position becomes permanent . . . It's all up in the air right now."

He's leaving us, or thinking of leaving, which to me is the same thing. My mom used to say he might leave, years ago—once when she thought he was having an affair, and another time when I was in first grade and she said they might divorce and she'd wanted to warn me in advance. Each time, I'd be worrying and writhing and shriveling from grief, and our apartment would seem like something pillaged. Back then, it never came to anything. But just the other week, she sat me down for a talk again: "Your father is unhappy."

"I want to go home," I say to him.

"What about your parallel parking?"

"I'm not *feeling* well."

"You're getting to be like your mother."

It doesn't occur to me at first that we're taking a highway, I-376 to Squirrel Hill. I'm following his directions—right, wait at the light, left—until suddenly there's a ramp and a yield sign. My feet become leaden with fear—I don't do highways—but there's no way to go back. I check the left mirror. There's a truck in the background, but I figure it's still far away.

My dad screams, and I almost hit the brakes. "Just fucking go!" he says. I press the gas pedal all the way into the floor. The car leaps like a horse, whatever I know of horses, which is nothing. I've never been on one. I can't be thinking of horses now. I can't be thinking of cars, speed, or death. Just the road. All focus on the road, one hundred percent.

We slow down a little before the Squirrel Hill tunnel. There's always a bit of a traffic around here, no matter what time it is. I can't relax, though, because the tunnel itself is treacherous, narrow, the walls closing in on you. My dad has warned me about tunnels. And then there's the Squirrel Hill exit, which has to be taken slowly. If you go above thirty here, you'll end up with your car smeared all over the barrier. And afterwards, I have to merge again.

It's finally over—the merging, the exit, the tunnel—we're not killed, we're safe. My dad tells me to turn into the Buncher's parking lot. He must be crazy if he thinks I can parallel-park after this.

My hands shake and my knees are jumping. Though he seems to be shaking himself.

"You fucking idiot!" he says. "That truck, why didn't you yield? He almost smashed us to a flat cake."

"It wasn't even close. Why did you scream? You *wanted* me to have an accident?"

"It's *my* fault now?"

"I was doing just fine until you screamed."

"That's it," he says. "I'm done with your driving."

"Sure," I say. "Quit. You're quitting everything. You've only been teaching me so you can leave for Kansas and lump it all on me— Mom, all our chores, the driving."

He laughs in a dry, ugly way. "Much good that would be. Don't worry, no one's counting on you. Besides, you'll *never* get your license."

He won't let me drive the rest of the way home, even though it's just a few blocks now. I don't insist. On Wendover Street, his old space is still free. He parks on the first try, as if to spite me. I stay outside. He goes in.

IT'S STILL LIGHT OUT, but the crazies from the building next door are starting to call to one another, squealing like desperate birds. I go up to Joe's car, and he opens the door for me. Vertinsky sings: *Your parakeet Flaubert is sad and says "jamais"* . . . "How did it go?" Joe asks me. What can I tell him? How is it going for you, Joe? Why are you here and not with your girlfriend upstairs? His hair is getting long in the back. He keeps glancing at his apartment windows, and his eyes brim with wolfish wretchedness. I can't help him, or myself. We're both stuck in here. "You want to go for a drive?" he says. I wonder if he knows what he's offering me. I can almost imagine it. The two of us parked on Schenley Drive, the rush of my breath against his, hurried unbuckling, unzipping. But where can it possibly lead?

"I've had enough driving for one evening."

Joe waves to me as I leave. I go around our building, climb up the fire escape. But I can't go in yet. I sit on the hard iron bars of the steps and listen to my parents. They are both in the kitchen, and my dad's getting himself a drink.

"How bad?" says my mom.

"You have no idea. I thought, *Mother of God, this is it.*"

"Shh, nothing happened."

"Nothing happened," he repeats. There's silence.

He says, "She's actually getting better. She's accurate and neat; she pays attention to her stop signs. I think she'll be good at it."

"Of course she will. She's your daughter."

"I just can't go back to it now. I need a break. Or maybe someone else ought to be teaching her."

"No rush," my mom says.

He laughs just a little. "Not anymore, not really."

"So you've decided then?"

"I can't jump around from city to city. I'm not a boy of twenty anymore."

"You might regret it."

"There will be something else," he says, "something here, perhaps something better. Besides, we aren't doing so bad."

"No," she says, "we're managing. Marina's got some people in Mount Lebanon, they're looking for cleaners, once a week. It's far, isn't it? What should I tell her?"

"Tell her we'll think about it."

It's gotten colder on the fire escape, but I don't want them to know I'm there. I arch my shoulders, hug my knees. They'll go for

a walk in twenty minutes, a gentle stroll along the better streets of
Squirrel Hill. By the time they get back, I'll have made tea and
some sandwiches. We'll sit at the living room table and talk of neu-
tral things: Joe, his Vertinsky tapes. "What's the matter with him?"
my dad will say. "Does he have nothing better to listen to?" My
mom will say, "I think it's sweet." The job in Kansas won't be mentioned. I almost prefer it this way.

In the meantime, the lessons continue. To my left is the road. To
my right is the curb. *What a wonderful thing, a sunny day.* The cra
zies sing "O sole mio!"

When the Neighbors
Love You

AT TWELVE, YOU WEAR brown corduroy overalls, and the neighbors love you. You go to Reizenstein Middle School in East Liberty and read books in English and in Russian. You translate the welfare letters your parents get and the other letters too—"Thanks but no thanks," "Should we have any openings," "We'll keep your résumé in our files." When the neighbors—your parents' friends—come over, you're allowed to hang around. You can participate in their conversations, you have things to say, you can quote from *The Great Gatsby* in the original and from *Père Goriot* in two translations. This impresses the neighbors; their own daughter doesn't read much. But when they start talking about their interviews, you know not to say anything. You go to the kitchen and wash the porcelain mother-of-pearl teacups your parents brought along from Leningrad.

—

AT SEVENTEEN, you are a senior at Taylor Allderdice High School, and the neighbors eye you with suspicion. You can feel their disapproval when you walk out of the house: they are watching you from their windows and you shiver and bring your shoulder blades together under your backpack. You wear severe metal jewelry and write with a ballpoint pen on the back of your hand. Your limbs are still coltish, and you lack womanly roundness, but your step has a sexy pliancy and you know that the boys at school notice you.

For the party, you wear your red spaghetti-strap dress and the tall, chunky sandals. You walk to the restaurant on Murray, weaving your way among slow-moving Orthodox families and loitering slacker kids. You love the orderly rumble of the street—the tinkling of restaurant doors, the restive energy of the traffic, a car screeching into a parking spot. Your parents say Squirrel Hill is changing, but you're comfortable here among these people and these shops. Borya Rivkin, your neighbor, waves at you from his jewelry store, the Malachite Box. Alya and Irina gossip on the stoop of their hair salon. On weekday afternoons, nameless women, shrouded in yellow windbreakers, tend the intersections, guard your step.

The party is the neighbors' anniversary; your parents are there, and your best friend, Vika, the neighbors' daughter, has pleaded with you to come. You told her you would be late—you have to work first, at the National Record Mart, and then go home and change—but when you get there, Vika is waiting for you on the sidewalk outside the restaurant.

"They're all drunk in there," she says. "Dancing."

You give her a quick hug and go inside to find your parents. The party is at the Panda Palace, but Vika's mother bought Russian food too; it's a combination of the two cuisines—sweet-and-sour chicken with chopped herring, steamed dumplings with a pickle.

The tables are pulled together in one long line, but the guests have already abandoned the tables. They are jiggling to "Hava Nagila," fingers linked—a staggering but joyful ring. In the corner near the entrance, the toastmaster, Roma, has set up his stereo system and a keyboard, which he uses for special sound effects.

"*Aaah,* here's the child," your mother says when she sees you. "Anechka, my sunlight, are you hungry?" She is looking all melted and flushed, lolling at the table, with her shoes slipped off. Next to her, your father is perfectly composed—he doesn't drink or dance, because of his heart condition.

You kiss them on the cheek. They ask if your shift was good, and you say, Yes, it's always good. They want to know if you're going out later tonight. You tell them not to wait up. They don't mind: it's a Saturday night, it's April, you are graduating in a couple of months. In September you'll be starting at the University of Pittsburgh. Your first choice was Boston University, and you've been accepted there too, but your parents said no.

Your mother tugs at your arm.

"Have you mailed the deposit?" she asks.

Toastmaster Roma sends a ripple of drums through the room, which means he is about to do one of his vocal-instrumental toasts. There's a swelling of voices, a stirring of feet, the toastmaster thumping into the microphone. In this bustle it's easy to miss a question. You try to look distracted.

"The *deposit,* Anya," your father says. "The check to Pitt. Did you mail the check?"

You tell them that, yes, you have sent the deposit. You gulp a whole glass of champagne. They look at you. You tell them you were thirsty. You go back outside, where Vika watches traffic while leaning against the prickly restaurant wall. You squat next to her, pull the stretchy red of your dress tight over your knees.

"I hate these parties," says Vika. "Let's get out of here, okay?"

You tell her, No kidding. You will call Maks, get him to pick you up. She says, Yeah, maybe we can all go dancing.

Twenty minutes later, after you've snuck another champagne, Maks pulls up in his Grand Prix. Next to him is Vitalik, riding shotgun, so you and Vika have to cram into the tiny backseat. You lean forward and wrap your sleeveless arms around Maks's neck. You kiss him on the side of his gorgeous square chin. You say, "Hi, baby."

"We want to go dancing," says Vika.

"It's not such a good night to go dancing," says Vitalik. The good clubs, he says, will be packed, and you can't drink there anyway, and the cover, the cover is ridiculous, and the music isn't all that good either.

You sink into the backseat and think about how much you dislike Vitalik, the pale back of his buzzed neck, his droning voice, the way he *explains* things. You think of the way your father *explains*—there is no sense in sending you to Boston, the school is too expensive, and the bachelor's degree is the same no matter where you get it, as long as you are willing to work hard.

Maks doesn't say where he is taking you, but the streets loop in the familiar way. When you get near the highway ramp, Vika sucks in her breath, but you don't go there, you stay in Squirrel Hill. Maks turns onto Monitor and parks by his house. His parents are away a lot, you hardly ever see them. You have a key to the house, to the back door that leads to Maks's room.

In the living room the four of you topple in front of the TV. You share a bottle of wine, and Vitalik finds a channel that shows a baseball game. He is trying to explain the game to Vika, but Vika pouts and hugs a cushion across her chest. She doesn't even see how hard Vitalik is trying, how he lists and lingers and sputters when he speaks. Maks disappears into the bathroom. When he comes back fifteen minutes later, he scoops you up and whispers that he needs to show you something, and Vika overhears and shoots you a jilted look. But Maks is antsy and unsteady, and when he touches you, you shiver and smash into his hard, drowsy kiss.

HE'S BEEN COMING to the National Record Mart, this boy David, from your AP English class. You've noticed him here before—idling in the R&B aisle, although he doesn't look like the R&B type. He is stocky and short, with brown hair and eyes, and an expression that says, *Go ahead, argue with me, try it.*

The Sunday after the party, you're working from one to seven, and he comes around three and leans over the counter.

"How you doing?" he says, and stares at you. You notice that the skin on his left cheek is bumpy, like after bad acne or smallpox. You've always thought he was a little dorky.

"I hear you're going to Boston University next year," he says. "You're Russian. One of those Russians."

You say, "I'm not going to BU." You walk out from behind the counter and go check on the two girls in Alternative Rock, who may or may not need your help. When you get back, he is gone.

But after your shift is over, he is waiting for you outside.

"You're not like the rest of them," he says, "the other Russian girls in school. They're always smoking in the back, and their clothes are really tight."

"It's just what people wear."

"I know," he says, "but hey, I mean *really* tight. They're like spilling out of it. You can practically see everything. And the crazy makeup?" He pauses to study you. "You don't wear much makeup, do you?"

Those other girls, he says, with their makeup and tight clothes, they stand in the back after school and men drive over and pick them up. Grown Russian men, with bulk and mustaches. Have you noticed? What's up with that?

You say you have no idea, you don't know them that well.

"So you're not going to BU?" he says, his face taking on a sweet, dismayed expression. "I thought you got a scholarship."

"Yeah, but not enough."

"Can't you take a loan? Can't your parents pay the rest?"

You press your lips together, hard.

"None of my business," he says. "I understand. But you *can't* go to Pitt. Pitt is for idiots."

"That's where I'm going," you say.

He tells you he is going to Harvard. He says it matters where you get your bachelor's: the quality of teaching is different, and then there are connections and opportunities. When he talks, his face becomes limber, full of vigorous intelligence, and you like that.

You tell him you want to study international relations, and he takes you to see an international movie at Manor, across the street. It's French, with long, strained pauses, gritty lighting, unattractive actors with pale faces and large feet. It's about rape. You hope that maybe David is bored. But when you glance at him, his face in the flickering movie-light is transfixed and tragic.

When you get home, your mother tells you Maks has called. You say, All right. She says, Aren't you going to call him back? You say, Maybe later. She says, It's eleven o'clock, and you say, Since when do you even like Maks?

He calls you again twenty minutes later and wants to know where you've been. You tell him the movies, French, nothing he'd be interested in. You open your top desk drawer, and there, under a pile of wrinkled Spanish quizzes, there is the check you were supposed to send to Pitt. You take it out and give it one long,

brave look—the folded corner, your father's small, sturdy handwriting—then you shove it back into your desk, deep, where
nobody will see it.

"Are you mad at me, baby?" Maks's voice on the phone is
scratchy and slow, which means he is probably drunk again. You tell
him you're tired and need to go to bed. He wants to take you out
tomorrow—just you and him, someplace special. You say, Okay.

In the family room, your father is watching the History Channel and your mother is sorting out buckwheat for porridge. She is
always making buckwheat porridge, because it's supposed to be
good for your father's heart. You sit on the floor and pull your
knees to your chest.

You say, "I'll go crazy if I stay here. I'll become a drug addict."

You father says, "Anya, please," in a voice so frail, so doleful, it
pinches your heart.

But you insist: "I can't go to Pitt."

He says, "You've sent them the deposit."

You look at your mother for support, but her face flutters with
alarm. Your father is staring into the TV again, and his lips are thin
and anemic. He has appointments with a cardiologist every two
weeks; he walks somberly now, with caution, like someone suffering from shortness of breath.

Your mother says, "Don't you have school tomorrow, Anya?
Please go to bed."

THE NEXT NIGHT, when you get to Maks's house, the living
room is thick with cigarette smoke and the gripping pot aroma
that cuts inside your throat. You'd smoked last year and the year
before, but this year you quit both cigarettes and pot. Vika smokes
sometimes, taking small, fearful puffs, as if she is expecting her parents to turn up and bust her.

"What up, G?" says Leonard, a boy with fat, rosy cheeks and blond wisps of hair.

"Qué pasa," says Vitalik.

Maks punches you on the shoulder, playfully, and goes to the kitchen. Maks's boys are lounging in the living room, doing nothing, smoking, watching MTV, exchanging their moronic gangsta non sequiturs. They are the kids from your school, the Russian kids, dressed to look like homeboys, with their pants low off their asses, *saggin'*. You know these boys, with their glasses, and pimples, and their newly straightened teeth. They've been smoking pot since junior high and doing other drugs too, and last year you noticed how dumb and spacey they'd become.

Vika sits on the edge of the couch, her hands clenched in her lap. "Where were you?" she whispers, like you had plans with her, not Maks.

Leonard plops next to Vika, loops his arm around her.

"Hello, chica," he says.

Vika giggles, uneasy—she likes the attention, but doesn't know how to take it. When Leonard puts his hand on her knee, she squirms away. He says, "Are you dissing me, gal?"

Besides you and Vika, the only other girl here is Zina. She is older and goes to Penn State, but when classes become a drag, she takes a drive to Squirrel Hill. She is a big, ugly girl, with short strawlike hair. She wears army boots and jeans that look painfully stiff. She likes to sit in the boys' laps, likes to get drunk and make them nervous and horny. She swears in Russian, which shocks and pleases the boys. They say nasty things about her, but they like it when she shows up, because she lets them feel her up and do other things to her too. You know this from Maks. You ask him how he knows, and he says his boys are telling him.

Maks brings the drinks from the kitchen: gin and tonic for you, a beer for Vika.

You say, "I thought we were going out."

"The guys just sort of showed up," he says, and places his palm over your hand. "What was I supposed to do?"

Your hand under his is cold and limp, like a dead fish.

"This is your idea of *someplace special*?"

His face hardens around the cheekbones. All the Russian girls are in love with Maks, but he is strange around them, almost shy. His hair falls into his eyes in a cool, asymmetrical way. Last year Maks installed a hot tub in his parents' house. Since then he's teamed up with his cousin and they've been fixing houses all over Squirrel Hill, installing hot tubs and new toilets, putting down new floors, painting walls, and laying new roofs. He tells you he makes enough money to have anything he wants.

Zina comes over to sit on Maks's lap, which means she is completely shit-faced, because Maks is off-limits. Leonard pulls her off by the waist of her pants. "Dance with me, beautiful," he says, and they start dancing, although it looks like he is humping Zina.

Maks says to you, "Relax. Next year half these jokers will be gone."

You tell him that maybe you too will be gone.

"You're not going anywhere," he says. He hugs you so hard you think he might crush your lungs. Like that's supposed to make everything better. His breath is hot and malty on your cheek. You push him off.

He says, "What *is* your problem?"

You get up to leave and Leonard stands in your way, and Vika says, "Anya?" in her small dollhouse voice. But Maks tells them, Let her. If she wants to, let her fucking leave.

The problem is that for a while last year you lived with Maks.

It started with your father losing his job—suddenly he was home all the time, shuffling between the bedroom and the basement, refurbishing something, rearranging the furniture, incessantly washing his coffee cup. The two of you were in each other's way. You took long showers and made the bathroom soapy and moist and jungle-like with steam. He took over your computer—tying up the phone line, looking for jobs. Which was more important, your homework or his jobs? And speaking of your homework, why did you wait until the last minute? Where were you last night? What were you doing on Murray last Thursday at noon?

It was so unlike him. He used to be your ally. You'd been best pals, planning chemistry experiments, looking through the illustrated encyclopedia of animals. But now all you did was fight.

Your mother took your father's side. They said, You cut school, and smoke, and your boyfriend looks like a porcupine. Your future? You have no future. You'll be a waitress, a lifelong babysitter, a cleaning lady (though who will want their house cleaned by *you*?). So you ran away and lived with Maks in his house on Monitor when his parents went to Russia for two months. You slept late, watched cartoons and made love in the morning, and in the afternoon Maks's boys came over and all of you got high.

Maks's parents returned in August. Of course they knew, his parents and yours, everybody in Squirrel Hill knew, and your parents, small and ashamed, began avoiding the neighbors. You remember the afternoon it all ended: the phone ringing at Maks's house, ringing for a long time and nobody wanting to pick it up, your mother's voice—*It's your father, it's bad*—and the bus ride to the hospital. They were too stoned to drive that afternoon; you had to take a bus.

TWO DAYS LATER you meet David on Forbes, by the National Record Mart. He gives you a tentative hug, stifled but eager, his fingers jabbing your back. He buys you an iced tea with tapioca, and you walk up and down Forbes, talking politely about colleges. Talking about anything else will make you feel guilty. You're still Maks's girlfriend, but what if Maks doesn't understand you anymore? David is tidy and square, in the JCPenney catalog kind of way. You could both be in Boston next year, looking preppy, unattainable, visiting Squirrel Hill together, on major holidays.

"Is this about money?" says David. "Because here's what you do. You say no to Pitt, yes to BU. You send them the deposit. When is the deadline?"

You tell David about the check in your desk—in your father's handwriting, payable to the University of Pittsburgh.

He says, "Fuck the check."

Thick lumps of tapioca slither through the loose plastic straw. They are cold and snail-textured against your throat, and you can't speak.

David says, "You apply for loans. Stafford Loan. Hebrew Free Loan. Your father's unemployed? 'Cause you may qualify for some need-based assistance."

You don't want to remember, but you do anyway—the ringing of the phone, the metallic rattle of the emergency room gurneys, the broken bottle of *volokardin* on the kitchen floor. You were good the whole year after that, gentle and obedient around your parents. You let them grill you on SAT words, let your father help you with algebra problems. You still came to Maks, mostly at night, when you knew his boys would be gone, but later you always went home. You thought you had redeemed yourself, had earned your right to leave. But when the letter from Boston came, your father said, "Makes no sense. Tuition *plus* room and board? Here we feed you and you have your own room." You started to argue, but then you saw your mother, the panicky splash of her hands, the quick spark of worry. You couldn't argue, you couldn't leave them a second time.

You tell David, "I'm sorry. It's not going to work."

He thinks you're joking, thinks you need a good shake, a pep talk of the sort they do on television. But you swivel out of his reach, you stop, so he knows it's for real.

He says, "What are you going to do? Wait till it's too late? Miss the deadline? *Not* go to college?"

"I don't know." You have a misty smile, and you look at David sadly, as if to say, *Forget me. I can't be helped.*

You wonder if David will try to follow you or walk you home. But he doesn't. On Murray, buses sigh near the sidewalks, douse you in their gasoline breath. Passengers disembark. Russians with hard, unhappy creases in their faces. Sandaled students returning from Pitt. From the murky insides of their hair salon, Alya and Irina scrutinize you, talk about you with slighting smiles. You want to slip into one of these buses, let it take you away, over the river and into another town, where nobody knows you, where the clusters of tiny white roofs are dotting the neighborhood hill.

BETWEEN SEVENTH AND EIGHTH periods you and Vika go downstairs. She has thick eyeliner on her top lids and underneath too. Shimmery lipstick. Blemishes peek through the layers of concealer, dark like bruises.

"What's the matter with you?" she says. "Did you and Maks have a fight?"

"I'm just tired of the Russians."

Vika sighs: "I know. Me too."

But you don't believe her. This year she is all about the Russians. She drags you to Maks's, and she hangs with the girls in the back of the school. At Allderdice, you either hang with the Russians or you have no friends at all.

Last year, Vika spent time on the Internet, on one of the Pittsburgh channels. It was like an anonymous support group; everybody was depressed there—*Julie's here! Hi, Julie! I'm depressed today. Aw, Julie! Me too.* She met a boy with the Internet handle *Sporty*; he took her to a private chat room and said he loved her, but when she met him in person, he turned out to be myopic and bipolar, and his face was the color of flour.

After that, she mostly stayed in her room and burned scented candles. She said, school was shit, and the Internet was shit, and nobody, not a single soul, gave a damn. You were going out—you were always going out that year—and you said she should come along. "With the Russians?" she said. "What do they want with me? Even the Russians don't want me."

Out of the corner of your eye you see David standing in the window, talking to a girl with partially green hair. You think how quickly he's given up on you, and it hurts, even though you were the one who walked away.

You say to Vika, "Listen. I might not be going to Pitt next year."

"You're kidding, right?"

"I don't know. I haven't sent them money yet. Just don't tell your parents, okay? Because they will tell my parents, and then—"

But before you can finish, you see that it's now dawning on Vika: you are deserting her. You were supposed to stick together, two college girls at Pitt; she had it all planned, from season tickets to fake IDs. She's been perusing the list of student clubs (arts, crafts, amateur athletics), scraping together a shaky case for joining a sorority. She is imagining her tipsy collegial activities now, the sweaty affection of frat movie stars, but you know it's never going to be like that. There will be the same stale afternoons in Maks's living room; Maks's boys, besotted by TV and pot. And Vika will end up with vapid and patient Vitalik, will get knocked up in three quick months, and there will be a wedding at the Panda Palace.

Vika is looking at you like you're her new enemy. "I can't believe this," she says. "This is so fucking unfair."

She grabs her books, slams the locker door, storms off. You watch her push through the flock of bobbing backpacks, clutched binders, honey-blond heads. She is so small among them, with her homemade brassy-blond streaks.

"What was that about?" says David. "A catfight? A Russian cat-fight?" He's in a yellow sweatshirt with a collar, his smug mouth stretching in a smile. You say you're sick of his talking shit about Russians.

"It was a joke," he says. "I'm sorry, Annie."

You pick up your backpack, but he catches your hand.

"Listen," he says, "I have an idea. You can't say no to something you've never seen."

YOU THINK: You were twelve and wore brown corduroys. You once read *Père Goriot* and *Eugénie Grandet*, but you don't remember the plots anymore. The neighbors called you *a clever girl* and *a darling.* You weren't supposed to hear but you did anyway, through the running water in the kitchen, where mother-of-pearl teacups lay in your hands like seashells. Your heart swooped at the praise and you imagined a brilliant future: articles, book jackets, scholarships to Europe. You were Anna Akhmatova, with her choker and rosary beads; you were Madame Curie at the Sorbonne, austere in her grief. You were in love with the handsomest of professors—British, possibly married, with a sarcastic crinkle around his eyes. But the romance, too, had an exceptionally happy ending, because you were a smart girl, a girl who made smart decisions, and nothing bad could happen to a girl like this.

David picks you up early Friday morning, and you don't tell anyone where you're going. He is driving a sporty yellow car. "Yours?" you ask, but he shakes his head. You've calculated that Boston is at least ten hours away; by the time you get there every office will be closed. But David says he knows people at BU. He says this is your unofficial tour.

"When do you think we'll be back?" you ask him.

"Stay through Saturday, go back on Sunday. We can stay in a hotel."

Two nights, you think. Two nights in a hotel with David, this dorky boy. He is driving and sneaking quick, thievish looks at you, and it makes you feel like you've agreed to something you didn't mean to agree to. Not a big deal, you tell yourself. You can manage David. You can manage your parents too. You will call and tell them you're going to Lake Erie with Maks. They'll believe that; you often go to Lake Erie. Unless Maks calls asking for you. So maybe you'll tell your parents you're going to Erie with the girls from school, American girls they don't know. But where does that leave you and Maks?

The drive is beautiful: wispy streaks of clouds, the sun soft and velvety through the glass. David's hands on the steering wheel are pale, with blunt, childish fingers. And suddenly, this crazy proximity, this smallness freaks you out. You think of Maks's hands, the white scar along his right forearm, his sunburns and scrapes, strained tendons and a busted shoulder. You tell yourself, you've just got to see the college; it doesn't mean you're leaving Maks. You don't stay anymore when Maks's boys are around. They bring him beer and drugs, and things get messy. They want to go up on the roof, race through Homestead at night. Maks says, Okay, whatever.

He laughs and spills beer down the front of his shirt. When you kiss him good night, he laughs again, but his eyes beam with mean, gleeful doom—he's letting you go.

David makes a stop near Harrisburg, and you call Vika. You'll ask her to please not be angry with you. You need to know if she thinks what you're doing is crazy, if your parents or Maks might find out. Because the truth is it's not just your parents, it's everything: movies at the Manor, desserts at Eat'n Park, the gossipy girls who always butcher your mother's haircut, the birthdays, the anniversaries, the way your parents shuffle softly to a slow waltz. And maybe it's better if you start off at Pitt, and later, after two years or so, transfer to Boston or wherever the better school might be.

There's a photograph you keep on your desk: you're thirteen, and it's you and Vika at the Jewish day camp. You both wear jeans and no makeup. You've got on a shirt with stripes, the one you used to call your prisoner's shirt. Your hair is longer and Vika's is shorter, and the two of you are sitting by the fountain, bound together by a pair of bronze frogs.

You come back to David. He is eating baby carrots from a ziplock bag. He's bought you a strawberry shake and a cheeseburger without fries.

"Are you ready?" he says. "We might hit some traffic in Connecticut, but I don't think we will."

The cheeseburger is in a crisp McDonald's bag and the shake is hoisted on a special cardboard tray. "Eat," he says. "Why aren't you eating?"

"I think I need to go home, David."

It's not a joke and he must understand this. You won't be persuaded this time. You're afraid of what he might do now—curse you or strike you or drive away and leave you here stranded.

He says, "Are you sure? Are you really sure?" And when you

finally look at him, you see that he's been fearing this since the moment he picked you up this morning. You see how he's struggling to act normal, how carefully he's folding the map he was studying a minute ago—matching the edges and smoothing the creases. And there's still the drive back ahead of you, all those uncomfortable hours. You want to tell him something kind, something his mom might say when his team loses at baseball or when he doesn't get the highest grade in math, but you don't say it, because you know it's not what he wants.

"Maybe you'll change your mind," says David, "you know, later?"

You take his hand and lace your fingers with his fingers. "Yeah, maybe I will."

WHEN YOU GET HOME it's three in the morning and raining. You unlock the door, sneak quietly into your room. Your jeans are heavy and wet and muddy at the ankles. You strip them off and sit in your tank top and panties on the edge of the bed. You can hear your parents breathing in the bedroom across the hallway. They've saved all your junior high trophies, all the ceramics projects, all the stories you wrote back in Leningrad. They've told everybody about your scholarship, too.

Softly, on tiptoes, you step across the hallway and stop at the entrance to their room. It's peaceful in here. They are breathing in unison now, except your mother makes a tiny whistling sound. Your heart fills with tender confusion, and you come closer until your parents stir.

"I mailed the check," you whisper.

They have no idea what you are talking about.

Among the Lilacs
and the Girls

TOLIK DREAMS OF SCHOOL. The hard wooden desk, initials whittled into its slanted top. Tall, boxy windows chilling the room. The blurry field of a blackboard chalked with formulas. He is taking a math test, he's been studying math, except now he learns it's biology instead, and he hasn't studied for biology. Time is running out, and he is failing. His teacher is approaching, but it's not the gray-haired hag he had in sixth grade. "Lina?" he says, surprised. "Is it you?" and then the bell rings.

It is five in the morning. He wakes up, and it's not the bell, it's the phone. Next to him, the sheets are rumpled and warm; the pillow in the dark is a dented outline of Lina's restless sleep. He passes his hand over it. He can hear her downstairs, fumbling, talking on the phone. He knows what they mean, these early phone calls—Lina paging her supervisor, the supervisor calling back.

She returns to bed, pulls the blanket to her chin, and he tries not to show that he is awake, listening to her breathe. She is not going to work today. He is thinking, *What is it this time, her head? her nau-sea? low blood pressure?* Her breathing is even, but he thinks he hears a little moan at the end of each breath. It's the second time she is not going to work this week.

THE ALARM STARTLES him at seven—he didn't think he'd fall asleep again. He brushes his teeth and follows the sizzling whisper of the frying pan downstairs. Lina is there in her loose orange housedress.

"What are you doing up, Lina?"

She is frying potatoes in vegetable oil.

"Making your breakfast, Tolik. What does it look like? What is it that you don't like *again*?"

The oil in the frying pan crackles and explodes.

"Nothing," he says. "I thought you were sick."

Lina is wielding two wooden spatulas. She hasn't showered yet, and her soft, sloping body under the orange silk smells sour and sharp like onions.

"Is Masha up?" she says. "I told her to get up twenty minutes ago. She'll be late for her classes."

He walks to the window and opens the blinds. The sky, low and gray, is swallowing Pittsburgh.

"Go see if she's awake," Lina says. She winces as she reaches up to get some plates.

"Why don't you go back to bed? What is it? Your head?"

"I'm fine," she says, and bites her lip, bloodless pale.

"I can see how fine you are."

"How about you take a shower now," she says. "Because if Masha gets in there first, you'll never get to go."

He curses Lina under his breath. Who needs this idiotic heroism? If you're sick, you stay in bed and get better. She has always liked everything heroic: Decembrists and their wives, the pioneer heroes of World War II. The sacrifice and the endurance. She taught *Children from the Underground* by Korolenko in her literature class. An idealist and fighter for human rights, Korolenko went off to save some peasants in Old Multan. They were accused of ritual killings; it was a famous case. Korolenko's daughter was ill and dying at the time. He knew if he left, he'd never see her again. But he left anyway. Lina thought it was noble. Tolik told her it was disgusting. You do not betray one of your own.

When he gets out of the shower, Masha is on the couch, waiting her turn, her arms crossed, her face a little blotchy. She is in her drawstring pants and a long T-shirt. She went out last night and returned long after midnight. He was awake, he heard the rambling of the Ford.

"Late night?" he says.

"I was studying."

He says, "Of course you were."

"Masha, eat first," Lina calls from the kitchen. "Your breakfast will go cold."

Masha twitches her shoulder and shuts the bathroom door.

He sits down across from Lina to eat, except Lina isn't eating. She is pinching her temples between her fingertips like she is hoping to squeeze out the pain.

"Eat something," he tells her. She shakes her head. "Of course you get these headaches and the blood pressure—you never eat."

"I can't eat," she says. "Can't you understand?" He catches a hint of hysteria, a quick flash of color on her cheeks, and he lays off, lets her sit there and flaunt her pain.

He thinks it must have started in their English class, five years ago, when they first came to Pittsburgh. They both did badly in that class. When they tried to speak they said nonsense. It didn't even sound like English. He took it better than Lina. Maybe it was her nervousness. Or maybe she wasn't used to being a student, a failure. In Moscow she got teaching awards every year.

They both dropped out of the English class after six months. They cleaned houses for money, took classes at the community college—CAD, Office Management, Microsoft Word. Eventually Lina got a job at a retirement home. She didn't even try to look for teaching jobs. But Tolik, who had been an engineer in Moscow, he tried. For a long time he tried.

AT WORK THEY LIKE his name, Tolik. He works at a car repair place in Homestead. They say, What's up, Tolik? Do you drink vodka, Tolik? They think it's funny. They are pronouncing it wrong, and he can never pinpoint which part of it is off. But he doesn't mind the name or the job. He tells them, Vodka? *Nooo!* Cognac! That's a joke they have there; that's how they communicate.

He checks the appointment book when he comes in today. Two inspections, one transmission job. He leans on the counter and twirls the blunt pencil in his callused fingers. It's still early. He wonders if Lina called Knutchek. He told her to. It's the second time this week she's staying home, and Knutchek better do something about that, or else Tolik will explain to him a thing or two. All the Russians in Squirrel Hill go to Dr. Knutchek, and that's made him sloppy and sure.

Joe, the owner, walks in from the cold, shakes off his jacket, rubs his hands. "Cold, ain't it?" Joe goes and turns on the little black-and-white TV they have there.

"How are you, Tolik?"

"Not so good. My wife sick."

"That's not right. Don't you take care of her, Tolik?"

"I take care? I take *good* care, don't worry. I tell her go to doctor, I am not the doctor."

They watch the TV. The reception is bad, and no matter how much they tweak the rabbit ears, the picture shakes.

"Snowstorm coming," says Joe.

Tolik thinks maybe the weather is to blame—the changes in atmospheric pressure, the sky heavy with snow. Even the healthiest man would get a headache with the weather like that. He wants to call home, but he is afraid to disturb Lina. Perhaps she is asleep. She better be sleeping. He will wait until after lunch, until one o'clock, and then he will call. She has made him lunch this morning: a bologna sandwich in aluminum foil and an apple. The bread has a faint chemical smell. Lina's hands always smell bitter, like medicine or chlorine. He wonders if the job makes her headaches worse, but she says it's not that.

Tolik isn't so sure. He thinks of the school in Moscow where Lina taught, the two white panel blocks with elongated windows like chocolate squares. In the fall it looked dismal; boys played soccer on muddy lawns. But in the spring the school disappeared into blooming lilac bushes; girls swooned over boys, crammed for the final examinations, looked feverishly for the lucky blossom with five petals. Lina existed there, among the lilacs and the girls, ruling them gently, scolding, consoling. Her classes stretched beyond the allotted hours, the girls lingered, giggled, unlocked for her their little souls. Tolik and Masha waited at home.

In the morning he watched her get ready for work. She dressed for *them*, the girls, the other teachers. Mascara, lipstick. She lined her lids soft blue, dabbed perfume behind her ears. She was like a girl herself, thin and professional in her quiet dresses. The edge of her skirt swirled around her legs as she clomped in her platform shoes, looking for her handbag, her metro pass, her keys.

On Teacher's Day, on her birthday, on the first day of school,

Lina came home bearing crumpled asters and long stalks of gladioli. They put the asters in vases, and the gladioli into buckets. The
brooms, Tolik had called them. *Not the brooms again! Couldn't you
leave the brooms at the school?* But she always brought at least some
of them home.

LINA IS ASLEEP when he gets home after work. Her lime-green
uniform shirt is folded on a chair. Unwashed clothes are heaped in
a pile on the floor, which means she has attempted laundry.

Masha is back from her classes; she is in her room and on the
phone already, speaking to some idiotic American boy. He goes in
without knocking.

"Did your mother call the doctor?"

"I don't know," she whispers. "Can't you see I'm on the phone?"

He snatches the phone from her and presses the off button.

"Dad! What the hell?"

"I'll show you *what the hell*," he says. "Your mother is barely
breathing and all you care for is running around with your tail in
the air." He tells her to go downstairs and warm up his dinner.

She slams the door behind her and stomps down the stairs, and
he's ready to kill her for making all this noise.

He doesn't follow her right away; instead, he sits down on her bed
and looks at the photograph on her dresser. It's from six months ago,
his and Lina's anniversary. Lina is in a pale coffee-and-milk satiny
dress. It must be a size too small—tight over her hips and tugging a
little around her belly. She and Masha had gone to Monroeville Mall
to look for that dress. It was low-cut with an off-the-shoulder jacket
that encircled Lina in a loose, silky hug. He could see the smooth,
creamy turn of her neck and the tender swelling of her collarbone
when she tilted her head up. She did something funny with the price

tag, said the dress was too expensive and she was going to return it after the party. He told her not to.

All of their Squirrel Hill friends came to the party—the women in square-shouldered dresses, their husbands in dark interview suits. They had rented a space at the Veterans' Club in Greenfield and hired a catering service. A singer, Roma, ran around with a microphone, orchestrated all the toasts, and sang loud Kiev songs—what did they have to do with Kiev? Lina danced in the middle of the room, cinching her waist, stamping out "Freylckhs" and "Seven-Forty." She danced like she'd never had a headache in her life, and everybody else danced around her, circling, crisscrossing hands. Other husbands watched her admiringly. Tolik watched too—though he mostly refused to dance—watched her face, blooming and young and vague like a watercolor. And then he got drunk, sat on the curb outside, cried a little, and scared Masha to death when he told her that the way her mother's health was going, this was probably the last time they would be celebrating like that.

BY SUPPERTIME Lina gets up. She still won't eat, but she is looking better—more color in her cheeks and she is trying to joke—and so he tells her to get dressed, they are going for a walk. She puts on black pants with an elastic waist and a blouse with a silk bow at the collar.

They cross Murray near Starbucks, where teenagers in puffy winter jackets and absurd baggy pants huddle together in the cold. They cut through the BP gas station and walk up Forward Avenue, passing by the Squirrel Hill movie theater and the bowling alley they've never been to.

He asks Lina if she's called Knutchek and she says no, she's feel-

ing better and going back to work tomorrow, so what's the point
of calling.

"You do this," he says, "neglect yourself, let your health slide
until it's too late."

"I'm fine," she says. "Can we talk about something else?"

He tells her that Masha's been getting out of hand, staying out
past midnight, hanging around God knows where. Ever since she
got that driver's license, she's been all over the place.

Lina says, "Where have I lost hold of her?" and he knows immediately it was the wrong thing to mention. He knows all of Lina's
tricks, this thing she is doing now, taking responsibility, plunging
into guilt.

They are going to see their friends, Marina and Kostya Kogan;
there's a book he wants to borrow from Marina. The Kogans have
just finished their supper when Tolik and Lina show up. Marina
offers to heat up something, but they say they've just eaten too, so
she puts together tea with éclairs from the Strip District and
chocolates from Three Bears.

Marina and Kostya are both programmers. Their house is new,
with Scandinavian furniture and blond hardwood floors. Tolik and
Lina bought their house last year and the floors are dark and mold-
ing under the musty carpets left by the previous owners. The four
of them sit around the table, drink tea and coffee. Kostya is talking
about budget cuts at his company, but he says he is not worried,
he's been laid off before, there are always jobs for programmers.
Tolik wants to ask if Kostya thinks he could learn programming,
but he doesn't want to ask in front of Lina.

Marina and Tolik go outside for a smoke. They stand on the
porch and Marina leans against the railing and stretches her back.
Her face is weathered and crude, but she's dressed in jeans and a
small sweater. The sweater clings to her limber body, rounds her
shoulders, sculpts her tight, delicate chest.

"Can I learn this computer stuff, Marina?"

"Sure you can, Tolik," she says. "What's the problem?"

"Age?" he says.

"You're not old."

She stubs her cigarette and breathes on her hands. There is still no snow, but in the past few hours it's gotten colder. He looks up at the inky nothingness, waiting for it to release its snow like the inevitable punishment. He drops his cigarette and slams his fist against the railing.

"What's the matter, Tolik?"

"They can't figure out what's wrong with her."

"Lina?" Marina squints at the living room window. "She doesn't look bad."

"You should have seen her this morning."

Marina touches his shoulder. She is wincing and smiling at the same time, a wretched, pitiful expression. "What *are* they saying, Tolik?"

He shakes his head: "Forget it." He says it in English. "Forget forever." It sounds American to Tolik, but Masha tells him Americans don't talk like that.

They go back inside. Lina is slumped over her empty coffee cup. She's telling Kostya how nobody in America is teaching real literature. Tolik catches a whiff of her breath, stale coffee and a tinge of rot, and he is embarrassed because everybody knows Kostya isn't interested in literature and because she no longer cares about her looks. She used to care, used to drive him crazy with her questions: *Am I fatter than Mashka's music teacher? No. Am I fatter than the TV girl who turns the letters on the Field of Miracles? No. Am I fatter than the woman with fake yellow hair who sat across from us on the train, and then got out at Sverdlov Square? Yes, for God's sake, Lina! Yes!*

He says it's time for them to get going, and Marina stands and says, Let me give you some of these éclairs. She comes back with a brown bag and the book Tolik wants. Tolik and Lina are zipping up their coats, making plans with the Kogans to do something this weekend. Marina says there's a concert at the JCC, a string quartet. No, please, not the string quartet, says Kostya, but Marina says yes. She is laughing and leaning against him and he is holding her, his hands wrapped over her waist, and Tolik thinks, *Why can't we be normal like this?*

On the way home, Lina is zinging with plans. She wants Tolik to drive her to IKEA on Saturday, so she can get something that Marina has—a coatrack, a curtain, a candle holder. They are walking down the hill and Lina takes short, bustling steps. She looks like a little barrel in that parka of hers, but he doesn't mind, everybody looks muffled up when it's winter. He takes her mittened hand.

Then she says she wants to take computer classes. And though Tolik knows better than to get angry at her when she is like this, he gets angry.

"Your head doesn't work," he says. "You can't lift it from your pillow all day."

"I'll manage," she says. "I don't earn enough and you have to work at that garage. If anything happens to you—"

"Nothing will happen to me." He has dropped her hand, moved away from her.

"But what if you get sick? I should be able to pull us through."

He spits. "Ulcer on your tongue. I'm not getting sick. Better worry about your own health." He stares at the green-and-yellow BP sign at the bottom of Forward. It is shaped like a road sign or a shield, but he always thinks of it as a horseshoe and the luck they don't have. He says, "Nobody needs your heroics, Lina."

He wants to tell her that he isn't about to waste their money, that the last time she took a course, an office management class, she got hysterical over her spelling and typing speed. She would never last at an office job, where everyone is backstabbing and mean, and there are no young and fragile lives to save. It was *his* idea in the first place, *he* wanted these computer classes, and if they do find the money, he should be the one to go. He has a better chance anyway— *Think with your head, Lina, think!*—he used to be an engineer, she a literature teacher. But he doesn't say anything, because already Lina is crying.

That night she cannot sleep at all. She sighs and tosses, and he feels her every turn. She sits up in the bed.

"What? What is it?" he says, sounding more groggy than he is.

"Nothing. Go back to sleep."

She sits there, rocking, unable to lie down. In the morning she finally sleeps, and he knows she is not going to work again.

THE DOCTORS CALL IT depression. He thinks that's ridiculous. What's depression anyway? Depression is not Lina's problem, her head is, her migraines, also her blood pressure, always too low, so she drinks coffee, which makes her feel even worse. That's what's making her crazy. Not depression. All those years in Russia nobody ever knew of such a thing.

They put her in hospitals here, Shadyside Hospital—when the headaches get bad; Western Psych—when she stops talking, eating, sleeping. At Shadyside, they run tests and find nothing. At Western Psych, they pump her with pills. She comes back dizzy with drugs, and so subdued, it's like watching somebody move underwater.

She is on antidepressants—whatever they are, he can't keep the names straight—and they work for a while but then stop working. He is told she needs therapy. His insurance doesn't cover it, but even if it did, therapy is a bad idea. Lina says she doesn't like it when strangers try to get into her soul.

—

IN THE MORNING it snows, and by the afternoon it snows so hard that Joe closes the garage early and sends everybody home. The first thing Tolik sees when he gets home is Masha. She is sitting on the sofa downstairs, her backpack at her feet, her body tilted forward like she's been expecting him.

"Your mother?" he says.

"I don't know," she says. "She's out of it. She's strange."

He walks past her, goes up the stairs and into the bedroom.

Lina is lying on her side, swaddled tight in a fleece blanket, her eyes open but unseeing. She doesn't stir when he comes in.

"Lina?" he says. "How are you?" He squats in front of her. Her skin seems so thin he is afraid to touch it. Her eyes—crazy, stalked—are looking through him.

She whispers something and he leans closer.

"What is it, Lina?"

"Tell Masha to give you your dinner," she says.

Even now she makes it sound like they're toddlers who can't take care of themselves. He shakes his head.

"Don't look at me," she says. She closes her eyes, and her face turns stony—her cheek-bones jutting, her jawbone sharp and small.

He now remembers she used to come from school like this, with her face like granite, her teeth clenched. She wouldn't let the pain show at school, only at home. You couldn't have a conversation with her when she was like that.

And then, when she was well, her students came to their house for tea, and Lina baked. Those high school girls, they all wanted to be teachers. What was it like? they said. He could have told them about the empty aspirin boxes, about the teeth marks on the back of Lina's hand. What should come first, one of the girls asked, the family or the school? Tolik walked out of the room. He didn't need to hear Lina's answer. The school, may it burn in blue flames, the school always came first. But now he thinks, maybe the school had kept her sane.

Downstairs Masha is waiting for him.

"How is she?"

"How do you think?"

They sit down and eat the borscht, and the taste is all off, there is no taste. It's like Lina has forgotten how to cook, everything she makes is rubbery and bland. It must be her medication, wrecking everything inside her, her taste buds, her sense.

"Should we take her to the emergency room?" Masha asks.

"Let's call Knutchek," he says.

He tells her to make the call, because her English is better. He listens on the other extension, covers the receiver with his hand and tells her what to say. The answering service picks up and Masha says it's an emergency and can they please page Dr. Knutchek.

When Knutchek calls back, she tells him the symptoms— faintness, headache, and slow, incessant tears.

Knutchek says something, and Masha turns to Tolik.

"He's asking if we think she is a danger to herself."

The doctors always ask that, and he and Masha never know what to say. They're looking at each other: How should they know? How can they?

She tells Knutchek Lina is weak, barely able to move, which probably makes her less of a danger, or does it? Who is the doctor here?

Knutchek tells them to wait, wait until morning, and then if she is worse, to call him again and he will call the hospital. He doesn't say which hospital, and Tolik isn't sure which one he means, although with all the talk about danger it must be Western Psych.

"Bezdelnik," he says about Knutchek, when Masha hangs up. "Deadbeat. The moment your mother gets well, I'm switching us to another doctor."

"That's what you said the last time," says Masha, and he tells her to shut up.

"Try to talk to her," he says.

They go upstairs and Tolik stands in the doorway.

She kneels in front of Lina's bed. "Mom," she says. "Hey, Mom." She touches her hand, so much gentler than Tolik; he doesn't know how to be this gentle.

Lina's eyes are weak and liquid; she doesn't seem to notice that tears are spilling along her cheeks.

"I'm a bad wife," she whispers, "bad mother."

They tell her it's nonsense, but she doesn't listen.

"*Obuza,*" she says. "Deadweight. I'm dragging you down."

She is crying as if she were sorry for them.

"Mom, we love you," says Masha. "You know that, right? It's just your depression talking. We need you, Mom."

She glances at Tolik—why isn't he helping?—then turns back to Lina.

"Let's think rationally," she says. That's what Lina's last doctor at Western Psych told them to say, the woman with the metallic glimmer in her hair. She said she favored the cognitive approach, believed it would work for Lina. It was her experience, she said, that Russians responded well to the cognitive approach. Her own parents were from Estonia. There was a book with exercises she told them to order on Amazon. They got the book from the Carnegie Library instead, and Lina spent a month copying the exercises in a notebook, filling out questionnaires, grouping her doubts and insecurities into neat little charts. That was a year ago.

"Let's think rationally," says Masha, but he can see it's not working. "Please," she says. "Listen to me, Mom. We *need* you." Her voice strains and Tolik becomes afraid for both of them.

"That's enough," he says. "See, she's calmer, she's falling asleep now." He grips Masha's elbow, pulls her up from the floor.

Masha pauses at the door. "She's not asleep. She's crying."

Tolik says, "She'll stop crying when we leave her alone."

Downstairs, they turn up the lights in the family room and try to watch reruns of a cop show, which they normally like. But now Tolik keeps thinking danger, and Masha looks startled every time wind slams the windows or flings itself against the corner of the house. Even though Lina is weak, the TV and the weather might be muffling the sounds from upstairs. "Do you want to watch this?" Tolik nods at the tormented detective on the screen. Masha says no, and they turn off the TV.

He thinks how much Masha has changed. It's not just her driver's license. She's gotten serious, intense. This fall she's cut her hair, and it's made her look graceful, with her narrow shoulders and the long stem of her neck. He worries when she stays out late, but it's normal, it hasn't affected her grades. She's been interviewing for jobs out of state, and he has a feeling she'll get them. He tries not to think of her going away.

Outside, the snow is falling in clumps, draping roofs, bandaging tree branches. The street stretches, white, pillowy, pretty. Safe like a fairy tale. On TV, they have already announced a state of emergency. Every year it happens and Tolik is amazed at this inability of Americans to deal with such a trivial weather condition. He gets himself a bottle of scotch from the top shelf in the kitchen, brings it into the family room.

"You want some?" he asks Masha.

She says, "What are you doing, Dad?"

He will only drink one shot. One shot is okay, he tells her. If he has to get up in the middle of the night and drive Lina to the hospital in this snowy mess, he will still be okay.

"*Americhka*," he says. "Just think, they declare a state of emergency over this."

She says, "I know. Ridiculous."

When these things happen to Lina, they become like a team. Masha makes insurance phone calls, speaks to the doctors. If she's not at college, he checks in with her from work every couple of hours. She gives him messages. She is tacit, efficient, and swift. At night, between seven and nine, they drive to the hospital together. Afterwards they have dinner at Wendy's or McDonald's. He can't imagine doing this without her.

"These doctors," he says, "they don't know anything. What do we try next, Masha? The needles? The bone-crackers?"

"Chiropractors," she says. "And acupuncture."

"Charlatans," he says. All these alternative wackos; he doesn't trust them a bit, but what else is there to try?

"That's what you said the last time," says Masha, and she is right, he did say it the last time. But then Lina got better, got stable, started eating again, and the new drug seemed to be working. He took her for a walk every night. He thought maybe they didn't need the wackos then, and the guys at the garage said, If it ain't broke, don't fix it.

But now it's broken again. All of them are broken. He can tell what it's doing to Mashka—she coils up, all tense. All those years they lived in Russia and knew nothing of depression. Laziness, he said. Nonsense. No depression, no drugs. But now it came after them and he feels it's contagious, this craziness. It's doing something to Mashka and he can feel himself getting crazy too. Everything becomes dull and tasteless like Lina's borscht, and the lights are low and yellow and grainy, like in a fever or a cheap movie, as if the voltage has suddenly dropped and he can hear the humming. Something gnaws at him and makes him afraid. That's how he felt when he was twelve and his father died, and it lasted a long time, forever—the photograph in the black paper frame, the hushed voices, his mother's steps in their hollow communal flat. He counted weeks until life got normal again, asking every Sunday before bed—*Maybe this week?* But he doesn't remember when it ended, all he remembers are the voices and the photograph, and every memory is in black and white. That fall never turned into a winter, and every Monday at eight-thirty he sat in class at his old slanted desk with ink spots and crooked initials, and watched the same rain streaking the window and the same shivering branch outside, and he knew that another week had passed but nothing had changed.

Masha is hunched in a chair, with her feet up, her arms clasped over her knees, her face half hidden. He tells her she's falling asleep. She shakes her head no, she isn't sleepy. She wants a tiny taste of the scotch he's drinking. He says, "Well, get yourself a glass." She brings a glass; he pours her a little. She sniffs at it and winces. "Drink," he says. "It'll make you sleep."

He can see how hard she is trying. She says she will stay up all night, just in case. He almost says it's stupid, but he doesn't. They clink their glasses and he says, "Nice to meet you." The wrong toast, but it will do. She shuts her eyes and drinks.

The Trajectory of
Frying Pans

SHE WAS IN HER early twenties, five or six years younger than me. She moved with a catlike suppleness through our dull office space (scratchy fabric of cubicle walls, coiled wires, the kitchen with its empty Pepsi cans assembled into a shaky pyramid for future recycling). She wore skirts—nobody in our office wore skirts—short, flared skirts, narrow, stretchy ones, knee-length with flowers that made you think of summer. In the kitchen, the guys nudged me. What a chick, they said. You Russians with your Russian chicks. Too bad she's married, right? Too bad for you, buddy.

They hired her in September, after Labor Day. The reason I remember is I always remember a long weekend, and also because on Labor Day I had gone to a barbecue party to meet a certain Alla Mayskaya from Kiev. It rained, the barbecue had soaked through the plastic tent, and Alla Mayskaya never showed up. Returning home, hungry and mad, I thought how this was the last decent holiday until Thanksgiving, and how the following week at the office would be listless and long—computer screens oscillating softly, the management conspicuously absent, my coworkers stumbling along with their coffee, exchanging sleepy recollections of their own barbecues.

But the following week at the office was not like that.

Her name was Nadya Shipilova, though having recently married an American, she was now changing it to Nadya Briggs, which kept causing problems at the payroll department and in our internal e-mail system. They had put her in a cubicle by the window, next row over from mine, and I could hear her phone conversations.

She made me remember Polina. They shared that awkward, long-limbed grace, except that Nadya's had a tinge of glamour, while Polina was a Turgenev girl (Asya or Jemma, *First Love* and *Spring Torrents*), leaning against a birch, hiding a book behind her back as I snapped pictures of her in Sokolniki Park.

I RAN INTO Nadya in the mailroom two days after she first showed up at the office. It was a Thursday. I never got mail at the office, but by Thursday you needed diversions—you drove from lunch the long way, you waited for the slow elevator, you made side trips to check out office supplies.

Nadya was trying to send a fax. She looked up when I came in, and I said hello.

"You know how this works?"

I said I didn't know but could try to figure it out. I regretted it immediately. I could have hidden behind a laconic *sure* or *nope*, but the long sentence gave me away.

"You're from Russia, no?"

I said yes, I was Mike, or Misha, or whatever; it really didn't matter after all these years, though here at work, *Mike* was probably more appropriate.

"I'm Nadya," she interrupted me.

"I know," I said, stupidly.

We both looked down at the fax machine, the scattering of cover sheets around it. I asked her where she'd gone to school.

She told me Allegheny College, Meadville. Before that? MGU —Moscow State University. She shrugged a little. "Where everybody went, I guess."

She guessed wrong. I punched a button that said RESET, and the fax machine began its even warbling. Some people went to MGU, and others went to the Institute of Petrochemical Engineering (also known as the Kerosene Institute). Some, with resounding Russian last names (ending in -*eva* and -*ova*), were sent on exchange programs to small liberal colleges in America, and others, like myself, with decidedly un-Russian swarthiness, dropped out after the first semester, sold furniture and books, and stood in line at the Department of Visas and Permits. To our coworkers, Nadya and I were equally Russian. They didn't know the difference, but I knew.

Before leaving the mailroom, I remembered how to work the fax machine: press 9 and then 1 to dial an outside number. I told this to Nadya in English. Then I threw in a terse *Take care*, one of those colloquial things that implied, *We are colleagues, you mean nothing to me.* If I said it quickly, it almost completely concealed my accent.

TWO THINGS HAPPENED the summer before: I got a letter from Polina, the first one after seven years; and I began dating again.

The dates were mostly blind dates, or half blind, as I called them whenever a relative or a coworker produced a picture in advance. I approached them systematically, developed a list of favorable locations—uncrowded restaurants with outdoor patios, small cafés with flickering candles and a New Age slant, museum rooms filled with pensive quietness and hollow footsteps.

I went out with Mila, the nicer of the twin sisters from Donetsk, and with Tanya Katz, who was studying to be a doctor. I took Zoyka Kamyshinskiy to the symphony. Sveta Metsler, a graduate student in Slavic Languages, invited me over for dinner. The results were disappointing. Mila worked as a realtor (she'd never finished college); Tanya Katz was separated (her husband, Petya, worked at my company); and Alla Mayskaya, when I finally met her, shortly after Labor Day, showed up with a small gold cross around her neck. The cross was what got me. I told my mother we didn't immigrate so I could date a chauvinist from Kiev.

When I didn't have dates, I stayed in my apartment, a top-floor studio on Forbes, above the Squirrel Hill Fitness Center for Women. It was a simple place: a futon always unfolded, three bookshelves, a TV sitting on a chair. At night, I microwaved the soup my mother dispatched to me in flimsy plastic containers. There was very little to do. I could read the *Wall Street Journal*. I could think of applying to business schools, of moving away. From my window, I could watch women in T-shirts and tight pants sweep in and out of the fitness center all evening long. Or else I could reread Polina's letter.

We had met in high school and fell in love around graduation exams. My memories were like blurred strips of a documentary: May, turbid air, drizzling rain. Polina in a loose red trench coat, stepping over puddles in her delicate shoes. Her face, upturned and lovely, somehow lightened by the rain, like poetry, wild and strange. There was a kind of reverence between us—that's what I remembered best—the love of a higher order or some other nonsense we believed in back then. A year later I left for America, and Polina stayed.

In the letter, she wrote that she had gotten married, happily, to an old college classmate, whom I'd never met. *Are* you *with somebody? You don't have to tell me*, she said. She hoped I'd too found happiness. She hoped that I'd write her back and that we could be friends—*The past is behind us now*—though she admitted she'd never told her husband about me.

I HAD BEEN LISTENING to Nadya all morning; I couldn't help it; her voice, her laughter, her throaty interjections scattered through the office in droplets, bright and girlish. What she said wasn't important. She was full of cheap American cheer: there was a furniture sale at Kaufmann's, dance lessons in Squirrel Hill, a black tabby cat at the Bethel Park Petco. Just before lunch, I heard her on the phone with her husband Dan—she called him *Danechka*—plodding through mushy Russian endearments, enunciating them. *Danechka* was learning Russian.

She stopped by after lunch, stood leaning against the side of my cubicle, one knee half bent below the flounce of her skirt, her shoe—its sole thick, with deep grooves—powerful and clumsy like a small tank. She said she was writing a loading script and wanted to ask me some questions about the database and the product. I said okay and nodded for her to sit on the extra—"guest"—chair. She did so gracefully, crossing her legs and arranging her skirt in waves of Mediterranean blue.

She said, "I saw you last night. You were with a girl, near the university."

I coughed. "An acquaintance from school."

It was like making bad excuses: everything I said came out clipped and unconvincing.

She smiled, and then produced her list of work-related questions. I had trained new employees before, and now I was prepared to unfurl for her my lecture. But Nadya was quick—I didn't expect her to be so quick. She asked me the right sorts of questions, specific and probing. If I lingered on something she'd already learned, she would chime in to let me know.

The girl she had seen me with was a blind date, Alina, dark-haired and pretty, with narrow shoulders and a delicate, knifelike profile. Her voice was full of raspy Ukrainian consonants, but I could learn to like those. She was an undergraduate, studying nutrition, and we had agreed to meet by Hillman Library on campus. It was five o'clock and the food trucks, usually sprawled along the curb, were packing up, ready to leave. I suggested a Middle Eastern restaurant on North Craig. Alina's eyes slid over me, dark and noncommittal. She was appraising me: one point for my tallness, another for my sweater (which revealed my good taste and good money), minus two points for my glasses and bookishness.

There was a bar, she said. She'd seen its happy hour advertised in the *Pitt News*. Besides, she had a class at seven-thirty.

I took her to the bar, a sweaty room packed with broad-faced undergraduates in laundered baseball hats turned backwards. We had to press against them as we made our way into a corner vacant enough for standing. I bought her a beer and got myself a glass of water—another point subtracted. I asked her if she liked her major. She said it was okay and looked past me, flashing a beguiling smile at someone at the other end of the bar.

Nadya sighed and shifted in her chair. Somehow we had gotten through all the work-related questions, and now, inexplicably, I was telling her about my date. She listened, sympathetic, engaged, but also amused. "You need a serious girl," she said. Her eyes, liquid amber, were flecked with quick humor.

I was glad I could amuse her. The rest of my coworkers missed

my humor. Women spoke to me with practiced clarity. Men per-
formed their careful jokes. *How you doing, Mike?* they said. *How's
life?* Life was shooting upward like a fountain, like a wrench hitting
you in the face. When I spoke, their faces took on a strained, con-
cerned expression, as if I were someone with special needs.

AFTER WORK, I drove to my mother's. She lived in a two-bedroom
apartment on Hobart. She'd never learned to drive, and though the
nearest supermarket was only a few blocks away, I took her grocery
shopping every week. The walk from my apartment to her place
took seven minutes—I had timed it one day.

I found her in the living room, standing on a stepladder, with a
hammer in her hand and two nails gripped between her teeth.

"What on earth are you doing up there?" I said.

She was with her best friend, Tamara, an older woman with
plucked eyebrows, who came over nearly every day to lecture my
hapless mother.

"I brought your mother a painting," said Tamara. She sat in my
mother's armchair, her shoes off, her legs thick in opaque medical
stockings. I was supposed to call her *Aunt Tamara*.

I turned to my mother again. "For God's sake, take that rust out
of your mouth."

She shook her head, and her black curls flopped and her big-
framed glasses slid down to the tip of her nose. She was like a girl
on top of that ladder, in the white turtleneck and black slacks she
wore to her accounting job downtown. She spat out the nails and
told me she was done. The painting was balanced on a precarious
hook she'd just hammered in.

"Is it crooked?" she asked.

"It's fine," I said. It was a pond, a sunset.

I helped her down the stepladder, and she kissed me on the forehead.

"How was your day?" she said.

"A normal day."

"Have you accomplished everything you wanted to accomplish?"

This was what she used to ask my father. The same tone, too, anxious to please and prying and also, somehow, patronizing. My father left before I entered high school. Their marriage had been a disaster, a string of loud, loveless fights, his temper flaring, the noise of broken furniture, the shards of ruined glasses.

She said, "I got you something." Her voice turned small. "A phone number. Tamara's niece."

She handed me a scrap of paper. It had a number with an unfamiliar area code, and underneath there was a name, Lariska.

"From New York," said Tamara.

My mother winked at her, and she responded by rounding her mouth into a lipsticked O of mock excitement. They waited for me to react.

"He's being shy," said Tamara.

"He's being coquettish," said my mother. "He's flirting without honeycakes."

I cringed, and my mother said, "You know I don't like it when you make that face."

They wanted some other reaction, enthusiasm or gushing gratitude. I remembered Lariska. She was plump, loudmouthed. I remembered she had slept around a lot.

"I thought you wanted this," my mother said, at once apologizing and accusing.

I had told her I wanted the dates. But when she hassled me and fussed and brought me these scraps of phone numbers, I felt smothered, a pitiful mess of a person. It was like being sick: nostrils itching, head filled with cement, and here's Mother, spooning the medicine, fixing the sheets, reminding: *There's no one else to take care of you.*

She had been watching my expression. "Why do you hate me so much?" she said. Her voice slipped into whisper, her lips twitched, and I thought she might cry. But she stopped herself—for Tamara—and her lips, now tight with control, contorted into a smile.

"Look at this painting," she said. "So pretty. Thank you, *Aunt Tamara.*"

Tamara bugged her eyes at me, but I ignored her. This was my mother's shtick, and we both knew how to play it. We played it well. I went up to my mother and hugged her. She tucked her chin against my shoulder.

"You're sure it's not crooked," she said, "the painting?"

"It's perfect," I said.

THE NEXT WEEK, I ran into Nadya at our cafeteria downstairs. We waited in line together. She was getting an egg salad sandwich if it didn't have chopped celery, or a turkey sandwich if it did. I was getting chicken, which came with yellow rice, so cold and hard it was like swallowing small pebbles.

"I saw you again," said Nadya. "With a girl, near the Carnegie Museum."

We had brought our trays to a small table in the corner.

"A different girl," she said.

"Ughu." With my mouth full, I made a sound like an eagle owl, which made her chuckle. "Affirmative."

"Another acquaintance?"

I shook my head. "A date."

"You must think I'm spying on you." Nadya leaned in, and her earrings dangled toward me and caught the light.

"That's right," I said. "That's what I think."

"Well, I'm not." She pulled away and straightened her back primly. "We live around there, Dan and I. Across from the museum. You know the apartment building? With a flower van always parked outside?"

I said I knew the van.

"But we're buying a house soon. So no more spying." She puffed up her lips in a flirtatious, sulky way.

"I'm counting on that."

I knew about the house and about Dan. He drove her to work every morning and picked her up at the end of each day. I'd met him once. He was young but shriveled, full of adolescent intensity, with a Ph.D. in computer science from Carnegie Mellon. The guys at the office had seen him too. They wanted to know why a pretty Russian girl like Nadya had to go and marry such a nerd. Those poor girls, my mother said, they understand what's good for them. Nobody wants to go back to Russia.

But Nadya's happiness was so convincing. I saw her in the morning getting out of Dan's car, quickly daubing her nose with powder, kissing Dan on the cheek, chirping something abrupt and sweet in his ear. And then she was walking toward the entrance, gathering her hair in a clip, clutching her small handbag full of to-do lists and important phone numbers, her face slack and distracted, a schoolgirl in love.

Nadya and I had finished our food but remained at the lunch table, slouched over the empty plates, our conversation clicking along like a plastic ball on a Ping-Pong table.

"Tell me about your date," said Nadya.

I told her this was an experiment—I was experimenting with dating. I told her about Polina's letter, and it nearly broke Nadya's heart.

"Are you sure you're ready?" she asked me. "For dating?"

"It's been seven years. I better be ready."

Was I melodramatic? I probably was. Half the time I believed in my grief for Polina. In a movie theater, for example, when the music welled up at the closing credits. In the fall, when the leaves whispered sadly and got caught in the brown hair of passing university girls.

"It was nobody's fault," I explained, making vague, expansive gestures. It was nice to pretend that Polina and I had been fated lovers, separated by distance, by sickness, by curse—the film version of *Great Expectations*. I described our feelings as refined and exalted, which was true and which had gotten us in trouble in the first place.

I didn't tell Nadya the truth.

Polina had wanted to come to America. To follow me, she explained, as if America were Siberia, and she, Polina, a Decembrist's wife or Raskolnikov's Sonya. I told her it wouldn't work.

The last time I saw her, back in Moscow, she came to me unexpectedly, simply showed up one evening and rang the doorbell. My mother let her in. We were scheduled to leave in two months and the whole apartment was in turmoil, books on the floor, furniture dismantled, my mother on the phone, in tears, battling with my father over the goddamn apartment. To sell or not to sell. And then Polina stepped into my room. Unnatural, unreal. She had that sickly look, her face drawn and pale, like she was suffering. I turned away. Outside it was snowing, and I stood with my face against the window pane and watched the spiraling of snowflakes, so slow and peaceful I could slip into unconsciousness. "Look at me," said Polina. "Why won't you look at me?"

The love boat crushed against everyday drudgery, wrote Mayakovsky in his suicide note, and I was no Mayakovsky and never owned a revolver. What I told Nadya was this: You love somebody or you think you love somebody, so you marry (if you're in Russia), or don't marry (if you're in America), but either way, you begin living together—small apartment, closed space, overflowing closets—and maybe for a while you're happy. But then, a month later or maybe two, you start to notice things—unswept bread crumbs, wet swirls of hair in the drain, the way she asks you questions at the movies, as if you've seen the film already. And after three months? You're fighting all the time, about money, laundry, spotty hygiene. Your rooms are small, you're pinched against each other. And it only gets worse after that, so after six months, you measure the trajectory of frying pans as she hurls them at you from the kitchen.

I stopped talking. The lunch hour was over and everyone had left. We sat alone in the unburdened cafeteria.

"That's not how it works," said Nadya.

There was something reproachful in her voice, something frosty and proper. Then it hit me: she was getting defensive. And for the first time I thought that maybe her own marriage wasn't all that solid. It pleased me for a moment, and then I felt bad for her.

"You're right. I don't know how it works," I said. "I've never really lived with anybody."

AND THEN IT WAS October and I was trying to date Sveta Metsler from Slavic Languages. We had met back in August but only gone out four times, due to Sveta's torturous suspicions. I called her to make dates, and later she called me to cancel them, because, she explained, I didn't *really* like her. She had a turned-up nose and light chubbiness, which I thought was sweet and earthy. But she hated it. She was angry at herself for her chubbiness, she was angry at Slavic Languages for being such a perfect yet impractical pursuit, and she was angry at America for anything she couldn't blame on Slavic Languages.

"Why are they so angry," I asked Nadya, "these girls I meet?"

"Maybe they all have a cold." She sniffled and pulled another tissue from a box on her desk. Nadya was fighting a cold.

I had brought her both DayQuil and NyQuil. "It's easy," I said. "You take one in the morning and one before bed, and everything assumes its rightful place."

"I can't," she said. "My heart starts pounding. I'm probably allergic." She sniffled again and blew her nose. "But tell me about your date."

Tell me about your date, she kept saying week after week. She avoided calling them by their names, perhaps out of forgetfulness, or maybe—I hoped—to point out their insignificance. The dates came and went, but Nadya was always there, in her cubicle decorated with family photographs and candy-colored greeting cards. We often worked together in that cubicle, twining a jagged line of code and jostling over her keyboard—a break of laughter, a friendly brawl. At noon we drove to lunch. When we returned, our office smokers, assembled outside, winked at us through their hazy cigarette clouds. Did Nadya notice how they winked?

Tell me about your dates, she said, and I told her as best as I could. They were nice Russian girls, my dates; they wore sexy button-down shirts, and their eyes were tastefully underlined in black. The moment I saw them I was smitten; I could forgive them anything in that first moment. But then we spoke, they spoke—recounting the years in America and the respective places of origin—and soon the conversations tapered off, revealing my high-mindedness, or their indifference, or something else, something small and shallow within us. And then we talked about the weather, our glances sailing past each other.

I tried to explain this to Nadya, and she groaned a little, like she thought I was one of those guys who never knew what they wanted and never wanted what they had.

"Okay," I said. "Maybe *I'm* the boring one. What do I know? Computers? Stock market?"

"You're not boring," said Nadya.

"Should I talk to them about the weather?"

She looked at me, quietly, sadly.

"That might be all right for starters," she said, "the weather."

At least, I thought, with Sveta Metsler I could talk about literature. But that was not what Sveta Metsler had in mind. She said she had to sleep with me: she was twenty-five and had never done it; that was the source of all her problems. We'd had dinner, pasta and shrimp with inexpensive red wine, which burned bitterly inside my throat, and later Sveta Metsler sat on the couch next to me and played with the top button on her blouse.

I didn't sleep with Sveta Metsler. Instead we kissed and cuddled and talked of figure skating and the stock market. She didn't want to talk about literature at all. She'd taken off her blouse grudgingly, as if I'd asked her to, and revealed her soft white baby-flesh with the red half-circles where the rims of her bra gripped her harshly.

That night, on the way home, I drove by the apartment building with the flower van downstairs. I paused on the other side of the street and looked at the windows, shaded and lit, unfamiliar silhouettes caught in their domestic dance. Which one of them was Nadya? A bus behind me honked—I was blocking its stop—and I slowly drove away. Even if Nadya came out at that moment, what could I tell her? What could I offer? She was up there, performing her courageous acts of love—fake love, green card love—and in the morning she would be at work, cheerful and breathless, hurrying to a meeting, gasping, exhaling her *okh*s and *akh*s, and later still she would be on the phone with Dan, calling him sweet Russian names he didn't deserve, persuading him every second that what they had was real, persuading all of us, persuading herself.

I called Sveta Metsler from work. I gave her the predictable excuses: She deserved something better. We were wrong for each other. It wasn't exactly untrue—there was some sense of honor involved in our negotiations—but mostly I was afraid that the reluctant compromise she had suggested would turn into routine.

"You should've given it a chance," said Nadya.

"Three months of living in the same apartment—"

She said, "The frying pans. I know."

I said we were all animals deep down. You had to really love each other before committing to the near-suicidal act of sharing your life.

"It doesn't have to be like that," said Nadya.

MY BLIND DATES slowed down. I began having dreams about Polina again, but it was a different Polina, pliant and approachable, warmed up and softened by Nadya's sexiness. She came into my room, and I wanted to tell her that I was sorry, but she laughed at me, the silver murmur, like it didn't matter anymore. Tell me about your dates, she said, and I woke up confused and desolate, and went to the kitchen to boil water for my morning tea.

At work every morning I waited for Nadya, but she was now often late. Her face was a little puffy, as if she had overslept or had been crying. She didn't look unhappy, but I noticed things. She was on the phone a lot, but she kept it quiet. Sometimes she took her calls in the conference room. Sometimes when I stopped by her

cubicle at lunch, she was still on the phone. She gave me a five-
dollar bill and covered the receiver with one hand. She said: Would
you be a sweetheart and get me something? A sandwich, you
know? I said I knew. An egg salad sandwich if it didn't have
chopped celery.

She and Dan had moved into their house, and Nadya's commute
was difficult. Dan couldn't drive her anymore; she had to take two
buses each way. She tried to be content about that, but to me she
admitted the truth: she was tired. She was starting to look sloppy
too, her hair tied in the back, her face makeup-less and raw. Instead
of skirts, she wore overalls.

I had listened to her conversations with Dan and I knew that
they were banal and thick with sugary sentiments, that in the end
they lacked the tender, flirtatious energy of our talks.

"Why can't he teach you to drive?" I said.

She rubbed her eyes. "I don't know. I've asked him before."

"You want me to teach you?"

She said, "That's sweet of you, but what's the point? Dan doesn't
want to buy another car."

She coughed a little, and I thought, *Here we go, not another cold.*
It was because of those buses, it was too much for her. She looked
weakened, feverish that morning. I thought of taking the rest of the
day off and driving her home. I had an image of her wrapped in
blankets, her hair tousled, an old-fashioned thermometer sticking
out from under her arm. I would stay with her until Dan came
from work.

I said it was a crummy situation, I was worried for her.

"Sometimes you have to compromise," said Nadya.

"What if it's wrong? What if you compromise and later, say, a
year later, you meet the one person you could love?"

I hadn't planned to say it, but once it was out I didn't want to stop. She looked at me, her face blurred with surprise and defeat and maybe—could it be?—hope. I wanted her to understand exactly what I meant, so I said, "Somebody you can talk to. The way we talk."

She said, "I'm pregnant." She waited a minute, to make sure *I* understood, and then something snapped in her. She turned away, slumped over her desk. I didn't know what to say to her. I stroked her shoulder and her back, feeling the corduroy strap of her overalls, the thinness of her blouse underneath.

They let us leave early that day. I drove Nadya home, a long, slow drive, stop-and-go in the traffic. She leaned her head against the passenger-side window, and we didn't talk the whole time. It worried me that we suddenly had nothing to say to each other.

Then we arrived. Nadya's pale yellow house looked pinned to the ground, scrunched under the flat, ample roof. It had one floor. Thick bushes, sculpted like urns, grew by the front door. A large stretch of short, withered grass sloped toward the road. There was no one around. No sidewalks or stores. We stayed in the car for a while.

"That's where you live?" I confirmed.

Nadya shrugged. "You want to come in? It's nicer inside."

I thought of Dan returning home. "Perhaps some other time."

She nodded quickly, as if to say she was sorry she'd asked. She placed one hand on the passenger-door knob and turned to thank me for the ride. It felt like I had just rejected her. I asked her to wait, and she did. A beautiful, excruciating minute—or ten, or fifteen. We were alone and quiet, some unseen threads drawn between us—restraint, attraction, doubt. Then I did something crazy: I leaned in and kissed her on the side of her mouth. "I'm so confused," whispered Nadya.

She said we had to talk, to discuss this, and though I wanted to talk right away, we agreed I'd come back on Sunday, when Dan would be out of town. I thought of Nadya as I drove home that night, and then inside my apartment, as I watched TV and ate soup cooked by my mother; and later when I turned the TV off I couldn't remember what I had just watched. I surveyed my apartment and imagined her there, looking at my books, sitting on the edge of my futon. This was all I could think of: the smell of her apple shampoo and how her knitted blouse felt slightly damp on her back when I touched her.

ON SUNDAY I was back at Nadya's house. I knocked and she opened the door. She'd been cleaning. I could tell it had been a productive morning for her. She wore jeans and an open-necked shirt, pink, scattered with small green flowers. I sat on the couch. The room wasn't at all like I'd imagined it. It looked chintzy, mismatched, with photographs pinned to the walls and fake plastic flowers. Nadya was poking around with a bottle of cleaning solution and a roll of paper towels. She was picking up things—Dan's things, I assumed—a pair of sneakers, a notebook. She said Dan had left in a hurry, a funeral in Harrisburg, a relative he hardly knew.

In my twenty-eight years I'd been to a funeral once. I guess you could say I was lucky, but the truth was I never knew most of my relatives. My parents were feuding, and this had divided our family. I wouldn't call it luck. It had been my grandmother's funeral, my father's side. I went with my mother; we took a bus to Vostryakovo Cemetery. It took us a while to find it, the plot and the funeral crowd. We got lost in back alleys, circuitous and muddy. Our shoes became covered in mud. We stood in the back. People looked at us strangely; they knew who we were, but no one talked to us.

Why did I think of it now? I was here, with Nadya, except she kept moving around. I couldn't quite focus on her. I thought what an awful house it was. The walls had a bleak, creamy color. The furniture smelled clammy and old. And Nadya was saying, *Dan, Dan, Dan*. Dan was sloppy; he left things behind him; she kept finding these horrible things: dried-up tea bags and calloused pizza slices. What's more, Dan was just like his father, whom they had seen in Philadelphia last month. "Two boots make a pair," said Nadya.

And now, I suddenly remembered my father's crystal shot glass, shaped like a boot. My father used to come home from work around eight, and we had supper in the kitchen. I was a fickle eater, which made my father mad. Most nights I was given a plate of buckwheat kasha with milk, and I splashed in it aimlessly. The wall where I sat was warm from the heating pipes inside it, and I liked to touch it with both of my hands. My father would tell me to behave myself. He'd look at my kasha and his face would go puckered. "Take it away," he'd say to my mother, and she'd take my plate away. "Who are you taking after?" he'd say to me, which meant I was done, I could run into the next room and watch the children's evening program on TV, which started at eight-thirty. Except sometimes I stayed and listened to my father's stories about his coworkers with funny nicknames, the Prince, the Big-Eared, the Eagle Man.

Nadya stopped cleaning and sat next to me on the couch. She was suddenly tired, she said. It happened all the time now. She leaned back on the cushions. Her eyelids were daubed blue, and I knew she had done it on purpose, for me. But it didn't look good; it looked pathetic. And it made me feel sad, the thought of her getting ready for me like that. "What is it?" she said. "What's the matter?" She reached to touch my forehead.

It was as if she were my mother. I angled away from her hands and her face. The sadness was gone, and now all I could feel was the tickling of violence. The ailment was in me. I wanted it, the screaming and the smashing, the broken plates and picture frames.

I had to leave before it happened. There were errands, I said, some shopping I promised to do with my mother. "Now?" she said. "But you've come all this way."

It took her a few minutes to recover, to understand. Then she figured it out. Her voice assumed its flippant office pitch. "Oh well," she said in English. "Thanks for coming."

IN DECEMBER, our company had layoffs, and Nadya was among the first ones to go, due to her lack of seniority. Our coworkers said it was a shame. They took her to a downtown restaurant with opera-singing waiters. The waiters entertained them with Russian "Kalinka" (at Nadya's request) and with something from Pavarotti. That's what our coworkers had told me. I myself hadn't gone.

We rarely spoke anymore, and when we did, it was about work. I thought she took our separation lightly. She'd cobbled up some last-minute office alliances. She went out to lunches a lot. I tried not to think of that day at her house.

On her last day, she stopped at my cubicle. She wore a dress made of clingy material, and her belly was starting to show now, a gentle swelling, so natural and strange on her otherwise spindly body. She brought me Russian candy, a gluey caramel, Moo-Moo. I thanked her and put the candy in my mouth. She smiled. There was a speck of caramel stuck to her tooth.

I wanted to tell her I loved her.

Instead, I told her I'd applied to business schools. "I know you'll get in," said Nadya. She seemed sincere, as if she understood how crooked I felt. "You need to get out of here," she said. And for a

moment I could see it too, the liberated version of myself, somewhere in a college town, in a wintry midwestern state.

I wrote to Polina that day. I'd never replied to her letter, but
now, months later, I had to. I told her I'd made a mistake, and
though it was too late to mend it, I wanted her to understand. I
wrote to her about my fears and my parents, the years in America,
my grad school plans. I even wrote about Nadya.

At night I dreamed about them. Two girls, all stalky lines and
flowing hair. We were in my old Moscow apartment, and I was
begging them to stay. They couldn't. Their shapes were getting
paler, their laughter faint. *The past is behind us*, they said. Snowflakes
spiraled down.

About Kamyshinskiy

AT 8 A.M. Alyosha Kamyshinskiy is going for a run. Before going, he stands in the middle of the kitchen and drinks a cup of coffee in one long gulp. The kitchen smells of garbage. Alyosha picks up a dry-erase marker. On the white refrigerator door he writes, "Clean the goddamn refrigerator."

Alyosha's daughters are asleep. They don't work and don't go to college. They sleep until noon, and the family dog suffers. The dog steals shoes—hides them under the couch, won't give them up. They live in a sprawling apartment with rotting floors and bad insulation. The windows don't lock. It is expensive, but the landlord allows dogs.

Alyosha Kamyshinskiy is a mild man. In his spare time he likes to look at art, read gentle poetry—a sleigh, a moonlit trail, the melancholy trot of a troika. Since he lost his job two months ago, there's been a lot of spare time. Every morning at eight, he goes for a run. He runs long and hard, and his sneakers hit the pavement in

a rhythmic, dependable pattern. Lines spin in his head. *White snow,*
gray ice . . . A blanket made of rags . . . City in the noose of a road . . . It
is a song, though not the kind of song Alyosha would ever admit
to liking. It's what his daughters listen to, glib Russian rock
bands—angular faces, angular lyrics. *Those who live by their own rules*
. . . And who will die young . . . The girls like songs about death. Their
mother died a year ago from cancer, but that didn't affect them the
way you'd expect. They sleep and gossip and don't work, while
Alyosha buys groceries and takes care of the apartment.

Alyosha Kamyshinskiy runs down Bartlett Road, across Murray,
all the way toward Schenley Park, and the song follows Alyosha.
Today, he thinks, today he will start living by his own rules.

AT 9 A.M. Kostya Kogan is leaving his wife, Marina. They are finishing their last breakfast together—cereal with milk and fruit, thin
shavings of strawberries and bananas. They each drink a glass of
grapefruit juice. The children have gone to school, and Kostya's
suitcase is packed, waiting by the front door.

"You can't come back," says Marina. She collects the cereal
bowls and takes them into the kitchen. The silverware rattles
sharply against the china. "This time, you cannot come back."

"You're kicking me out?" says Kostya. He follows Marina into
their birch and stainless steel kitchen, leans against the smooth
veneer of the kitchen island.

"You're leaving us," explains Marina. "You're leaving us for the
woman who used to dance with a snake at Moscow Nights. Do
you want a sandwich before you go?"

"Do I want a sandwich?"

"Of course you want a sandwich. You think the Sinitsa woman
will make you a sandwich?"

She reaches for the metallic refrigerator door, and the children's photographs, affixed with bright plastic magnets, wink at Kostya. Mishka is in third grade and having trouble with math. Verka is turning thirteen in two weeks; she likes ice-skating and rap. In the Kodak photographs their faces are the succulent color of apricot.

"Turkey or ham?" says Marina.

"At least don't sell the house," says Kostya. "At least till the children finish school."

"I can't afford the house," says Marina.

"I'll pay the mortgage," Kostya tells her. "Just promise you won't sell."

Marina wraps the sandwich in wax paper and adds a small carton of orange juice. She puts it all in a brown paper bag.

"I couldn't live without you," says Kostya. "You know that's why I come back."

"This time you don't." Marina strokes his cheek. "I'm late for work. Let yourself out." She kisses him quickly on the lips. "You're having a baby with the Sinitsa woman," she reminds him. "And don't forget, you have two shirts at the dry cleaners."

AT 10 A.M. Seryozha Rodkin tries to sleep. This week he works the night shift, which would be perfect if only he could fall asleep. He turns the pillow and pulls the blanket over his head, but the sun seeps in through the thin wool fabric, and he can hear Olya's TV tweeting downstairs. He tries to breathe, tries to count. He has to call a cab for Olya's four o'clock appointment at Magee-Womens. His car is in the shop until next Tuesday. He is thinking about this now. About cabs and how they are sometimes unreliable. Also about the bus schedule he needs to check for later, when it's time to go to work.

At half past ten, Seryozha gives up and slogs downstairs. The lack of sleep gives him a wobbly, hungover feeling—diffused headache, weakness in the stomach. On the living room couch, Olya is watching soap operas and napping during commercial breaks. Her head is wrapped in a turban she's made for herself, because, she said, all the wigs they had seen were obscene and expensive. She thinks the turban makes her look like a collective-farm girl, but Seryozha disagrees. It is a nice turban. Besides, collective-farm girls wear kerchiefs.

Seryozha fixes the fleece blanket over Olya's feet.

"You go back to bed," she tells him. "Checking on me again?"

"Couldn't sleep," he says, and goes to collect the mail.

He comes back with two bills, cable and electric, and immediately sits down to write checks. This is what Seryozha does in the morning when he cannot sleep. When there are no bills left, he goes over bank statements and sorts through receipts, adding them up, anticipating the next credit card balance. From her couch, Olya jokes that he should get trained in accounting. He says he is too old to get trained in anything. He tries not to show how fidgety he's become in the four months since her cancer came back. The numbers help. The numbers keep his mind in order, his hands occupied. He records balances in a special notebook, his handwriting round and sturdy.

"Hey, bookkeeper," says Olya. "Have we saved enough for California yet?"

THE DOORBELL AT Seryozha Rodkin's house has a harsh and unpleasant ring. At 11 a.m. it jolts Olya out of her sleepy reverie over a series of Gerber Baby commercials. "Who's that?" she says, and places her hand on her chest where her left breast used to be.

Seryozha goes to check. It could be anybody, thinks Seryozha.

A postman with another package from Alex in San Diego. An activist with a petition. A neighbor who wants to park in their driveway. A thief? A murderer? Those are the least of Seryozha's worries. He stands on tiptoes and tries to see through the diamonds of insulated glass.

Outside, Kostya Kogan waits with a suitcase, shifting his feet, kicking at the doorstep, trying to peer into the window.

"It's Kostya Kogan," Seryozha reports to Olya.

"Send him away," she says.

Seryozha opens the door and looks at Kostya and the suitcase.

"So it's true? You and the Sinitsa woman?"

Kostya shrugs, sways uncertainly. "You know me, Seryozha. Marina's everything to me."

"You need a place to stay?"

He shakes his head. "I'm moving in with . . ." He makes exuberant hand gestures, like he can't remember the name.

"Sinitsa?"

"Yeah."

Olya comes out of the living room, her fleece blanket wrapped over her shoulders like a cape. Kostya bounces toward her: "Hey, Olya! How're you doing, Olya?!"

She says, "I was just going upstairs."

BY ELEVEN-THIRTY the fickle October sun manages to warm up the sprawling apartment of Alyosha Kamyshinskiy. The rooms fill with the low rumble of domestic noises: the teakettle gurgles; the dog, stretched on the sunlit kitchen floor, sighs in her sleep; hesitant, muffled music starts up in one of the bedrooms. And on the other side of the bathroom door, there is the lazy dripping of the water. Alyosha Kamyshinskiy wants to take a shower.

"Is it possible to use the bathroom in this house?"

He knocks, and leans his ear against the bathroom door.

"I'm talking to you, Tatyana."

"You always need the bathroom," says Tatyana. "You always need something. Can I have any privacy in this house?"

"I'll show you privacy." Alyosha's voice stiffens meanly, and he bangs on the door with his fist.

"You come and go," says Tatyana. "You don't tell us. How should we know when you come and when you go and when you need the bathroom? We live here too."

"And the rent?" Alyosha shouts. "Who's paying the rent?"

"The unemployment office?" Zoyka, his older daughter, calls out from her room.

Zoyka's door is locked; she's been on the phone for the last thirty minutes, and Alyosha needs to use the phone. He knocks on Zoyka's door, and the dog wakes up and scuttles from the kitchen, barking. The dog has a thing about doors.

"Is it possible to use the phone in this house?"

Zoyka doesn't answer, and Tatyana doesn't answer, but the dog attacks Alyosha's ankles and bursts into spasms of hard, wheezy cries.

"To hell with you all," says Alyosha. He pulls a blue windbreaker over his T-shirt, still wet in places from his run. He'll find himself a pay phone. They'll cry, they'll beg him, they'll regret this later. He reaches for the front door, and the trembling dog, its pink-and-black gums furious and bared, lunges at his feet.

"WHAT'S HAPPENING TO Kamyshinskiy?" says Kostya Kogan. It's almost noon, and Seryozha is making an organic lunch for Olya. She is cooped up in the bedroom upstairs and won't come down. Seryozha knows it's because of Kostya. But Kostya won't go away.

He's taken a day off on account of his leaving Marina, and now the poor slob doesn't know what to do with himself. *Why don't you go to your woman?* Seryozha wants to ask him, but he doesn't have the heart. Instead, Seryozha's making scrambled tofu on veggie pita.

"You want some?" says Seryozha.

Kostya shakes his head. He says he wants scotch. And a cigarette. But Seryozha tells him to relax.

"Kamyshinskiy runs," explains Seryozha. "I always see him running."

"I know," says Kostya. "Plays tennis, too. I saw him with a racket. He was wearing shorts."

"Can you blame him? The man wants to live healthy."

"The man wants to die healthy," Kostya answers grimly, and makes a spitting sound. "You know he's getting out. Now that Irina's gone . . ."

Seryozha winces. He doesn't like to think of Irina's being gone. They had the same diagnosis at the beginning, Irina Kamyshinskaya and his Olya. "Don't gossip," he says.

"It's not gossip, it's a fact," Kostya says. "Tonight he's flying to Chicago. He says it's for an interview."

"So, good for him."

"There're no interviews on Saturdays."

"What do you want from me, Kostya? You want some scrambled tofu—have some. You want the Sinitsa woman, then go to her. What do you want me to say?"

"Nothing," says Kostya. "Nothing. All I'm saying, we don't know shit about Kamyshinskiy."

ALYOSHA KAMYSHINSKIY finds a pay phone in the lobby of Poli's. By twelve-thirty the ladies from the nearby retirement community have arrived in pastel trousers and tailored peacoats. They give Alyosha funny looks—is it because he hasn't showered? Alyosha tries to ignore the ladies; he dials the number, waits to be connected. It's a disgrace that a man can't make a phone call from his own home.

"Galochka?" he says into the phone. "Is it you?"

"Of course it's me, silly. Who did you expect?" The voice on the phone is measured, slightly mocking. Galya Razumovskaya is twenty-seven. She lives in Chicago, teaches American history to undergraduates. She is writing her Ph.D. dissertation.

"I wanted to tell you about my flight. It's at nine forty-five. US Air."

"I know," she says. "I have it written down."

He imagines Galya in her room, in the apartment she shares with Hilda, another graduate student. Galya's room is tidy, with pink checkered curtains and a pink bedspread. He is picturing her on the bed, studying, a pair of small wire-rimmed glasses perched on her straight little nose. She is shy about the glasses, refuses to wear them when Alyosha is around. The phone is wedged between her shoulder and ear. She is underlining something in a textbook, her mouth half opened, her girlishly thick lower lip . . .

"Are you sure this is wise, Alyosha? You visiting again so soon?"

"Galochka, my fledgling, please don't worry."

"All right," she says.

A miracle. No one ever says *all right* to Alyosha, everybody argues, only Galochka agrees. They could get a nice apartment in Chicago, a two-bedroom apartment. One room will be Galochka's office; she will spend her days reading history books, writing her dissertation. Alyosha will get a job, and she won't have to teach anymore—teaching makes her tired. In the evening she'll make him dinner and tell him about the smart things she's read that day.

Together they'll go to see art movies at Galochka's university. Galochka likes art movies. Or maybe it's Zoyka who likes them. They are the same age, Galochka and Zoyka; they used to be in school together in Leningrad, and Galochka came over after school sometimes, an intelligent, mature girl—a little on the heavy side— with dreamy brown eyes. Alyosha noticed her even then, but they met really met six months ago in Chicago, by accident, when Alyosha was attending the wedding of his second cousin.

"Bring along your jacket," says Galochka. "The weather is changing."

She is so thoughtful, so sensible. He will bring his jacket. He wants to bring her so many things: soft, silky things; French perfume in a carton box with that fragile scent that makes him think of April and snowdrops. But he is afraid of these small frivolities— he is a serious man with grown-up children; Galochka doesn't expect this from him. So instead he is bringing her a slim book of poetry by Igor Severyanin, his guilty pleasure.

> *Pineapples in champagne! Pineapples in champagne!*
> *So extraordinarily delicious, so sparkly and piquant.*

"Do you miss me?" he says. "Do you miss me, baby?"
"I will see you at the airport, silly. Nine forty-five."

KOSTYA KOGAN ROAMS on Murray Avenue, hauling along his suitcase. It's after one o'clock, past his lunchtime, and he has forgotten his paper bag lunch at Seryozha's. The Sinitsa woman is waiting for Kostya in the small apartment in Greenfield, on a small street behind the old Giant Eagle, and Kostya will go to her eventually. Of course he'll go. But it's not time yet.

They call her *the Sinitsa woman*; they make it sound almost dirty. Sinitsa is her last name. It means a kind of bird. She used to dance with a snake at Moscow Nights, the Russian restaurant, which opened two autumns ago and went bankrupt in less than a year. She came onstage in the scant trappings of a belly dancer. There were spangles in her makeup, and the snake lay over her naked shoulders like a shawl. That was how Kostya first saw her. A tall, light-haired woman, with plump arms and a white, round belly. "Enough to hold on to?" Borya Rivkin used to joke, he owns a jewelry store on Murray.

When Moscow Nights closed, Sinitsa got a job as a cashier at the Edgewood Kmart. She's like everybody else now: speaks crummy English, buys oranges on sale. At home, she is soft and unfocused, forgetting her appointments, misplacing her keys. Kostya scolds and soothes and cajoles her, and she yields, foolish and pliable in his hands.

Borya Rivkin's store is on the other side of Murray. It's called the Malachite Box. Kostya crosses the street, squints against the window. Inside, Rivkin, starch-collared and courtly, is circling around an American customer, showing off his good English, adjusting the mirror in front of her. Kostya wants to go in, wants to say, *Hello, Rivkin! What's new in Rivkin's life?* But Rivkin might only nod, look down at the counter.

They have loyalty to Marina, and Kostya can understand that. It almost makes him happy, because she needs it and because he wants what's best for her. It's not the first time that Kostya is leaving, but Marina never told anyone before. Loyalty is good, thinks Kostya. But why can't they have a little loyalty to him, too? They have loyalty to everyone, especially Kamyshinskiy. Kamyshinskiy with his soulful eyes, with small poetry books stashed in his coat pocket. They think he is a saint. But Kostya knows Kamyshinskiy's scheming; there's something cowardly in Kamyshinskiy's soulful eyes.

—

ALYOSHA KAMYSHINSKIY comes home and begins to pack. He packs an electric razor, three pairs of underwear, an extra sweater. In the kitchen Zoyka and Tatyana are arguing in muted voices, which means it's about him. There's the smell of something cooking in the kitchen, possibly chicken soup. Maybe they are feeling guilty.

They drift into Alyosha's room, hang by the door, quiet and unobtrusive at first, like shadows. They watch him as he's folding his pajama bottoms.

"Going somewhere?" says Tatyana.

"Chicago. For an interview."

"Where's your suit?" Zoyka comes closer and looks into his bag.

"My suit?" he says.

Zoyka senses his hesitation and bristles with power. They both do, Zoyka and Tatyana.

"Your interview suit."

"I was going to wear it. It wrinkles easily."

"Your interview is on a Saturday?" Tatyana drawls uncertainly. Everything about Tatyana is uncertain. She makes no money, but wears nice clothes (long chenille sweaters; black pants tucked into tall, velvety boots). Alyosha doesn't know where the clothes come from. He doesn't ask, and Tatyana never volunteers.

"Maybe if you stayed in college, you'd know more about interviews."

Talking about college is the quickest way to get rid of Tatyana. She plucks at the plaited bracelet of her Seiko watch, and her face turns wistful with the thoughts of better places. It's the look she gets before bolting for the rest of the day.

"Zoyka," she says, "you wash the dishes."

"It's your turn," says Zoyka.

"Zoyka, please. I'm late. A person is waiting."

"Who?"

"It's not important," Tatyana says. "A date."

"It's one-thirty in the afternoon," says Zoyka. "I want to know who's waiting for you at one-thirty in the afternoon."

"You don't know him," Tatyana says too quickly, and her cheeks turn the color of brick.

"Dad, tell her! I'm not doing the dishes."

Alyosha cringes. "Can't you two resolve this between yourselves?"

Alyosha doesn't like to get involved. *Girl stuff*, he calls it. A young man who used to call for Zoyka is now calling for Tatyana. Tatyana is rarely home. Sometimes Alyosha has to take a message. Other times it must be Zoyka who answers the phone, brittle and unhappy Zoyka, who is looking more and more like her mother. But what can Alyosha do?

"Why can't you be mature about this?" says Tatyana.

Alyosha wishes she had stayed in school. He barely remembers the young man's name. *Girl stuff*, thinks Alyosha. Hasn't he fed them, educated them, stuck around through his own wretchedness so they could have a stable childhood? Hasn't he, in the end, brought them to America? The girl stuff turns Alyosha's stomach, but he can't be responsible, can't afford to interfere.

"I want you to clean this pigsty," he says. "And I don't care which one of you does it."

Zoyka pitches her eyebrows like two poisonous exclamation marks, her mother's facial expression.

"Clean the goddamn place!" yells Alyosha. "How many times must I tell you!"

When they leave, he goes to look for his interview suit. It's in the back of his closet, a black suit, appropriate for funerals, anniversaries, and job interviews. Should he wear it? He feels the stiffness, the dusty smell of naphthalene. The suit requires a shirt, a tie, a pair of black shoes that need polishing. Alyosha would have to pack his jeans and sneakers. Also another sweater. He might need a larger bag.

He leaves the suit hanging in the back of the closet. Stupid comedy, he mutters. The girls have figured it out anyway.

AT TWO-THIRTY, Olya is coming down the stairs, rubbing special antibacterial lotion on her hands and her elbows. She says the treatments have made her skin dry and cracked. The house now always smells of her lotion, the strange mix of fruit, medicine, and cleaning solution. When Seryozha leaves the house, the smell clings to his shirt.

"Are you ready, old lady?" Seryozha comes over, takes her hand, reaches for a kiss. They have a four o'clock appointment at Magee-Womens.

"Is he gone?" says Olya. She's looking around for Kostya.

"Do you see him?"

"Don't let him come here again."

She's lost weight since the operation, and her face is now thinner. She puts on extra makeup before leaving the house. The spots of blush. The pink of lipstick. She goes crazy on mascara, and her eyes in the thicket of black lashes are big, tough, and frightened.

"He's our friend," reasons Seryozha. "We can't turn our backs on Kostya."

"He's the one who's turned his back," says Olya. "He's made his choice. We have to cut him off."

Seryozha pulls her coat from the closet, but Olya shakes her head and says it is too warm, she wants her leather jacket. Seryozha has checked the Weather Channel and the little thermometer outside the living room window, but he doesn't argue, he never argues, he does what Olya says.

"Remember in the English class?" says Olya. "Marina, Kostya, Borya Rivkin, the Kamyshinskiys . . . Kostya isn't worth the soles of Kamyshinskiy's shoes. That poor man, the way he used to fuss over Irina."

Seryozha wonders if he should tell her what he knows about Kamyshinskiy.

She says, "They were the best. The cutest couple."

"Come on! We were the cutest!" He hugs her quickly. "We *are* the best."

He decides he shouldn't tell her. She will only get upset.

"We'll have him over sometime," says Seryozha, "Kamyshinskiy and the girls."

Olya's face sharpens and pales behind the protective pink of her makeup.

"Not now. Maybe when I'm feeling better."

Seryozha looks at her. "No rush."

She ties a silk scarf around her neck, and Seryozha says he has to see about the cab.

"Let's take a bus," she pleads with him. "We've got plenty of time."

Seryozha hesitates.

"Seryozha, please!" says Olya. "I need fresh air. I need a walk."

PASSING BY THE Café 61C, Kostya Kogan has a sudden, inexplicable urge to go home. His home, Marina's home. Just for one more day. He will tell Marina that he got locked out, that he's lost the keys to his new place. He will tell her the suitcase was heavy. It is tempting. Kostya leans against the low iron fence that separates the little sidewalk tables from the people traffic and thinks.

Marina will come home around six, six-thirty, if she stops by the Giant Eagle on her way. She will put her keys on the shelf, hang her handbag on the hat-and-coat rack, every motion exact and automatic. In the dark her face will seem arid with fatigue. Maybe she'll pause before the mirror, her back to the living room, the tight, braced-up back. The kids are clamoring upstairs—at least three hours before their bedtime—and she can't crumple yet. Instead, she'll touch her hair, tweak her lips; she'll pinch herself together. Then, in the mirror, she'll notice Kostya in the living room armchair, with the suitcase at his feet. And for a moment she will think that he came back, that he has changed his mind.

Somebody coughs behind Kostya, on the other side of the low iron fence, and then a voice—a young and forward voice, wavering around the edges—asks him, "Can you give me a light?"

Kostya turns and sees Tatyana, Kamyshinskiy's younger daughter, sitting at an outdoor table alone, twirling a cigarette in her fingers.

"I don't smoke," says Kostya.

He walks around the little fence and sits across from Tatyana. She is lean and languid, and her eyes are hidden behind shades. Her hair is brown and shiny with reddish streaks. It's cut bluntly just above her shoulders, and in the front it's long, hiding half her face. That's how she is, Tatyana, she hides. And twirls, twirls that unlit cigarette in her fingers.

"How's your father?" Kostya asks her, because it's the right thing to ask and because she is his friend's daughter.

"My father is a dog," says Tatyana. "How are *you*, Kostya?"

She uses the polite form of *you*, but it doesn't sound formal; it sounds shy and a little flirty. And then there's the way she pronounces his name, *Kostya*, softly, tentatively, like she's trying it out. Kostya is younger than her father, seven or ten years younger. He has seen her with younger men and with older ones too. She is always there, at the 61C, smoking and reading and drinking coffee. Sometimes there are those men. And now there's Kostya.

"My father's moving to Chicago soon. Did you know? He will live with his new girlfriend, who's twenty-seven. They'll have babies."

"I'm sorry," says Kostya.

"Don't be. I'm glad he's going. I only wish he'd done it sooner. You have no idea what it was like living with him and my mother. Fortunately, *she* is gone."

"You don't mean it," mumbles Kostya.

"You think this is some shitty kind of grief? God, they hated each other. They hated me and Zoyka, too. Because of us, they were stuck together. That was noble or something. To be stuck. Somebody must have told them that. Or else they'd read it in some shitty parenting magazine."

"Listen," says Kostya, "your father is my friend . . ."

"You don't need to counsel me, Kostya. I like you. Do you like me? Did you know my father's girlfriend is twenty-seven? Did you know she went to school with Zoyka? It's like fucking your own daughter, right? How old is your new girlfriend, Kostya? Will you have many babies with her?"

She is almost shouting at him now, and the people at the other tables begin to notice. Kostya delicately coughs. Tatyana stops abruptly, stares at the table, drops her cigarette, then picks it up again.

She says, "I'm sorry. It's not your fault."

She is suddenly looking small and flat. She keeps her head down, her face hidden again by that slack, luminous hair, and Kostya thinks she might be crying. He is afraid to reach over; it's too intimate a gesture. A hug would be too intimate too, given the circumstances. Instead, Kostya takes the unlit cigarette from Tatyana's restless, hopeless fingers. He goes inside the coffee shop and gets her matches. Back at the table, he lights the cigarette and hands it to her.

She says, "Thanks."

"Can I have one?" says Kostya.

She gives him a cigarette. They sit across from each other and smoke.

"You're a good man, Kostya," Tatyana tells him, using the polite form of *you*.

SERYOZHA AND OLYA miss the bus. First they miss the one that stops at the corner of Phillips and Murray, in front of the hardware store. It shows up early and passes by without pausing—no potential passengers in sight. Seryozha and Olya see it as they round the corner.

"See? Unreliable," says Seryozha. "Cabs and buses, all unreliable, but buses especially so."

They walk to the other bus stop. It's a long walk, and part of it is uphill. Several times Olya asks if they can stop. Just for a moment, she says. Seryozha regrets listening to her, regrets not getting a cab. It's windy, and Olya's silk scarf does nothing to protect her throat. Lately with all the treatments, Olya has become susceptible to respiratory infections. She is gasping, and Seryozha feels he's torturing her.

Seryozha did not want to come to America. The children went ahead, but Seryozha, who had a job with security clearance, said no way. They had an apartment in a durable old building near the Voykovskaya metro station; they had a car and a garden plot, and Seryozha said he hadn't been working for nothing. He said that if Olya wanted to go, the door was open, she could have a divorce. It happened one morning, after weeks of Olya tormenting him with America. He said it in a hard, icy voice and went off to work, and it must have seemed odd, because normally he was reasonable, almost meek, and Olya was the one lording it over the household. After that, Olya began writing letters—too many letters—and recording the minutiae of their life on audiocassettes. She marked the days between the monthly calls from Pittsburgh—where the children lived—marked them with a pen, on the calendar in the kitchen. And how could Seryozha know that in less than a year she would get sick?

The other bus stop is at the corner of Forbes and Murray, by the Episcopal church. Seryozha and Olya are still a block away when they see two buses cross at the light, stop briefly, disappear.

"What? Now they go in packs?" says Seryozha.

By the time they get to the bus stop, it is three-thirty and they have missed all the buses.

"Now what?" Olya asks, almost happily. Seryozha suspects she's been wanting to miss her appointment.

"We can't miss it," he says. "I won't have you miss it."

He tries to flag a cab, but there are no cabs around. He flags every car. That's what they did in Russia: when they couldn't catch a taxi, they caught a private car. But here private drivers don't stop, don't care about earning extra dollars.

"Maybe we should go home," says Olya. "Reschedule for later?"

But just then a car stops, a red Corsica, and Alyosha Kamyshin-skiy rolls down his window and asks if they need a lift.

"Are you going to—"

"Yes," says Kamyshinskiy. "Get in." He knows where they are going.

—

IT IS QUIET IN Kamyshinskiy's car. He doesn't have tapes, doesn't play the radio. Seryozha sits next to Alyosha, and Olya is in the backseat, next to a large duffel bag. It's the kind of bag you take on a weekend trip, the kind you carry with you on an airplane. Olya adjusts her turban. Nobody asks any questions.

"HOW ARE THE GIRLS?" asks Olya. They are passing by Carnegie Mellon University, and Seryozha points at the new construction site. Those rich bastards, says Seryozha. They're building and building. Kamyshinskiy nods—*The girls are doing fine.*

JUST AFTER THEY TURN from Bellefield onto Fifth Avenue, they hit a small traffic jam. Olya fidgets in the backseat. "How is the job situation?" Seryozha asks Alyosha. Kamyshinskiy shrugs and doesn't mention Chicago. He checks the rearview mirror, catches Olya's face, switches into another lane. He is quicker than the buses; he doesn't need to make stops.

OLYA SHOULDN'T WORRY; Alyosha knows where he is going; he's been there many times before. They drive some more and turn where they are supposed to turn, and then there's a building with the fractured façade—jagged lines, squares of glass, the entrance shaped into a jutting corner—Magee-Womens Hospital.

OLYA AND SERYOZHA go inside, but Alyosha doesn't leave immediately. He is sitting in the car and watching the glass entrance, a wheelchair left on the sidewalk, the doors sliding back and forth, a corner of the vestibule barely visible. He didn't think he'd ever come here again. It was a year ago, but it doesn't feel like a year.

He says, The girls are fine. Don't do shit around the house, and Tatyana has dropped out of the university, but otherwise they are fine.

He says, I have a job interview in Chicago.

She doesn't believe him. She never believes him. He can tell by her face, indifferent, shrunken, the color of wax.

She says, Who are you trying to fool?

He says, I might get married again.

She laughs: That poor little girl? Appliqué, blotting paper, math homework. Didn't she used to have a gerbil?

Alyosha remembers that he mustn't argue. They've had all of their arguments already. She was in pain, delirious on morphine. She was unlucky all her life. Wrong husband, talentless children, mediocre jobs, not enough money. Never enough money. And then . . . to come to America, the dream of all dreams, and to lose it all on the American hospital bed.

He says, I have to catch my flight.

She says, What are you waiting for? Go. You will move to Chicago to live with the girl, and Tatyana will live with the boy she has stolen from Zoyka. You'll stick Zoyka with the old, crazy dog, and you know how few apartments take dogs. That terrible, expensive apartment. But you know Zoyka: she will stay in there, alone. She will have nightmares. You will help her with the money at first, but eventually she'll have to get a job, something with typing, entering numbers into a spreadsheet. She won't like the people there—too provincial, small-minded, she'll say. She won't like the job or the room. She'll develop an allergy to the carpeting. I've always had allergies. Maybe that's how it starts. Bad genes, weak immune system, not enough sunlight. Something simple: an allergy, a nosebleed, a lump.

It's not my fault, says Alyosha Kamyshinskiy. She *is* twenty-seven. I can't stay around forever.

But who will be around to take care of Zoyka?

BY SEVEN O'CLOCK the streets are dark and wet. The neon signs light up above the shopwindows, reflected in the puddles. The green sign of the Barnes & Noble, where Zoyka Kamyshinskaya is looking for self-help books on love. The red sign of the West Coast Video, where Tatyana is renting a movie. The orange sign of the Burger King in Greenfield, where Kostya Kogan is smoking outside, just a couple of blocks away from the little apartment where Sinitsa is waiting for him.

And miles away, at the Pittsburgh International Airport, Alyosha Kamyshinskiy is waiting for his plane to Chicago, trying to lose himself in the thin volume of poems by Igor Severyanin:

> Pineapples in champagne! Pineapples in champagne!
> I turn the tragedy of life into a reverie-farce.

"Kamyshinskiy is in love," says Olya.

They are walking slowly from the bus stop, counting the puddles.

"You knew?" Seryozha is surprised. "Gray in his beard; devil in his ribs. Are you upset?"

"No," she says. "And Kostya left Marina. What is America doing to us, Seryozha?"

"It's not America. It's them. America just gave them space. Remember how we all used to live? Those apartments, those square meters, nothing to rent, nowhere to move? Remember the coupons for soap and sugar? Dear guests, you can either wash your hands with soap—"

"—or drink your tea with sugar," says Olya.

She is quiet for a while.

"Take me to California, Seryozha. I want to see the kids."

He says yes, once the treatments are over, and the doctor permits.

But she is still uneasy, he can tell from the way she doesn't lean on him, from the tension in her wrist.

"I'm not leaving you, if that's what you're worried about," he says.

"Look at me, Seryozha."

"You're not getting rid of me so easily. And if you meet a handsome clerk at the Kmart, well, tough, I don't want to hear about it. Even if he can dance with a snake."

Olya softly smiles, as if to herself, as if she is not completely convinced. But she lets her sleeve cling to Seryozha's sleeve. They don't have to talk about Kamyshinskiy yet.

"You knew this about me, Olya."

They are counting puddles. On a night like this, in the dark, you can pretend that this is a big city. Traffic swishes by. The footsteps are impersonal and quick. On a night like this you can pretend nothing has happened yet. Olya squeezes Seryozha's hand. It's just the two of them in the rainbow of fluorescent shops, in the round dance of streetlights. Many years ago.

Home

I WENT HOME FOR Lariska's wedding. My parents met me at the Pittsburgh International Airport. They looked like twins in their enormous matching parkas. It was March and cold. My father's mustache was tinseled with ice; my mother's hair appeared orange. I had seen them two months before, for New Year's, but now they seemed changed and aged, and also shorter. We hugged, and they took away my bag. There was the smell of my mother's old perfume and my father's breath, smoky-stale. Five minutes later, we were still lumped together in this awkward three-person embrace, even as we scooted through the concourse and into the mini-train that took us to the parking area. "You're home," my mother said.

In the car, we listened to the radio. Usually there were tapes, Russian guitar or popular arias, but this time it was nothing but weather-and-traffic and some occasional high-pitched alerts, followed by cleanly spelled telephone numbers. When we went into

the Fort Pitt Tunnel, the radio stopped. On the other side was
Pittsburgh. It met us with a jolt of electricity and the wet glint
from the rivers. I could never properly describe it, the way it spilled
in front of you, the lighted tips of its buildings, the disco blue of
the new stadium. It seemed impossible not to like it.

We drove to Squirrel Hill. My parents had a house there, a
mousy, nondescript thing, brick with yellow siding, two diminutive
windows peeking from above the gabled porch. Inside, the carpets
had rotted, and the kitchen counters were green and scratched.
They'd been renovating it slowly. Last time, it was the master bedroom: new hardwood floors, wallpaper with big glowing flowers.
They wanted me to like it, but it just made me depressed.

This time, they showed me nothing. They flipped on the lights
everywhere, and when I asked them if anything was new, they just
shrugged, and then my father went to take out the garbage.

They put me in the guest room. There was a narrow bed and a
narrow bookcase with my father's books on masonry, pipe fabrica-
tion, and rigging of EOT crane. The wallpaper had thin vertical
stripes. My mother perched on the edge of the bed and watched
me unpack.

"You want some hangers?" she said.

I told her it was okay, it was just jeans and some sweaters.

"And the dress?" she said, and when I didn't answer, she added,
"For the wedding?"

"It's not that kind of wedding," I said.

I'd been planning on wearing a black skirt and a black button-
down shirt. Synthetic, stretchy, wrinkle-free. But my mother said
you don't wear black to a wedding. "We'll go shopping at the
mall," she said.

I said, "Fine, if you want to."

"It's not for me."

She looked at me, and I could tell she was wondering what kind of person wore black to a wedding. An unhappy person.

"You want some tea?"

"I'm just tired," I said. "Do you mind if I go to sleep?"

She told me she was *utterly* opposed to it. Then she kissed me and went to get some towels from the closet.

It was strange how little my parents knew about me, how little I told them. They knew where I worked, where I lived, what car I drove, from whom I bought insurance. But they'd never met my boyfriend, and they didn't seem to know I even had one. Every once in a while they visited me in Boston. I took them to Gloucester for seafood or, if it was winter, I showed them ice sculptures at Frog Pond. We'd drive through Brookline and I'd point out Tom's house. Tom, they always said, which one is he? And each time I'd explain that he was the friend who'd helped me pick a DeWalt cordless drill for my father's birthday. Ah yes, they'd say. They always remembered that drill.

THEY WERE GONE when I woke up next morning. There was a note left for me on the floor: *Dear Masha, There's oatmeal in the cupboard + your special tea from the Russian store. Miss you!!! Back at 4:30. Your mother.* They started early. My father worked at a steelmaking facility, and my mother was a nurse's aide at a retirement home in Greenfield. Their days off were Mondays and Tuesdays, and except for New Year's, they worked on all holidays. Today was Thursday.

I brushed my teeth. In my slippers and bathrobe, I shuffled through the house. I opened drawers and cabinets, I looked through yesterday's mail, I checked my mother's prescriptions on the dresser, rolled up and held together with a rubber band. The rooms smelled thinly of heart medicine. Nothing seemed different.

Downstairs, I poked through leftovers, which looked like small corpses encased in aluminum foil. I found a stray bag of Lipton tea. I watched two sitcoms on TV and a show about rich high school kids in California.

My mother called at eleven-thirty. She asked me how I'd slept, what I'd eaten for breakfast, and whether I'd called Lariska yet.

I said I hadn't.

"What are you waiting for?" she said. "She knows you're here."

"*How* does she know?" I said.

"I spoke to her mother. They're expecting you."

My father called an hour later.

"You're here?" he said, as if he thought he might have dreamed my arrival last evening. "You talked to your friend yet?"

"Lariska?"

"You've got other friends around here?"

The answer was, I didn't.

I'd known Lariska since our first year in Pittsburgh. Had we had other choices, we might have picked other friends, but, as the saying went, in a fishing lull, even a lobster is a fish. It was an odd sort of friendship. I was quiet, and she was brash and impatient. She always tried to cram some sense into my head, and since I didn't think her own life was so great, I was tiring of her lectures.

She worked for a consulting firm in New York, a job I considered glamorous and lonely. Gleaming shoes, rolling luggage, sunlit airports. I, too, used to be a computer programmer. I'd worked for an insurance company, nine to five, no travel required. It wasn't a bad job—it had its moments of creative sparkle—but I didn't love it and I wasn't great at it, and after five years, I stopped. I was in grad school now, at Harvard, studying Slavic Languages and Literature, surviving on loans and a small TA-ship I got for teaching Intermediate Russian Grammar to undergraduates. I was poor and my career prospects were uncertain, but I loved it. I lived in West Newton, behind a tiny movie theater. There was a fitness club across the street, and a restaurant, where I ordered big plates of homemade pasta. Tom came over a couple times a week. On Wednesday nights, he brought takeout sushi, and we ate at my tiled kitchen table, jostling and elbowing each other, and bumping our knees. On Saturday nights, we went out.

When I told Tom about Lariska's wedding, he seemed to think it was a good thing.

"You want to come with me?"

His face blurred into something impersonal. "We had an agreement," he said. He coughed a few times, the way he did when something made him nervous. "Maybe if this was next year."

I gave him a look like *Who are we kidding?*

We'd met in a language seminar at Harvard. He was finishing his dissertation on Byzantine culture, and we'd agreed he had to focus on his work. Once he was done, we'd drive across the country; he'd meet my parents in Pittsburgh and I'd meet his in Colorado; we'd rent an apartment together, somewhere near Harvard. It had seemed like a good idea at the time. How long could it take him to finish? I figured, a year at most. We were young. Our relationship could languish for a while. But now, it had been two years and he was nowhere near being done. He needed more time. He'd lost weight, developed insomnia and maybe an ulcer. He only slept a couple nights a week. The nights we were supposed to meet, he often canceled, and when we did meet, he was restless and distracted, and wouldn't stay over, because, he said, he couldn't breathe.

He'd convinced me to go to Pittsburgh. He said it was good for my work: "You're gathering material." He said he'd drive me to the airport. It was ridiculous: my area of study was early twentieth-century émigré literature. As far as I knew, there'd been no émigré writers in Pittsburgh. I figured he just wanted me gone. I took a cab, and called him from the airport. He was free to hole up in his poor apartment, steeped in the "second golden age" and covered with the maps of Mesopotamia.

I FOUND LARISKA in her parents' living room, standing on a makeshift platform. She was in a new strapless gown from David's Bridal, and her mother was crouched underneath, pinning up the hemline. I almost missed her there at first, lost in the white swirls of organza.

"Masha!" the mother said. "How timely! We decided on green for the bridesmaids."

"Am I a bridesmaid?" I said.

"Don't mind her," said Lariska. "Wear whatever you want."

Lariska's parents lived on Monitor, in the cluttered two-bedroom they'd occupied since they'd first come to Pittsburgh. Except now they owned the whole house, renting out the second floor. Her father was still unemployed, but her mother had taken computer classes for Russians, and now had a job with Mellon Bank. Besides programming, she did something with stocks, and she wanted to buy another house. In her kid-size sneakers and slouchy pullovers, she was a tiny, flitting thing. I called her *Aunt Sasha*, and Lariska, who'd taken German in college, sometimes called her, jokingly, *Mutter*.

She finished with Lariska's hem and stepped aside to study it. She told Lariska to stand straight.

"Does your mom have a sewing machine?" she asked me.

"I don't know," I said. "Should I check?"

"I'll call her myself," said Aunt Sasha. She grabbed Lariska's cell phone and said she'd be right back.

Lariska looked at me and frowned. "It sure took you a while," she said. She was like a Christmas tree in that dress, with her arms spread apart and the pins sticking out. "I thought you were coming this morning," she said. "I had to go look at flowers. I could've used your help."

The key with Lariska was to always change the subject.

"Where's your husband-to-be?"

"He's gone to D.C. with his mother."

"Now?" I said.

"It's their last mother-son fling."

"Sounds disgusting."

"I'm kidding," she said. "It's actually easier without them around."

"I thought they were supposed to help."

She shook her head. "His folks have given us some money, which they're not even supposed to. Anyway, my dear *Mutter* has it all figured out, the dress, the catering, the flowers. She's a genius, my *Mutter*. And the place, wait till you see the place. We got really lucky."

Luck wasn't what I'd call it. She was marrying Zhenechka, her distant cousin. They'd met in Pittsburgh for the first time, and she immediately liked him. Back then, he'd been involved with someone else, but Lariska had gone ahead and briefly conquered him—i.e., she'd got him into bed—which, of course, hadn't stopped him from sleeping around. Now, nine years later, she called it luck and fate. She'd run into him in New York. They'd been dating six months. He was finishing medical school.

"Why such a rush, is what I'd like to understand."

"I beg you," said Lariska. "You and everyone else. It's not like he and I just met each other." She jumped up and down and tugged at her neckline. "Where the hell is my mother?"

"Talking dresses, I guess."

"Look," said Lariska, "I'm sorry about the dress. Green's such a weird color."

"I thought it didn't matter," I said.

She made a pleading face.

"Who are the other bridesmaids?"

"You're going to love it," she said. "It's Mila and Yana."

The Donetsk twins and I had never liked each other. "Why does it have to be them?"

"What can I say," said Lariska. "They're always around."

YES, THE DONETSK twins were still around, as proof that some things didn't change. Mila had gone back to college, after a short stint in real estate, and Yana had just had a baby. They still milled about with their numerous cousins. Colleges, marriages—it was all a communal effort with them. A chance American might worm his way into their base, but the twins remained fundamentally Russian. My parents liked to mention them: how they'd seen them at Giant Eagle, how the twins had seemed polite and serious, and why did I think I was so much better than them? "Of course," said my father, "you think you're smarter than everyone else. You're at *Harvard*!"

My father didn't like the idea of Harvard. He lamented the loss of my old job at the insurance company. Couldn't I keep it while doing my studies? He wondered aloud about tuition and debt. He questioned the security of academic jobs. He questioned their value. Nor did he like what I was studying. "You don't even live among Russians," he said.

"I used to."

"Not in years. It's all different now."

I said it wasn't what I studied anyway, and besides, Squirrel Hill never really changed. New signboards here and there. A couple of new Russian stores. Young people got married, old people got hearing aids. Every once in a while, someone's teenager would do something extravagant, like get busted for drugs, or join the Peace Corps. Otherwise, it all remained the same: my mother's eggplant recipe, house renovations, New Year's parties. The safest career in Squirrel Hill was still in computer programming.

The only way to change was to escape, the way Lariska and I had escaped, to New York or to Boston. Except now, Lariska was going back. It was as if we had learned nothing. What kind of life did she imagine for herself, with her cagey, begrudging Zhenechka, his dreary friends, his meddling mother?

And as for my mother, she was already fussing in the kitchen by the time I got back from Lariska's. My father, too, was back. We ate dinner in the living room, with the plates in our laps and the coffee table crowded with bread and herring, three cans of Old Milwaukee, and a bowl of salad. Neither of us had much to say. We swiped pieces of herring, we clinked our beer cans. The TV was on, and we watched the local news, something about a fire in Homestead. My father drove through Homestead every day, on the way to work and back. It was a poor area, mostly black. "Your friends," he said, pointing at the TV. We'd argued in the past about poverty and race, his opinion being that the problem was people's laziness, and that liberals like me were to blame. He didn't like liberals. He didn't like conservatives either.

Lariska's parents were the same. We used to call it *the immigrant mentality.* But now Lariska was changing, becoming more like them. She had her Zhenechka. They were planning to move back to Pittsburgh. She'd already spent a good hour today talking to me about taxes and property values.

My mother asked me if I liked Lariska's dress.

The dress, I said, was preposterous, and so was the whole idea of

the wedding. Like most Russian men, Zhenechka had antiquated
views of family. He'd cheated on Lariska, and he would cheat on
her again. For a person of his background, cheating was normal. "I
give it six months," I said.

My father said, "Like you know."

"I know enough to avoid the Russians."

"Sure," he said. "You just study them in college."

He collected our plates, stacked them on top of the dishwasher.
"I'm going to take a nap," he said. "I recommend you do the same."

It went like this every time I came home. I'd learned to keep
quiet whenever he tried to provoke me, but it didn't always work.
The last time, he said I was *intolerant*. I'd gone to a New Year's party
with them, but I wouldn't dance or play my mother's parlor games.
"When did you get so boring?" said Borya Rivkin. He was one of
my parents' friends. "Girls your age shouldn't be so boring." His
own daughter, Vika, was eight years younger than me and engaged.
The wedding would be in October.

"Don't let them get to you," Tom said. "Don't let them trample
your accomplishments." He was extra gentle with me after the
New Year's break. He took me ice-skating at Frog Pond, and then
we went out for crêpes. There, wedged in a row of small breakfast
tables, we sat holding hands, and he told me that one day we'd have
a home of our own.

NEXT MORNING, my mother and I went shopping. She'd called in
sick at work, and my father had said I could take the old Ford,
which he'd been keeping for my mother, even though they both
knew she would never touch it.

"Does it still run?" I said.

"Flies like a bird."

It didn't fly, but it got us to Ross Park Mall, and my mother did a commendable job navigating. I was wary of being alone with her. I thought she might ask if I was seeing someone, and then I'd have to lie or give her my usual answer—that she'd know if there was something *serious* going on. Tom and I didn't seem very serious now. After the day at Frog Pond, he'd all but disappeared in his work. We fought a lot, and admittedly I was the one who started it. It was as if I wanted to upset the balance. I didn't think the balance worked.

We fought the last time we'd gone out. We'd had a dinner with our friends from Tom's department. They lived in Cambridge, in a beautiful house, with shiny wood and built-in cupboards and shelves full of sculptures and books. They'd been married awhile, and I'd always admired them. The way they listened to each other. The way they worked in their adjacent studies, taking breaks to make love or have supper. Their names were Jim and Marla, and at dinner they announced that Marla was expecting their first child.

It didn't go well with me and Tom. Before the party we'd gone to our favorite cheese-and-wine shop, where we spent half an hour selecting wine and tasting samples. We'd spoken in fake French accents and acted like snobs. But then there was the telltale pause at the checkout when we glanced at each other and reached for our separate credit cards. Though what really ticked me off that night was John and Marla's announcement.

On the way back, I said, "What are we waiting for?"

Tom was driving. I knew he'd drop me off and then go home to Brookline.

I said, "By the time you get done with your work, there will be nothing left of us."

He said, "You're just making it worse."

My mother asked me nothing. Because it was March, the stores were carrying their summer inventory. There were halter dresses in "cyan," front-twist dresses in "gumdrop green," and swirl-print dresses with large geometrical patterns. There was nothing in there for me. My mother was starting to say that perhaps we should try David's Bridal, and I was thinking that Lariska would have to do with two bridesmaids instead of three. But then, at last, we found it. It was in the back of a smaller boutique. Draped neck, flutter sleeves, crinkled silk. The color, pearly and elusive, was listed as "tossed leaf." It was about twice as much as what I'd budgeted.

"Don't worry," said my mother. "It's on me."

"Did you get rich all of a sudden?"

But she'd already got out her checkbook.

"Dad will kill you when he finds out."

We were at the register now, my mother double-checking the name of the store, tracing out her signature, logging the amount.

"I work too, you know," she said. "It's not just your father."

She bought me the dress, and I took her out for coffee and ice cream, the proper kind. The menus were done in Italian cursive and listed no prices. The servings were tiny. The ice cream came in shiny metal cups. My mother dunked each spoonful in her coffee. She called it *café glacé*. As a young girl, she used to order it in small basement cafés in Leningrad. Later in Moscow, where she'd moved after she'd married my father, she taught me to make a home version. It involved instant coffee and a brick of *plombières* for forty-eight kopecks. But it was never as good as in Leningrad.

"Remember how good it was?" she said.

She looked well. Her face had filled out, assumed a warm, complacent color, and I could see none of the little red spots that appeared around her eyes after one of her headaches. Her depression was under control. The only thing was, she felt hot all the time, a sign of menopause. She'd already taken off her parka, and now she was unbuttoning the top of her cardigan.

"I'd like to live somewhere that's not so hot," she said.

"Pittsburgh is hot?"

"In the summer. And in the winter it's all ice and snowstorms."

"Where would you go?"

She shrugged and looked into her coffee cup. "We don't talk like we used to," she said after a pause. "You don't confide in me."

I said, "I don't confide in anyone."

"I know. It must be lonely."

"Maybe a little," I said. "But basically I'm fine."

For a moment I thought I might tell her the truth, but then the impulse passed.

"And you?" I asked. "Dad's bullying you like always?"

She smiled. "We have our problems."

IN THE EVENING, we ate toasted sandwiches and watched a James Bond marathon on TV. I was supposed to call Lariska, but the thought of going back there, to the house teeming with her relatives and Zhenechka's relatives, was more than I could handle that day. She called me herself, at seven. "You're coming over?" she said. It was her last night as a single lady, and the Donetsk twins were bringing tequila and pot. "Come on," she said. "Make an effort."

It felt more important to stay with my parents. Despite what my mother had said, they didn't seem unhappy. They were a little gentler with each other. They yelled a little less. If my father saw a good joke on the Internet, he'd show it to my mother; if she was playing solitaire on her computer (the easy kind), he'd stand behind her chair and tell her which card to pick up next.

I thought we would spend our evening together, doing some

family thing, playing hangman, or watching the "Song of the Year" tape, or maybe catching the rest of the James Bond marathon. But after dinner, my mother went upstairs to lie down. My father said it was my fault: what was I thinking dragging her from store to store? And the coffee, didn't I know that coffee was bad for her? Or did I do it on purpose?

The two of us were on the porch, in our coats and slippers with socks. My father was smoking.

"You're wrong," I said. "You're wrong and you know it."

"Sure," he said. "I'm wrong. Your mother's wrong. Your friend is wrong for getting married. How can it be that everyone is so wrong? Or maybe it's the other way around, ah? Did it ever occur to you? Maybe it's *you* who's wrong? Maybe that's what you should think about."

I told him to leave me alone.

"You're already alone," he said. "You can't even talk to your parents. Is it the Russians' fault? Is it their fault you're not good enough for Americans?"

I said it wasn't true.

My mother came downstairs to check her blood pressure. She was in a nightgown, but she claimed she felt better. Instead of going back to bed, she settled in an armchair in the living room.

"Let's have a drink," she said. "The three of us."

My father said, "Not with your headache."

I said I wasn't in the mood.

We had stopped talking altogether. We watched the local news. That morning, a woman and a dog had been killed on a highway. They'd been asleep in their car, parked in the dirt patch that separated traffic on I-79, and it looked like they were maybe homeless. In the morning the dog got out. When the woman awoke, she saw it was dead on the side of the highway. She went to get it, and a pickup swiped her too.

My father said the woman was an idiot because you never walk across a highway.

"That's what you're saying now," said my mother. "You'd do the same thing."

"Never," he said.

"Not even to save your dog? Or a child?"

"It was dead! Dead!" said my father. "There was nothing there to save."

AND WHAT IF MY father guessed the truth? What if there was something faulty in me that made Tom reluctant? I watched CNN, I ate out, I read American books. I'd quit my job and gone back to school, which was something most Americans admired. But I lacked their boldness and fluency, their flippant resistance to gloom. My father said I'd *never* be quite like them.

It was the morning of Lariska's wedding, and it seemed like I hadn't slept at all. I felt emptied and beaten and left with an old broken trough, like the greedy old lady from one of Pushkin's fairy tales. Except I wasn't even greedy.

Lariska rang the bell at ten o'clock. It looked as if she hadn't slept much either. She was pale and forlorn, with her hair pulled back and a couple of pimples along the side of her jaw. She looked like one of the Orthodox girls who went to Hillel Academy—too young to get married.

"You never called," she said.

I told her I'd been busy.

"Busy with what? You're just sitting in here."

The world, I said, didn't revolve around her. Besides, she had the twins to entertain her.

Lariska groaned.

Outside, it was spring, the sky blue and ebullient, everything thawing, dripping. A splendid wedding day, except never before had a wedding seemed like such a bad idea. We walked to Schenley Park, the streets trim and comely and full of well-made, sturdy houses, a perfect place to settle down with your doctor husband. In the winter, she'd bring her kiddies to the skating rink, which now stood half melted and neglected. We loitered around it.

"Is Zhenechka back?"

Lariska shook her head. "Not exactly."

"You're sure he's coming to the wedding?"

"Give me some credit," she said.

The rule was, if it's bad in the beginning, it'll never get better. She'd told me this herself.

"I said that? Really? I don't remember."

"You don't have to do it," I said. "You don't have to pretend. If you're not sure—"

"But I'm sure," she said. "Don't you get it? I've been sure for years, since the first time I met him. There was a dinner party at his parents' house. It was April, we'd just got here from Leningrad, and they'd invited us because we're related. I sat across from him. I closed my eyes and I could see it all: the two of us together, the rest of our lives."

I'd never seen her so sentimental. Ten years ago, this would've been me. But now I knew it was simpler than that: Love either worked or it didn't. And in the beginning it did. Tom's face, so pale, so thin, the needled lines of his first wrinkles, our autumn trips across New England, spiked apple cider and the opulence of leaves. The windows are half open, and Tom's hand is warm on my knee. He's saying I have this windswept, sultry look, and he can hardly stand it, the way I look, the way the leaves are swirling ahead of us.

Lariska stretched out her hands. They trembled a little, and the fingers were red.

I said, "Wedding jitters?"

"It's so dumb," she said.

I gripped them in my hands, and we stood like that for a minute.

She said, "I'm sort of envious. I think you're really brave. I wouldn't have the nerve to drop my career and start something else. It's what we always dreamed of, isn't it? I know you think I'm settling, retreating—"

I didn't, I said.

"I wish you'd understand it's not like that. I need you to believe me. Can you try? Can you promise me that?"

We hugged, which was something we never did. Her coat was torn at the shoulder and smelled of cigarettes. Her cheek felt cold against my cheek. She was late for her hair appointment.

After she left, I went inside the pavilion where kids had birthday parties and pizza. It was empty—the parties didn't start till later, and besides, there wouldn't be much skating that day. I stepped out onto the deck. An older man sat out there, at one of the big wooden tables. He asked me if I needed to sharpen my skates. "Three dollars," he said. "Best price in town." I thanked him. I told him I didn't have skates. I had to make a phone call. "Go ahead," he said, and then excused himself.

I got out my cell phone. It was on days like these, days scrambled by sunlight and insomnia, that I found myself feeling foolishly hopeful. Or maybe Lariska was to blame.

"It's you," said Tom. "Are you back? Are you home?"

He could never remember my plans.

I said, "I'm coming back tomorrow."

He said he'd been sick with a cold. It was bad. He wanted to call me, but he didn't think I'd want to talk to him. He wondered how the wedding went.

"It hasn't happened yet."

"I wish I could go," he said. "I'd love to meet your parents and your friend. Of course, I'd get everyone sick with whatever I have. I've done no work in three days. Has it been three days already? Is that when you left? Three days ago?"

"Honey, you're making no sense."

"That's certainly nothing new."

I told him to go back to bed and that I'd see him tomorrow.

"Come straight to my house," he said.

I said I'd take a cab from Logan.

RUSSIAN WEDDINGS ARE not like American weddings. There are no ushers inquiring which side of the family you belong to, no seating arrangements, no receiving line. They are confusing and disorganized, with the guests puttering in the hallway and poking into wrong doors; and some boys, who look like they're still in high school, scurrying around with car keys and rolling up their sleeves; and somebody's mother saying, "But what about parking?" The parking, in fact, is difficult, because the wedding is at the Mellon Institute on Bellefield, which might be the reason why the minister is late and why he leaves his car outside with the emergency lights blinking. He's nondenominational. His hair is long and he makes a long speech about the importance of commitment. He tries to say something in Hebrew. It sounds all wrong and it makes the groom wince. The groom, as a kid, had studied at Hillel Academy. It's hard to imagine that he's ever been a kid. He's portly, unpleasant, but the bride, of course, doesn't see it. They share a kiss. The stereo plays "Freylekhs." The guests want to eat.

Or maybe every wedding is like this?

Except it wasn't so bad. There was a trellis strewn with pretty flowers, and a carpet that led up to it, and the bride had a tremulous smile, and the music was sweeping. The ceremony ended, and we filed into the room next door, where the tables were shaped in a long L. There was a giant chandelier and a blackboard.

"A blackboard," said my father. "Whoever thought of that?"

"I don't see it bothering anyone else," said my mother.

"Did I say I was bothered?" he said.

I asked them to please not fight in public. They weren't, they said. They were having *a dialogue*. And no one cared anyway.

"You worry too much," said my father.

I'd arrived with Lariska, an hour in advance. I'd gotten ready at her house, and it was only just before the ceremony that my father finally saw my dress. "Not bad," he said. "A little mousy in color."

"It's green," I said, and he just raised his eyebrows.

We were seated across from Lariska's acidic Aunt Tamara. "Are you related to anyone here?" she said. We weren't. We were only related to one another, and soon we'd be going our separate ways. For now, we were solicitous and quiet. My mother passed the eggplant and the sprats. I helped her with the salad. My father poured us some vodka and some lemonade.

I hadn't been the only one perplexed. No one knew exactly what to say, given the couple's spotty record. There were quick, awkward toasts, followed by the clinking of glasses, and a speech by Aunt Sasha, in English, for the benefit of the out-of-town American guests. "Enough," said Lariska's aunt. "Enough of this peacocking and playacting!"

"You're writing this down?" my father said. "These are your Russians."

The room, of course, was full of them. There were new arrivals and my parents' old friends; ailing women, widowed men, separated computer programmers. Borya Rivkin and his daughter

Vika. Aunt Sasha's friend from Mellon Bank, Natasha, remarried and pregnant, with her new husband hailing from Spain and her son now finishing high school. Tanya Katz, reunited with her husband, Petya, and pregnant as well. A girl in a red spaghetti-strap dress stood by the blackboard with her mother. She was chalking a chemical formula. "Remember them?" my mother said. The girl's name was Anya. Her mother did accounting, and her father had died from a heart attack last April. The girl was in Boston, in grad school, studying chemistry, following in her father's footsteps.

Before dessert, the twins came over to chat. During the ceremony, we'd hardly had a chance to acknowledge each other. Now I saw they had lost some of their old rambunctious charm. They looked pinched and tired, and their dresses didn't match. Mila had midterms, and Yana had stayed up with the kid, who'd been crying and crying. It was hard, they said, but also gratifying. It was just the two of them now. Their parents had moved to Chicago. So many changes, they said. They'd heard that I'd, too, made a change, and they wanted to say they were glad, they were proud. "Harvard," said Yana. "It doesn't get better than that."

And then it was time for the couple's first dance. They weren't great dancers, especially Zhenechka, who'd always been a little lumpish, and also nearsighted. But you could tell he was doing his best. He held Lariska tenderly and tried not to step on the edges of her dress, and whenever he blundered, she smiled at him. They were trying. And maybe not everything was a mistake. Maybe we *had* learned something, and next time we'd do a little better, if only we gave it a chance. Lariska and Zhenechka were dancing. Under the shining chandelier. In small, shuffling steps. Forever and ever. In sickness and in health. Mismatched like the rest of us. More beautiful than anything. And I had no words to describe them.

Acknowledgments

MY DEEPEST GRATITUDE to everyone who helped bring this book to life. To my wonderful agent, David McCormick. To my wise editor, Jill Bialosky. To everyone at W. W. Norton and at McCormick and Williams.

Thank you to the Lynne and Ed McCreight family for the James C. McCreight Fellowship at the University of Wisconsin Institute for Creative Writing, and to everyone at the institute for their support and friendship, especially Ron Wallace, Ron Kuka, Jesse Lee Kercheval, and Judy Mitchell.

Thank you to George Saunders for being the most amazing mentor and friend. I couldn't have done without you.

Thank you to all my professors and classmates at Syracuse University and especially to Chris Kennedy, Mary Gaitskill, Gary Lutz, Arthur Flowers, Bob O'Connor, Adam Levin, and Keith Gessen.

I am immensely grateful to Grub Street, Inc. for encouraging me to write and for letting me teach. Steve Almond, Chris Castellani, Eve Bridburg—you were there for me in the beginning and you've been with me since.

Thank you to everyone at the Bread Loaf Writers' Conference. Thank you to Michelle Wildgen, Amber Dermont, Stuart Dybek, Natalie Danford, Jacob Knabb, and all the editors who have published my work.

Special thank you to my fabulous, talented writers' group: Jami Brandli, Jane Roper, Jessica Murphy, and Morgan Frank. You are my inspiration.

Thank you to all the friends who were with me along the way: Nancy Baker, Rebecca Curtis, Sarah Harwell, Sheila Hoelscher, Andy Lee, Mark Lubinskij, Irina Mukhanova, Rita Mae Reese, Heidi Lynn Staples, G. C. Waldrep, and Konstantin Zhovinskiy.

Most of all, thank you to my family. To my husband, Ian Fraser. To my sister, Juliya Litman. And to my parents, Mariya and Josef Litman, for bringing me to America.

THE LAST CHICKEN
IN AMERICA

Ellen Litman

READING GROUP GUIDE

A CONVERSATION WITH ELLEN LITMAN

Why is The Last Chicken in America *told in stories?*

The core of the book is a series of stories about Masha, a newly arrived immigrant whose experience is closest to mine, and her family. However, I wanted this novel to be about not just one family but a whole community. I wanted to write about immigration from the point of view of characters who had come to America at different times in their lives and followed different paths: a retiree who, after many years of separation, joins his daughter; a divorced mother who is starting to feel estranged from her old peers; a high school graduate who desperately wants to move away from Squirrel Hill but perhaps isn't ready to take the plunge. Stories seemed like a natural way to give voice to these characters.

Are the stories autobiographical?

Yes and no. My family and I did emigrate from Russia. I did live in Squirrel Hill, attend the University of Pittsburgh, and shop for food at Giant Eagle. Much of the book is influenced by my experiences of coming to America, being a part of an immigrant community, and trying to assimilate. The feelings and conflicts I describe are often real (at least for me), but the situations and characters are fictional.

Why "the last chicken"?

Readers will probably recognize the line from the argument Masha's parents have at their local supermarket in the title story. (They are arguing about poultry, among other things.) I initially chose "The Last Chicken in America" because it seemed like a funny and unexpected line, and also (full disclosure) because a teacher pointed it out to me and suggested it would make a good title. Over the years, though, as I thought about the story and worked on the rest of the book, the line echoed more and more the experiences of my characters. The Russian immigrants in the book come to America ("the land of plenty") and find themselves in a world that is infinitely smaller than the one they'd left behind or the one they had imagined. In this new immigrant world, the resources seem limited. Every job prospect and every relationship may be their last chance for security and happiness. The larger America, with more choices and chickens, exists somewhere, outside the bounds of this world, but it might take them a while to find a way there.

DISCUSSION QUESTIONS

1. Though several dozen characters are introduced in the stories that make up *The Last Chicken in America*, Masha and her parents appear in the first and last stories, and several stories in between. Why do you think Litman chose to make these three characters the backbone of her "novel in stories"?

2. How does Squirrel Hill serve as both a trap and a source of cultural comfort to the characters in the stories?

3. How does Alick compare with Masha's boyfriend in the final story? What does Masha's choice in boyfriends say about her evolution as an American—and as a young woman?

4. In what ways are the characters' struggles in the book similar to the

hardships faced by many Americans? In what ways do the characters have a distinctly immigrant experience?

5. How does Dinka treat her father in the story "What Do You Dream of, Cruiser *Aurora*?" Are there other instances in the book where the traditional roles of parent and child seem to be reversed? Why might this kind of role reversal occur?

6. At the end of "What Do You Dream of, Cruiser *Aurora*?" Liberman describes Mira as "a lovely and powerful vessel." What do you think he means by that?

7. In the story "Charity," Masha and Pamela exhibit two very different attitudes toward religion. What are they? How is the tension between the more secular Jewish immigrants and the conservative Jews both exposed and suppressed?

8. In the final story, "Home," we learn that Natasha has met a second husband, a Spanish man. How does this change your understanding of Natasha and her experience in the earlier story?

9. Why does Masha's relationship with Victor sour in "The Russian Club"? How does their breakup illuminate the difference between being a visitor and being an immigrant? What does this story say about the barrier between cultural curiosity and immigrant hardship? What rifts in the Russian community are exposed in this story?

10. Why do you think Litman chose to write to "you" (i.e., in the second person) in the story "When the Neighbors Love You"? How is Anya's choice between Maks and David similar to her choice between BU and Pitt?

11. What is the meaning of the story title "The Trajectory of Frying Pans"? Why can dating be particularly challenging for young immigrants like Misha?

12. How has Masha's relationship with her parents changed by the

final story, "Home"? How has her understanding of the immigrant experience changed?

13. In "The Russian Club" Victor writes, "For a true Russian person, immigration is death. A Russian poet can't survive in immigration." Do the experiences of the immigrants in this book bear out this notion?